Of Octopuses and Men

MISHA BELL

♠ MOZAIKA PUBLICATIONS ♠

Published by Mozaika Publications, an imprint of Mozaika LLC.
www.mozaikallc.com

Cover by Najla Qamber Designs
www.najlaqamberdesigns.com

Photography by Wander Aguiar
www.wanderbookclub.com

ISBN: 978-1-63142-737-4
Paperback ISBN: 978-1-63142-738-1

CHAPTER

One

THE QUIVERING purple tentacle slithers in between the girl's legs.

I dart a wary glance at my grandmother.

Figures. While most grandmothers might have a heart attack seeing something like this, mine is watching with fascination, like a rookie gynecologist.

A second tentacle joins the fun.

Grandma's fascination heightens, now matching that of a rookie proctologist.

I swivel my head from the TV to her and then back. Finally, I cautiously ask, "Grandma... why are we watching tentacle porn?"

With a slight frown, she presses the pause button. "It's called *hentai*. They draw these cartoons in Japan."

Seriously, Japan? Eating raw octopus isn't enough? Now you have to corrupt my already uncomfortably sex-obsessed grandmother?

I sigh. "Why are we watching hentai?"

She waggles her perfectly groomed eyebrows. "This is something your grandfather and I enjoy. Figured it would be up your alley."

Cthulhu help me, if TMI could turn into a person, it would be my grandma. She's even worse than her daughter—my mom. "Why would you think tentacle porn is 'up my alley?'"

She glances at the large aquarium by the window, the one housing Beaky, my BFF who just happens to be a giant Pacific octopus. "You really love that thing, and you've been going through a dry spell, so I—"

I clear my throat loudly and pointedly. "Are you suggesting I get into bestiality?"

I do love everything to do with octopuses. Since I'm a marine biologist and one of eight sisters, it's only logical. But that doesn't mean I want to have sexual relations with them.

She shrugs. "Like I said to my scatophiliac friend at bingo the other day, I don't kink-shame."

I pinch the bridge of my nose. "I don't have a 'sex with octopuses' kink. I'm not even sure there *is* such a thing."

She grins. "It's called Rule 34. If you can conceive of it, there's a porn of it."

I purse my lips. "If someone has sex with any living being without their consent, I reserve the right to shame them. And I don't care if they molest an octopus, a goat, or a cockroach."

Grandma nods to Beaky. "You keep saying how

smart he is. Maybe he could do sign language with his tentacles?"

She's just as difficult to argue with as my sister Gia. Which is fitting, considering Gia was named after her. I try anyway. "Beaky and I are just friends."

"You can be friends with benefits."

Ugh. "We're strictly platonic."

"Well… I was cleaning your room and stumbled upon your tentacle dildo." To my shock, she looks bashful as she says this—a definite first.

I flush the shade of red Beaky turns when he's trying to look menacing. Then I recall that Florida is famous for sinkholes.

Can one swallow me right now?

"I got that on a lark, Grandma. Besides, octopuses don't have tentacles. You're thinking of squid and cuttlefish."

"Oh?" She studies the tank in confusion. "So what do you call those eight appendages?"

I walk over to the tank and grab its remote control. "Arms."

She blinks at me. "What's the difference?"

I know I'm going into my marine biologist mode in front of the wrong audience, but I can't help myself. "If the suckers are all over—"

"Suckers?" She waggles her eyebrows.

"Ugh, Grandma, stop. Like I was saying, if the suckers are all over, it's an arm. If they're only at the tip, it's a tentacle. Arms also have finer control, while tentacles are elongated and—"

3

"Okay, okay, I'm sorry," she says.

I narrow my eyes. "Sorry that you suggested I have relations with my octopus? Or sorry you snooped in my private drawer?"

Her grin is as mischievous as a naughty kid's. "Sorry I asked."

With a huff, I activate the motor under the aquarium, and the whole thing begins to roll. "In case it's not clear, Beaky and I are going for a walk."

Waving goodbye, my grandmother resumes her porn, looking just as fascinated as before.

Hey, I'm not judging. I watch and re-watch *Aquaman* whenever I feel frisky.

The anime girl moans in the squeaky, high-pitched voice that's characteristic of the genre. Do Japanese men find childish voices sexy?

Fine. Maybe I'm judging a little.

Having outstayed my welcome, I guide Beaky's motorized tank into the dining area, where I find my grandfather sitting at the table, lovingly reassembling a sniper rifle. Like my grandmother, he's in great shape, especially for an octogenarian. With his thick hair and muscular arms, he could donate testosterone to younger men.

He looks up from his gun, a smile twisting his weathered lips. "Ah, Caper. What are you up to?"

I grin. My name is Olive (my parents are evil in their hippie-dippie-ness), and when Grandpa calls me Caper, he means "little olive," which makes me feel like a little girl again. Obviously, I'll never tell him that his nickname for me is botanically incorrect: capers are the flowers of a shrub, while olives are a tree fruit from an altogether different species.

"Taking Beaky out for a walk," I reply, nodding at the tank.

Grandpa squints at the glass, and Beaky chooses that exact moment to make himself look like a rock—as he does every time Grandpa tries to look at him.

Grandpa rubs his eyes. "Is there really an octopus in there? I feel like you and your grandmother are trying to make me think I'm going senile."

"No. It's Beaky who's messing with you."

I can't blame my grandfather for not spotting my eight-armed friend. When it comes to camouflage, octopuses blow chameleons out of the water. Also, if a chameleon was literally in the water, no amount of camouflage would save it from becoming an octopus's lunch.

Grandpa shakes his head. "Why?"

I shrug. "He's a creature with nine brains, one in his head and one in each arm. Trying to puzzle out his thinking would give anyone a headache."

Grandpa squints at the tank again, but Beaky stays in his rock guise. "Why do you walk him, anyway?"

"To keep him from being bored. What he really needs is a bigger tank, but for now, he'll have to make do with a change of scenery."

"Bored?"

"Oh, yeah. A bored octopus is worse than a seven-year-old boy hopped up on caffeine and birthday cake.

In Germany, an octopus named Otto repeatedly shorted out the Sea Star Aquarium's entire electrical system by squirting water at the 2,000-watt overhead spotlight. Because he was bored."

Grandpa lifts his bushy eyebrows. "But don't you make puzzles for him? Let him watch TV?"

I nod. Making puzzles for octopuses is actually what I'm famous for, and how I got my new job. "Toys and TV help," I say, "but I still get the sense he's feeling cooped up."

Grunting, Grandpa delves into his pocket and pulls out a handgun the size of my arm. "Take this with you." He thrusts it at me.

I blink at the instrument of death. "Why?"

"Protection."

"From what? We're in a gated community."

He thrusts the weapon at me with greater urgency. "It's better to have a gun and not need it."

I don't take the offering. "The crime rate in Palm Islet is ten times lower than in New York."

Grandpa takes the clip out of the gun, checks it, shoves in an extra bullet, and snaps it back in. "It would give me peace of mind if you took it."

"By Cthulhu," I mutter under my breath.

"Bless you," Grandpa says.

"That wasn't a sneeze. I said, 'Cthulhu.'" At Grandpa's blank stare, I heave a sigh. "He's a fictional cosmic entity created by H. P. Lovecraft. Depicted with octopus features."

"Oh. Is that him in your grandmother's sexy cartoons?"

"Absolutely not." I shudder at the thought. "Cthulhu is hundreds of meters tall. He's one of the Great Old Ones, so his attentions would rip a woman apart as quickly as they would drive her mad."

"Fair enough." Grandpa attempts to shove the gun into my hands again. "Take it and go."

I hide my hands behind my back. "I don't have any kind of license."

"You're kidding." He regards me incredulously. "Tomorrow, I'll take you to a concealed carry class."

I fight a Cthulhu-sized eye roll. "I'm kind of busy tomorrow, starting a new job and all."

With a frown, he hides the gun somewhere. "How about this weekend?"

"We'll see," I say as noncommittally as I can before grabbing my handbag from the back of a nearby chair and pressing the remote button again to roll the tank into the garage.

My grandparents, like other Floridians, prefer to leave their houses this way, instead of, say, through the front door.

As soon as my grandfather is out of sight, Beaky stops being a rock, spreads his arms akimbo, and turns an excited shade of red.

"You should be ashamed of yourself," I tell him sternly.

We are the God Emperor of the Tank, ordained by Cthulhu. We shall not bestow the glory of our visage upon the undeserving. Hurry up, our faithful priestess-subject. We want to taste the sunshine on our suckers.

Yup. Ellen DeGeneres talked to a fictional sentient octopus in *Finding Dory*, while my real one speaks to me in my head. And I'm not alone in having these imaginary conversations. Ever since my sisters and I were kids, we've given animals voices. In my mind, Beaky sounds like nine people speaking in unison (the main brain and the eight in his arms), and his tone is imperious (octopuses have blue blood, after all). Oh, and his words come out with that faint gargle-like sound effect used in *Aquaman* when the Atlanteans spoke underwater.

I open the garage door.

It's super bright outside, despite the ancient oaks that provide plenty of shade.

With a sigh, I take a big tube of my favorite mineral-based sunblock from my bag and cover myself with a thick layer from head to foot. The UV index is 10, so I wait a few minutes, and then I cover myself with a second layer. I do this furtively in the garage to avoid my grandparents teasing me about taking a job in the Sunshine State while being paranoid about sun exposure.

And no, I'm not a vampire—though my sister Gia looks suspiciously like she might be, with her goth makeup and all. Avoiding the sun makes legitimate scientific sense given the harmful effects of UV rays, both A and B, as well as blue light, infrared light, and visible light. They all cause DNA damage. This issue got on my radar a couple of years back when Sushi, my pet clownfish, developed skin cancer, probably due to her aquarium being by a window. I've been careful ever since, even going as far as gluing a triple layer of UV-protective coating over Beaky's tank.

Now, do I realize that I worry about the sun a tad more than anyone who isn't a paranoid dermatologist? Sure. But can I stop? Nope. I think some level of neurosis is programed into my DNA, at least if my identical sextuplet sisters are anything to go by. But hey, when I'm in my eighties and look younger than all my sisters, we'll see who has the last laugh.

Sunblocking finished, I throw on a lightweight zip-up jacket that's coated in UV-protective chemicals, a wide-brim hat, and giant sunglasses.

There. If I were really taking this too far, I'd be wearing one of those Darth Vader visors, wouldn't I?

My heartbeat picks up as I follow Beaky's tank out into full sun, but I calm down by reminding myself that the sunblock will do its job. When the tank rolls down the driveway and onto a shady sidewalk by the lake, my breathing evens out further.

So far so good. Now I just hope I don't get too many annoying questions from nosy neighbors.

A pair of herons take flight nearby as we stroll along the lake shore. Beaky stares at them intently and changes his shape a few times.

We wish to taste those things. Be a good priestess-subject and deliver them to the tank.

I pat the top of the tank. "I'll give you a shrimp when we get back."

We both spot a raccoon digging in the grass by the lake, likely looking for turtle or gator eggs.

We wish to taste that too.

"I'll give you a shrimp without the puzzle," I tell him.

Usually, I put his treats into one of my creations, making the meal extra fun for him, but if he's worked up an appetite by watching all the land animals, I don't want to delay his gratification.

A five-foot alligator slowly crawls out of the lake.

Yup, we're definitely in Florida.

Spotting it, Beaky picks up two coconut shells from the bottom of his tank and closes them over his body, appearing to the world—and to the gator—like an innocent coconut.

"That thing can't get you in the tank," I say soothingly. "Not to mention, it's scared of me. Hopefully."

The statistics on alligator attacks are in our favor. In a state with headlines like "Florida man beats up alligator" and "Florida man tosses alligator into Wendy's drive-through window," the gators have learned to stay far, far away from the insane humans.

Because Beaky doesn't read the news or check online statistics, his eye looks skeptical as it peeks out from the coconut shells.

I return my attention to the sidewalk—and spot him.

A man.

And what a man.

He could've starred in *Aquaman* instead of Jason Momoa. If I were casting the leading man for my wet dreams, this guy would definitely get the role.

The thought sends tendrils of heat to my nether regions, specifically the part I privately think of as my wunderpus—in honor of *wunderpus photogenicus*, an amazing octopus species discovered in the eighties.

By the way, I once took a picture of my wunderpus, and it's also *photogenicus.*

But back to the stranger. Strong, masculine features framed by an impeccably trimmed beard, cyan eyes as deep as the ocean, a tanned, muscular body clad in low-riding jeans and a sleeveless top that shows off powerful arms, thick, blond-streaked hair that streams down to his broad shoulders—he'd look like a surfer if it weren't for the broody expression on his face.

Beaky must've forgotten about the gator because he's out of his coconut and looking at the stranger with fascination.

Figures. Aquaman has the power to talk to octopuses, along with other sea creatures.

I realize I'm also gaping at him and tense as he gets closer. Unlike back in New York, where it's customary to pass a stranger without acknowledging their existence, here in Florida, everyone at the very least greets their neighbors.

What do I say if he speaks to me? Do I even dare open my mouth? What if I accidentally ask him to have his way with me?

Wait a second. I think I've got it. He's also walking a pet, in his case a dog of the Dachshund breed, a.k.a. a hotdog dog, the most phallic member of the canine species. All I have to do is say something about his wiener—the one wagging its tail, not his Aqua-manhood.

When the man is a dozen feet away, he seems to notice me for the first time. Actually, his gaze zeroes in on Beaky's tank, and his broody expression turns downright hostile—jaw clenched, mouth downturned, eyes flinty. The insane thing is, he looks no less hot now. Maybe more so.

What is wrong with me? No wonder I end up dating assholes like—

His deep, sexy voice is the kind of cold that can create a wind chill even in this humid sauna. "How much for the octopus?"

I blink, then narrow my eyes at the stranger, my hackles rising like spikes on a pufferfish. He wants to buy Beaky? Why? Does he want to eat him?

This *is* the state where people eat gators, turtles (even the protected species), bullfrogs, Burmese pythons, and key lime pie.

Gritting my teeth, I point to the tail-wagging dog at his side. "How much for the bratwurst?"

A sneer twists his full lips. "Let me guess… a New Yorker?"

Aquaman? More like Aqua-ass. "Let *me* guess. Florida man?" I can picture the rest of the headline: "… steals octopus in tank and tries to have sex with it."

Given what my grandmother said about Rule 34 and where I am, it's not that far-fetched. I once read an article about a Florida man who tried to sell a live shark in a mall parking lot. What's sex with an octopus in comparison?

His thick brown eyebrows snap together. "The stories you're alluding to are about transplants. They're never about actual Floridians."

"Oh, I've read what you're talking about," I say with a snort. "'Florida man receives first-ever penis transplant from a horse.' I'm pretty sure the article said that the brave pioneer was born and raised in Melbourne—that's two hours away from here."

Oops. Have I gone too far? Everyone does seem to carry a gun here. And since I found him attractive earlier, with my dating track record, he might well turn out to be dangerous.

Instead of pulling out a weapon, the stranger rubs the bridge of his nose. "Serves me right for trying to argue with a New Yorker. Forget the news. That tank is too small for that octopus. How would you like to live your life inside a Mini Cooper?"

I suck in a breath, my stomach tightening. "How would *you* like to be walked on a leash?" I jerk my chin toward his wiener, whose tail is no longer wagging. "Or to be forced to ignore your screaming bladder and bowels until your master deigns to take you for a walk? Or to have your reproductive organs messed with?"

He glowers at me. "Tofu isn't neutered. In fact, he—"

"Tofu?" My jaw drops. "As in, a tofu hot dog? Talk about animal cruelty."

The veins popping out in his neck look distractingly sexy. "What's wrong with the name Tofu?"

Before I can reply, Tofu whines pitifully.

"Great job," the stranger says. "Now you've upset him."

"I'm pretty sure you did that." *By naming the poor dog Tofu.*

"This conversation is over." He turns his back to me and tugs on the leash. "Come, Tofu."

Tofu gives me a sad look that seems to say, *I don't like it when my daddy and my new mommy argue.*

With a huff, I roll Beaky's tank in the opposite direction.

CHAPTER
Two

AFTER A FEW MINUTES, my blood cools a bit, and I realize why I got so upset. Aqua-ass was right about Beaky needing a bigger tank. It's been a source of stress and guilt for me for the past few weeks.

I haven't always had Beaky. The seaquarium I worked at in New York went bankrupt seemingly overnight, and they couldn't find Beaky a new home. So, I took him in. Unfortunately, I didn't have space for his original tank in my tiny apartment, and they gave me this one, which I then motorized. In my defense, Beaky could've ended up in worse conditions, or even been put to sleep. His well-being is the main reason I took the job that starts tomorrow—the job that risks my skin, literally, since the odds of melanoma are so much higher here in Florida.

My hope is that Sealand, my new employer, will let me house Beaky in one of their large tanks. When I brought up this issue during the interview process, they said it's something the owner *should* be able to accommodate, and that I'd have to speak with him after I start.

Which reminds me… I take out my phone and check my email.

Nope. Nothing from Octoworld—the place I reapply to on a daily basis. Working at Octoworld is a dream of mine, since, as the name suggests, they specialize in octopuses, while Sealand, like so many other places, cares more about the mammals of the sea, like dolphins.

Don't get me wrong. I don't hate dolphins, but it does grate on my nerves when they're all anyone wants to talk about as soon as they learn that I'm a marine biologist. Of course, they do so at their own peril. I like telling people little-known facts about dolphin behavior, like how they sometimes kill porpoises for fun, and how they often play with (read: torture) their food (they're particularly cruel to octopuses). Occasionally, they also kill newborns of their species, and, last but not least, they can be sexually aggressive, sometimes even toward humans.

Realizing I've made a full circle around the block, I roll the tank over to my grandparents' house. I don't want to risk bumping into Aqua-ass again.

When I step inside with the tank, "All by Myself" by Céline Dion is blasting from my grandmother's phone.

"Did Grandpa leave?" I shout over the music.

"No, why?"

I grin. "Never mind."

She pauses the music. "How was the walk?"

I feel my face pinching. "I met one of your wonderful neighbors."

Grandma looks like she's on the verge of jumping up and down with excitement. "Which one?"

I sigh. "He wasn't actually wonderful. I thought you'd learn to pick up on sarcasm by now."

Her excitement wanes. "Who was it?"

"A guy in his late twenties or early thirties. Long hair. Asshole."

Should I mention that he is so annoyingly hot Grandma could substitute him for tentacle porn?

She looks thoughtful. "Is it the young man who lives in that house with all those solar panels?"

"I have no idea what house he lives in."

Grandma points out the window. "There."

I look. Yep. There's a roof covered completely in solar panels. If that's Aqua-ass's house, he must really dislike paying electric bills.

"Poor man. I bet the HOA is on his case." Grandma shakes her head.

Oh, no. Not another rant about the homeowners' association. Based on what I've heard from my grandparents so far, dealing with the HOA is less fun than petting a goblin shark.

"What's his name?" I ask Grandma, in part to change the topic and in part because I feel a morbid curiosity.

"I'm ashamed to say it, but I have no idea," she says.

"We say hello to each other all the time, so I feel like I should know."

"Oh, well. It doesn't matter." I can keep referring to him as Aqua-ass, though now that I think about it, that sounds a bit like it might have something to do with diarrhea.

Grandma's eyes gleam. "Did you like him?"

"No. The opposite."

She pouts. "Why not? Do you have a boyfriend in New York?"

Must seem calm. The last thing she needs to know about is the restraining order against my idiot ex. "I'm very single."

Her smile is mischievous again. "Maybe you can start fresh here in Florida? Find love. Put down roots."

"Right. Sure. Anything can happen," I say, and fake a yawn. "I'd better get ready for tomorrow."

I doubt Grandma wants to hear the truth: that I've decided to be a loner, like an octopus. An octopus's idea of romance is a dinner date, where after having sex, one of the participants sometimes *ends up* as dinner. If I'm a loner, I don't have to share my blanket with anyone. And I can have sex with anyone I want—without the cannibalism part. Also—and this is key—I can focus on my career.

If I want to score that job at Octoworld one day, I'll need a good reference from Sealand, my new employer. That means I should go to bed early, so I can make a good impression tomorrow.

After I guide the tank to the guest room where I'm staying, I give Beaky the treat I promised him earlier.

We accept this offering, priestess-subject. Still, if you can make it so we can taste that tofu hot dog entity, we'll put in a good word for you with Cthulhu, blessed be his tentacles.

I smile and am about to offer him a cuddle when I see a noodle-like strand coming out of his siphon.

Eek. He's pooping. Double eek—Hulk, Beaky's green anemone tank mate, is now eating the poo. I know I can't shame an animal for their nature, but still. As a human, it's gross seeing the Hulk munch on Beaky's poop noodle.

The octopus cuddle will have to wait.

Unfortunately, when I get into bed, I'm wide awake. I guess I'm anxious about my first day at the new job. Carp shit. Why does this always happen when you need sleep the most?

I count octopuses in my head.

Not a wink.

Getting my laptop out, I put on *Finding Dory*—a movie that always seems to calm me down.

Even that doesn't help.

Should I watch something else?

I peruse my collection.

When it comes to fiction, I have a passion for the sea, just like in my real life. Well, more of an obsession. Fine, I'll admit it, if an FBI profiler saw these titles, she'd conclude that I want to become a mermaid, and that wouldn't be far from the truth. When I was little, I wanted to be an octopus, but as I got older, I decided that being a mermaid is my dream.

I grin as I recall watching *The Little Mermaid* for the first time. I hated that movie. If it were up to me, the two romantic leads would swap storylines. Ariel would stay a mermaid, while the hot prince Eric would turn into a merman for her. Is it incestuous of me to picture the resulting hero looking like King Triton, Ariel's father, when he was young? Oh, and this goes without saying, but the villain of the story would not look so much like an octopus. Ursula would be Ariel's wise teacher instead, and the villain would be a dolphin.

Few people know this, but there was originally going to be a dolphin in that story. However, Disney dropped the idea—probably because the dolphin was too sexually aggressive.

I yawn.

Yes, that's a good sign.

Maybe it will happen now?

I close my eyes, but sleep evades me for another hour.

Crappity carp. Maybe I should do something active? Like go for a swim? The beach is just a walk away, and I could bring my mermaid tail with me...

But no.

It's already two a.m. I have to wake up at eight. Even if I fell asleep right this second, I'd barely get enough zzzs to function.

I sigh. Why can't we humans be like whales and sleep with one half of the brain awake?

Oh, well. There's a tried-and-true sleeping aid I can resort to.

I take out the tentacle dildo.

Yep. I'm going for an orgasm. Maybe two.

The key thing is not to think of Aqua-ass as I come.

Aquaman, sure. Young King Triton, also acceptable. Even the Silver Surfer, a villain from *Fantastic Four,* would be preferable to my grandparents' annoying neighbor.

Nope.

Major fail.

Just as I reach the peak, the hard muscles and long hair that flit through my mind's eye are not fictional. They belong to the man I was trying not to think about.

Aqua-ass.

I mutter curses under my breath. Something is officially wrong with me. Hopefully, I can at least sleep now.

Blissed out, I close my eyes and drift off.

CHAPTER
Three

I WAKE up to a ray of sun on my face.

Fuck me with a sea urchin. I'll have to start putting on sunblock before bed.

I grab my phone to check the time.

Carp on a cracker.

The battery is dead.

I jackknife to my feet. The phone was supposed to be my alarm, so if it's dead, I might already be late for my first day.

After zooming through my morning routine, I hurry into the kitchen and check the time on the microwave.

Okay, if I skip breakfast and break the speed limit, I can make it.

Grandpa walks into the room. "Morning, Caper."

I flash him a smile. "Please tell me the car I'm borrowing is ready to go."

He nods. "Oil changed the other day and gas tank

full. I even left a Glock in the glove compartment—you don't need a license for that."

Since I'm late, I'm not going to argue about the gun thing with him.

"Have you eaten?" Grandpa asks.

I shake my head. "I'll grab something when I get there."

Frowning, he opens the fridge and pulls out a lunch box covered with stickers of mermaids and octopuses. "Your grandmother had a feeling you'd be in a rush. There's lunch in this, but you can have it for breakfast."

A warm feeling floods my stomach. That's my old lunch box; they've kept it all these years.

I take the box and kiss him on one stubbly cheek. "Tell Grandma she's the best. And so are you."

"I'll do that. Run."

I rush into the garage, then race down A1A—a scenic road I don't even get to enjoy due to the hurry.

I make it to Sealand with just a minute to spare.

A woman is waiting for me. She's a young, pretty blonde with precancerous skin and a fake smile that makes her look like a dolphin.

"Miss Hyman?" she asks in a too-cheerful tone, considering the early hour.

I fight the urge to cringe. "Miss Hyman" sounds like a tired prostitute yearning for the good old days of being a maiden. Not that my full name is much better. "Olive Hyman" makes me think of a virginal membrane with a Mediterranean flavor, something you'd serve with a side of vinegared placenta.

I extend my hand. "Please call me Olive."

Her hand is clammy when she shakes mine. "I'm Aruba."

And that's all it takes to have that Beach Boys song stuck in my head again. If someone else at this place is named Jamaica, Bermuda, Bahama, or some variation of "pretty mama," I'll jump into a shark tank.

"Mrs. Aberdeen is sorry she can't meet you here herself," Aruba says. "She's dealing with an emergency."

Rose Aberdeen, who was insistent I call her Rose, interviewed me for this job. She's an aquatic animal behaviorist—or fish shrink, as she put it—and also the de facto HR department here at Sealand.

I arch an eyebrow. "I hope everything is okay."

"Yeah. A drunken man somehow got into the pool at Otteraction. He got bitten and started bleeding everywhere."

"Oh, my. What's Otteraction?"

She looks at me as if I've just asked whether water is wet. "Otteraction is our otter attraction." You can almost hear the unsaid *duh.*

Wow. I can see *that* headline: "Florida man tries to eat otter." Or have sex with otter? It could've gone either way.

"Are the otters okay?" I ask. As far as I'm concerned, the human deserved to get bitten.

"Peanut was traumatized, but Mrs. Aberdeen is on it."

I snort. "Can you imagine what the man will say to his wife when she goes, 'OMG, what happened?'"

Aruba stares at me with an uncomprehending expression. "No. What?"

"You should see the *otter* guy."

Her tiny nostrils flare. "You think this tragedy is funny?"

"No... sorry. Never mind. I didn't get much sleep last night."

She shakes her head, slowly. "Come. Let me give you a tour."

I follow, staying on my best behavior.

Sealand turns out to be at least double the size of my old workplace, with a larger variety of animals.

Not surprisingly, as the last stop, Aruba takes me to the dolphins, and her smile turns genuine for the first time today. "These are my charges."

"Ah." The expression on my face is the kind people paste on when a friend shows them a picture of their new baby or pet. "Do you train them?"

Her eyes glaze over. "I prefer to think they train me."

I bet those manipulative sneaks do just that.

"I didn't see any octopuses," I say.

"It's octopi," Aruba says.

"No. It's not. Only some words of Latin origin get that ending, like how alumnus becomes alumni. Octopus is of Greek origin, so that rule doesn't apply. If you were to give it a Greek ending, you'd get octopodes—but please don't use that. Life is complicated enough."

Her forehead creases. "Whatever you want to call them, we do not have them and hopefully never will."

"Why?"

"We had one once," she says, her words dripping with disapproval. "She escaped and ended up here, in the dolphin enclosure."

My heart sinks. "Oh, no. Poor thing. What happened?"

"It was horrible." Her forlorn expression wins her a few points in my book. "We lost Flipper."

I blink a few times. "Someone named an octopus Flipper?"

"No. That bitch's name was Athena. Flipper was the dolphin she choked to death."

I puffer-fish, crossing my arms over my chest. "Did Athena perchance choke Flipper as he tried to eat her?"

"Dolphins eat octopuses in the wild all the time."

Yeah, but those dolphins are hungry. The ones here are probably fed better than I am.

I clench my teeth. "I take it Athena didn't survive?"

"Who cares? Poor Flipper. He—"

I tune the rest out because the last thing I want is to choke Aruba. That's not the first impression I want to make here. To change the topic, I ask, "Do you guys have dolphin shows for the public?"

Even though I'm not a fan of dolphins—especially after the Flipper story—I still don't love the idea of turning aquariums into circuses, or *circusi* as Aruba would probably call them.

To my surprise, she shakes her head. "Dr. Jones

doesn't approve of such things. I train my babies to behave when they participate in research—that sort of thing."

Ah, the mysterious Dr. Jones. He was too busy to interview me, but he's been mentioned often and reverently. Based on what I've heard, I picture him with the brain of Einstein and the body of Davy Jones from *Pirates of the Caribbean*: a beard reminiscent of an octopus, a crab claw for one arm, and tentacles for the other.

"Do you think I'm going to meet Dr. Jones today?" I ask. He's the one who'll make the decision about Beaky's residence, so I'm eager for the get-together.

Aruba's smile turns fake once more. "I highly doubt it. He's always very busy on Mondays. Tuesdays too. It took me two months to meet him—and my job is more useful than yours. No offense."

You can't just say shit like that and add "no offense" at the end to make it seem better. Even dolphins know this.

"Your job?" I ask. "I take it you're not just a trainer, then? You're a researcher too?"

She drops the dolphin smile. "Anything is better than making toys for goldfish."

Why do people think the word "toys" is insulting? Puzzles, toys—I don't care what they're called as long as they make sea creatures happier.

"Olive is a renowned enrichment expert," a familiar voice chimes in, startling me. "She is to be treated with respect."

I turn to see Rose—apparently Mrs. Aberdeen to Aruba.

"The dolphins don't need enrichment," Aruba says. "They have me."

I take in a deep breath and let it out slowly. "Sounds like you are the enrichment, then. If every aquarium could afford to dedicate a human to entertain every animal, I'd be out of a job—and glad for it."

"Sadly, we can't afford that solution," Rose says to me. "How about we head over to my office and discuss what we *can* do."

I nod, and we leave Aruba behind as we walk into a small building with a roof gleaming with solar panels. I guess this is a staple here in the Sunshine State.

"Take a seat." Rose gestures at an office chair opposite a weather-beaten desk.

I sit. "I heard about the emergency."

"Yeah. It was otter chaos."

I snort. She must be the one who came up with the name Otteraction.

She proceeds to tell me that the otters are fine, and the human too, and I mention my "otter guy" bit, which gets a much better reaction this time.

"So, to business." She dives into her desk and pulls out a bundle of khaki and white. "You can start wearing this tomorrow."

She hands me the bundle.

It's an outfit consisting of a polo shirt and shorts that I've seen everyone here wearing.

My breathing shallows, and I have to remind myself

that this is nothing at all like when my ex would tell me what to wear. Uniforms are the norm at places like this. My last employer was the exception, not the rule.

"Okay. I'll put this on tomorrow," I say as calmly as I can.

She gives me a laptop next. "It's all set up for you."

"Thanks." I log in as per her instructions. "Should I spend today getting to know your intranet?"

She waves it off. "Not much to see there."

"What should I do then?"

She scratches her chin. "I've spoken to Dr. Jones about you, and his vision is that you and I work on two sides of the same problem."

"Oh?"

"I'll focus on enrichment that trains the animals we plan to release, with your engineering help when needed. Meanwhile, your focus will be on making the lives of our charges more fulfilling and fun while they're here."

Wow. I like the way Dr. Jones and Rose framed this, especially because this task is where I shine, at least when it comes to octopuses.

"That sounds great," I say. "What are you guys doing now?"

She gives me a long list. A lot of it is standard and boring stuff, like giving ping-pong balls to the fish and using tubes, tunnels, air bubbles, and so on.

"What's my budget?" I ask.

"Why?"

"There are some cheap fun things we can do, like

adding mirrors to tanks, but if you can afford it, a submersible computer tablet could be a great toy for most species—that, or at least a TV outside the tank. My octopus enjoys both."

What I don't mention is that Beaky's favorite app is Tinder. He uses his arms to swipe left and right on random dudes on my account, but since I'm not ready to date, I ignore all the resulting messages and dick pics. The latter might actually be what Beaky is after, as they may remind him of something delicious, like geoduck clams.

"Does that work with fish?" Rose asks.

I nod. "At the last place I worked, there was a Pacific blue tang who seemed depressed. After I donated my old tablet to use in her tank and set it up to play some carefully selected content on a loop, she really perked up. Some fish also like music and—"

"You have a decent budget." She turns her laptop to show me the sum. "To go beyond this, you'd need to talk to Dr. Jones, as he ultimately makes the budgetary decisions."

"Great. That amount can get me started. How about I have a look around to see if there's any low-hanging fruit?"

"Perfect." She stands up and extends her hand. "I can tell we'll have fun working together."

I give her hand an enthusiastic shake. "Before I go… I wanted to talk to you about my octopus."

She lets go of my hand. "I assume Aruba mentioned the Flipper-Athena fiasco?"

"She did, but I'd like to remind you that octopus-proofing enclosures is my specialty. My octopus hasn't escaped once—nor have any of those in the tanks that use my designs."

She looks at her desk. "How about you make your case to Dr. Jones instead?"

Carp. I thought this was just a formality, but now I'm beginning to seriously worry.

"In that case, can you introduce me to Dr. Jones? I'd like to speak to him now."

She pales. "Dr. Jones is a very busy man. You have to make an appointment."

I sigh. "Who do I talk to about that?"

"HR."

I frown. "Isn't that you?"

She pantomimes putting on a hat. "It is now." Plopping back down, she types away on her computer. "Today, he's booked all day," she mutters. "Tomorrow too. Ah. Here. How about eleven a.m., two days from now?"

"Sure," I say, hiding my annoyance.

This means two more sleepless nights.

"Great." She gestures for the door.

I'm about to leave when she clears her throat.

"Since I still have my HR hat on, I should mention that we have a very strict policy against employees fraternizing."

I almost tell her it's not a problem because I didn't like any of the guys I saw on the tour, but instead, I go with a noncommittal eyebrow lift.

"You should especially keep this policy in mind when you work with the otters."

"Sure." I leave her office, suddenly overcome with the desire to check out the otter habitat.

It was the only stop not available on Aruba's tour—and now I think there was a reason besides "otter chaos."

Yep. Dex is the name of the guy who works with the otters, and he is definitely cute. He's not my type, though. In fact, he reminds me somewhat of his charges, not to mention their close relative, the weasel.

"Frozen ice blocks with fish are their favorite toys," Dex tells me when I ask him about current otter enrichment. "As far as non-edible things, they really like playing Frisbee, getting sprayed with a warm water hose, and playing with floating plastic toys and hollow coconut shells."

I smile. Beaky likes that last one also. "Have you tried using a laser pointer to play with them?"

He rubs his small hands over his whiskers. "You mean like the ones people use with cats?"

"Yeah. I tried that at the last place I worked, and the otters loved it."

His eyes widen. "That's such a great idea. I'll get one and try it tomorrow. Can't wait."

"Cool. Hope they like it. Now if you'll excuse me, I'm going to go check out the rest of the exhibits."

And more importantly, I don't want Rose to see me here and think I'm already testing that most sacred HR rule.

Dex thanks me for the idea again, and I scram. Finding a shady spot, I reapply my sunblock and finally eat my lunch for breakfast.

Even though it feels a little nutty to do this on my first day at Sealand, I check Octoworld for new job openings. Sadly, there are none.

With a sigh, I do what I often do after this: check out the social media pages of Octoworld's founder (and my idol), Ezra Shelby. Ezra is a legendary marine biologist and is to octopuses what Jane Goodall is to chimpanzees.

I frown at Ezra's most recent educational post. Being a fan of *Finding Dory*, I'm not sure how I feel about what it says:

First things first (spoiler alert): Finding Nemo *starts with male and female clownfish tending to their eggs, and then the female is eaten by a barracuda and all but one egg disappear.*

I stop reading for a second to catch my breath. That scene caused me psychological harm and is why I highly prefer the more cheerful sequel about Dory.

Now, let's talk about how things would've proceeded if the movie was based on real marine biology, Ezra's post continues. *For the moment, let's forget that male clownfish eat damaged eggs, so Nemo, with his tiny fin, might not have been born in the first place. But assuming he was born, Nemo would've been an undifferentiated hermaphrodite, as all the young members of his species are. With the female gone and no other clownfish around, Nemo's father would've become a female. Thus—again, if there were no other clown-*

fish around—Nemo would grow up a male and then mate with his father—

I chuckle. As much as I respect Ezra, she needs to give Pixar a break. Sea creatures don't talk to each other either; it's poetic license. Though there are *Mormyridae*, also known as elephantfish. They have huge brains and do communicate with each other via electrical signals, as well as—

A videocall lights up my phone.

It's Blue, one of my sextuplet sisters.

I pick up.

Though our faces are identical, Blue's short hairdo makes it impossible to confuse us the way people did when we were little.

She's holding her cat, Machete, on her lap, which makes her look like a Bond villain—a comparison she might appreciate because she's a super-fan of that franchise.

"Hey," Blue says. "How's your first day going?"

I smile. Blue is currently my favorite sister because she let me crash with her right after I left my asshole ex. She also made sure he'd think twice before coming anywhere near me.

"See for yourself." I pan my phone so she can see the otter and the manatee exhibits in the distance. "I'm surrounded by Florida, for better or worse."

She grins. "I'm guessing you're single-handedly keeping some lucky sunblock manufacturer in business?"

I roll my eyes. Being my fave doesn't mean she can

tease me and get off scot-free. "Do you have any idea how many herons I've seen since I arrived?"

Her grin drops, and I feel a tiny pang of guilt. Unlike my perfectly reasonable avoidance of sun damage, Blue is afraid of birds—even the cutest ones, like penguins.

"How many?" She squeezes her monster cat, and he hisses at her before jumping away. "A siege?"

I shake my head. "If a siege is what you call a bunch of them, then no. It was just a pair, and from far away. I'm pretty sure Beaky wanted to eat them."

"How is he?" she asks. "Have you gotten him a bigger tank?"

I tell her that I haven't yet. Then she asks about our grandparents, and I bring her up to speed.

"Well, keep me posted," she says. "Oh, and heads up, I heard from Fabio that he and Lemon are planning to vacation in Florida soon. Guess where they'll be staying?"

Carp. The answer is with my grandparents, obviously.

Fabio is our childhood friend who happens to be a porn star, and Lemon is another one of my sextuplet sisters. Ironically, given her sour name, she's got the sweetest tooth of us all.

"Sounds like my style is about to be majorly cramped." I wipe a bead of sweat from my brow with a napkin.

"You have style?" Blue peers at me intently.

I pretend like I'm listening to a distant sound. "Did I just hear someone go, 'Mine, mine, mine?'"

She cringes, which means she got the reference to seagulls—the reason she still hasn't seen *Finding Nemo* to the end.

"I'd better go," she says.

"Yeah, thanks for checking in," I say and hang up, only to instantly get another call.

It's my dad, calling without video—like a caveperson.

"Hi, Dad," I say.

"Thing Five," he says, using his nickname for me. "You're on speaker phone. I've got your mom here too."

"Hi, Mom."

"Namaste, sunshine," she says. "How are you feeling?"

I'm glad we're doing this without video, so she can't see me cringe. Between the breakup with my ex and my move to Florida, I'm officially the child my parental units have decided to worry about.

"I'm great." I force a smile onto my face in the hopes of making my voice more cheerful. "Everything is awesome."

I know I sound like that song from *The LEGO Movie*, but if I'm not peppy enough, Mom will dish out a ton of unsolicited advice, most of it orgasm-related.

"Good to hear," both parents say, though Mom sounds less convinced than Dad.

"What's up with you guys?" I ask, praying to Cthulhu that they accept the change of subject.

"Not much," Dad says. "Unless... did we tell you we're also going to be in Florida?"

"Oh?"

Is anyone in my family *not* coming to the Sunshine State?

"Yeah, we're going to be visiting my parents," Dad says.

Whew. A different set of grandparents. I love Mom and Dad, but having them, Lemon, Fabio, Grandma, and Grandpa under one roof would make me want to shoot myself with one of Grandpa's guns.

"Hope you have a great time," I say.

"Yeah," Mom says. "We have a lot planned."

They share their itinerary with me while I finish my meal.

After I hang up, I feel rejuvenated, so I spend the rest of the day getting to know the sea creatures whose lives I hope to make more fun in the near future.

I see a lot of easy wins. Some critters might benefit from something as simple as a Mr. Potato Head, while others might like LEGO bricks. In a few cases, some of the animals just need a more interesting way to get their food.

As I head home, I almost feel good about my new job. If I get Beaky's fate sorted out, I might actually enjoy working here... even if it's not Octoworld.

———

A Tesla is blocking the driveway when I arrive. My grandparents must have friends over for dinner.

I park on the street and sneak into the house through the garage. There are voices in the kitchen that support my "friends" theory.

Tiptoeing into the guest room, I change into something comfy and toss Beaky a crab trapped inside a new puzzle of my own design.

The God Emperor accepts this offering, priestess-subject. We shall let the world revolve around the Tank for one more day.

I wait to see if Beaky solves the puzzle instantly—something that has happened in the past.

Nope.

He coils around it, his gaze intense.

"Have fun," I say, and head out of the room.

As I approach the kitchen, I hear three voices: those of my grandparents and another, a vaguely familiar male one.

Wait a second.

It can't be. Can it?

As I step into the kitchen, my eyes no doubt resemble those of the bubble-eye goldfish.

It's as I thought.

For some unfathomable reason, Aqua-ass is here, at the dinner table.

CHAPTER
Four

MOUTH OPEN, I gape at him, taking in the long, gold-streaked hair, the wide shoulders, those full, sexy lips...

Was he *this* freaking hot the other day? No, couldn't have been. For one thing, he's dressed nicer today, in a pair of khaki pants and a white polo shirt that highlights the strong, tanned line of his throat and accentuates the bulge of his powerful biceps. Despite my intense dislike of the man (and hopefully not because of it), I want him to drag me into the guest room and fuck me hard, like a dolphin.

"What the hell is he doing here?" I ask no one in particular.

Grandma grins at me. "You made me realize I was being a bad neighbor, so I rectified the situation."

I should've known. There was that gleam in her eyes when I talked about Aqua-ass.

Speaking of Mr. Ass. He looks up from his plate,

and his cyan eyes narrow on my face. "*This* is the granddaughter you said would be joining us?"

Why is even *that* sexy? By Cthulhu's mighty wings, someone better give that Olive-ravishing dolphin some Viagra.

Before any of my horniness shows on my face, I turn away demonstratively. "Enjoy your dinner. I'm out."

My grandmother gasps theatrically, as though living in Florida has made her internalize the famous Southern hospitality.

A scraping sound makes me look back.

Aqua-ass is on his feet now. "No. She should eat with her family. I'll leave."

I roll my eyes. "*She* is still here."

Grandpa stands up, his face stormy. "Gia worked on this food all day. You're adults. Can't you at least pretend to be civil for an hour?"

Carp. He's got a point.

Even Aqua-ass looks chastened—and these aren't *his* grandparents.

Fine. I won't be shellfish. But can I have dinner with this guy without slapping—or licking—his gorgeous face? Or my grandparents doing something that makes me want to die of embarrassment?

Unlikely, but I don't have a choice.

"I'll stay if he promises not to mention my octopus." Despite the guilt, the sentence comes out petulant.

Aqua-ass sits back down. "No octopuses at all. We

can also avoid mention of all sea life, just in case that offends your delicate sensibilities."

"Deal," I say. "We can also skip talk of hot dogs and tofu."

He smirks. "No need. I can handle talking about my pet."

Grandpa sits back down with a sigh, muttering something like "children."

I don't reply to Grandpa's jab because my genius counterargument is "he started it." Instead, I smile prettily at our guest. "What about news stories?"

The smirk wanes. "What about them?"

"Could you handle it if I quoted some actual news here at the dinner table? It's a family tradition."

"No, it's not," Grandpa says.

"The opposite might be true," Grandma says.

"It's fine." Aqua-ass runs his hand through his long, sun-streaked hair. "We can talk about whichever news stories you want."

Am I staring too much at his hair? Moving quickly, I pull out my phone and look up a few stories I can taunt him with.

Just as I glance up and open my mouth to quote some, Grandma speaks up. "How about we eat before we talk?"

As if waiting for this moment, my treacherous stomach makes a noise that sounds like "feed me" in whale speech.

Fine.

I scan the table for something to shove into my

mouth, something edible that is not Aqua-manhood, which is what my wunderpus would opt for.

To my chagrin, today is my grandparents' weekly Fish Day—something Grandpa's doctor recommended. Sucks. I was craving serious meat, but as the name implies, Fish Day means they only have roasted salmon on the table—useless to me, since I follow the motto of the shark support group from *Finding Nemo*: "Fish are friends, not food."

The good news is that Grandma has made some of my favorite side dishes: quinoa with mushrooms, rice pilaf with dates, and tortilla chips with salsa and guacamole. There's also a big salad here, but I avoid it. The last thing I want is to give Grandpa a reason to make olive-oil-related jokes at my expense.

I'm not sure if Aqua-ass is trying to copy me as a form of subtle teasing, or if he simply doesn't like salmon, but his plate has all the same items as mine.

When she hears me crunching on the chips, Grandma nods approvingly. "Good girl. Let me introduce the two of you." She gestures at Aqua-ass. "Olive, meet our neighbor, Oliver. Oliver, meet our granddaughter, Olive."

"Yes, I know what you're thinking," Grandpa says to me before I can react to the intro. "He's even more olive than you."

I groan, nearly choking on my chips.

"I like the name Oliver," Grandma says. "Reminds me of *Oliver Twist*, one of my favorite movies."

Oh? I thought her favorite movie would have

naughty tentacles in it. Come to think of it, someone who's never heard of Charles Dickens's classic tale might think the word "Twist" is referring to some kind of twisty tentacle.

Oliver's cyan eyes gleam with amusement, which makes me wish he could twist me... in bed.

"I was named after my grandfather," he says.

Grandpa looks wistful. He, my dad, and my other grandpa are all disappointed about the lack of boys in our huge family.

"One of Olive's sisters is named after me," Grandma says. "And Gia's twin is named after their other grandmother."

"Right," I say, keeping the bitterness out of my voice. "Whereas I and my litter of sextuplet sisters were named on a whim."

Oliver's eyes widen to the size of two lakes, but before he can ask anything, Grandpa chuckles. "It wasn't a complete whim. I seem to recall your parents were at the Olive Garden when they brainstormed all of your names. There might've been a dirty martini with an olive involved."

I hope that's a joke, though I can easily picture this happening. I have a sister named Lemon, and her name could've come about thanks to a glass of water served to my dad. Honey might've gotten her name because that's what my mom wanted in her tea. Pixie, Blue, and Pearl could owe their names to a waitress with a pixie haircut and blue eyes who wore a pearl necklace that day. After all, both of our parental units like *The Usual*

Suspects, especially the part where surroundings were used for inspiration.

"So… you have eight granddaughters all together?" Oliver asks, incredulous.

Good for this Florida man. He can count. At least to eight.

"Yep," Grandma says, beaming with pride. "The pair of twins and the hexad of sextuplets."

Should she be testing a Florida man's intelligence by using fancy words with Greek roots like "hex?" And since she went there, shouldn't she have said "dyad" instead of "pair" for consistency?

"What about you?" Grandpa asks Oliver, who looks like he's still digesting the weirdness that is my family. "Any siblings?"

Recovering, he nods. "Two brothers."

Interesting. I wonder if they have jaws as chiseled as his. And eyes as—

Grr. Must get a grip. Seriously, why am I lusting after this particular guy so badly? There are plenty of other, more polite fish in the sea.

Stuffing my mouth with food, I ignore my grandparents' follow-up questions for Oliver. Instead, I sneak a peek at my phone to read some stories about his peers. The hope is that they'll tamp down on my overactive libido.

"Easter Bunny beats up Florida man"—and there's a video of this. "Florida man masturbates into stuffed animals at Walmart." Lovely. Another tried to shoot a puppy, which is bad enough, but then in a twist that is pure Florida, the puppy inadvertently landed a paw on the trigger and shot the man instead. Another man set his home on fire with a bomb he made from a bowling ball. Another stole an ambulance from a hospital and drove it into the mud. Yet another Florida dude slashed an 88-year-old woman's tires for sitting in his favorite Bingo chair. But my favorites are: "Florida man proudly claims he was the first person to vape semen," and "Florida man dances on patrol car in order to 'escape vampires.'"

"What's so funny?" Grandma asks.

Carp. Busted. "I was just reading stories about Florida men." I lock eyes challengingly with Oliver's cyan gaze—a miscalculation because now I want to go snorkeling in it.

Grandma claps her hands excitedly. "Do they talk about how amazingly attractive they are? When we first moved here, I thought there must surely be something in the water."

Hey, at least she didn't say she wishes they had tentacles.

I check Grandpa for any sign of jealousy, but he's busy clearing his plate—which I hope doesn't mean they have an open marriage.

"No," I say. "These articles are about crimes." I recite the ones I just read, and then I add, "Oh, and Florida men must really not like cars." I point at my screen. "One fired a musket at them while dressed as a pirate, while another guy got naked and threw rocks at them." I see Oliver wince, so I tack on, "Speaking of naked—

they often are, like the one who humped a tree and then punched a deputy."

Good going. Now I'm picturing the Florida man in front of me naked, which would result in a story along the lines of: "Unfairly delicious Florida man takes off clothes; all surrounding ovaries spontaneously combust."

"It's always warm here." Oliver puts down his fork next to his now-empty plate, his eyebrows pulled together into a broody expression that belies his surfer looks. "Makes it more likely that idiots will get naked. Also makes it so that people are outside in public more, which leads to more crime. I bet when it's cold in other states—which is most of the time—they hump their house plants instead of a tree outside."

Cthulhu curse him. He's managing to look sexy during a debate. I want to smooth that pleat between his brows with my finger and then lick said finger. "I don't think the weather accounts for the sheer number of these articles."

He sighs. "That has more to do with the Sunshine Law."

I perk up. "Does it require people to wear sunblock? I'd be all over that."

"Don't get her started on sunblock," Grandma says to Oliver in a loud, conspiratorial whisper. "Not if you ever want to go home... or step into the sunshine again."

Grandpa chuckles. "The Sunshine Law is for transparency. It allows regular citizens easy access to public records."

Oh, no. If we start Grandpa on local (or any) politics, we'll still be here when Cthulhu awakens.

"That's right," Oliver says. "That law means lazy reporters have instant access to arrest reports and mugshots."

Do I want him more when he's smug or grumpy?

I glance at my phone. "Did I mention the story where a knife-wielding Florida man tried to rescue his imaginary girlfriend from a garbage truck?"

Oliver looks at everyone but me. "We're also the third-largest state, and more people means more crime."

"Depends on the people," I say. "Did I mention the one where a Florida man shot his sister in the ass with a BB gun because she gave him a penis-shaped birthday cake?"

Grandma smacks herself on the forehead. "I totally forgot about the cake."

She leaps to her feet and rushes to the fridge. Pulling out a cheesecake, she brings it ceremoniously to the table.

I help myself to a large piece while Oliver ignores the treat and serves himself a big heap of salad instead.

"I got this at the bakery," Grandpa says. "What do you think?"

I taste the cake. "Yum. It's not as good as the ones you can get in New York, but—"

Oliver groans, making us all look at him—another

mistake on my part because my hormones might not be able to take much more of this. "That's such a typical New Yorker statement."

I scowl at him, more to hide my urge to nuzzle my face against his beard than because I'm mad. "It is?"

"We have the best pizza," he says with the most fake New Yorker accent I've ever heard. "Also, the best bagels. And hot dogs. Not to mention the museums. Oh, and pizza. Did I mention the best pizza?"

"Well…" I cut another sliver of cheesecake with my fork. "Is it our fault those things actually *are* superior in New York?"

As I stuff the cheesecake into my mouth, I can't help but wonder what this cake would look like if it were shaped like Oliver's Aqua-manhood. Something tells me I wouldn't want to shoot anyone's ass over it with a BB gun.

Oliver downs his water glass, managing to look frustrated in the process. "Do you know which state New Yorkers move to in droves?" he asks. "Fifty thousand just last year."

I make a circle with my fork. "I'm guessing Florida?"

He nods. "And do they ever go back to New York? Sadly, no."

"We wouldn't go back," Grandma says.

"No way," Grandpa says.

"Traitors," I say, making it sound like a cough.

Oliver forks a piece of romaine lettuce into his mouth and crunches into it with the kind of gusto people usually reserve for cake. "Where did you get such juicy lettuce?" he asks. "I'd like to buy some for Betsy." A warm smile curves his full, yummy lips as he says the name. "She's a lettuce connoisseur."

Grr. It takes all my willpower not to ask, "Who the hell is Betsy?" The surge of jealousy I feel is as irrational as the lust that's been fogging my brain. Still, a part of me hopes that Grandma will ask the question for me.

Given the limited info I've received, Betsy the Lettuce Connoisseur sounds thinner than I am and vaguely French. Is it wrong that I already hate her properly-nourished-with-fiber guts?

"You can't buy this lettuce. I grew it myself," Grandma says, and beams with the exact same pride as when she told him about my sisters. "The trick is the soil. You need to mix equal parts peat moss and compost, then add in some perlite, worm castings, and MYKOS."

Seriously, Grandma? All you had to do was ask about Betsy.

The warm smile is back on Oliver's face. "I'm not sure I can grow it in the quantities Betsy likes, but thanks for the tip. I've been wasting my compost on my lawn. Maybe it's time I start a garden."

He composts? Why doesn't Betsy? Is it sexist to assume this means they don't live together?

Come to think of it, if they lived together, wouldn't he have brought her with him to this dinner?

Grandpa frowns. "If you start a garden, make sure

it's behind your house, or else the HOA will be on your case."

"Really?" Oliver puts his fork down. "Over a garden?"

Well, that was a big mistake. For what feels like an hour, my grandparents take turns bashing the evil that is their HOA.

At some point, Oliver takes advantage of a lull in the HOA tirade and stands up, unfolding his tall, muscular frame and making me drool anew. "It was a pleasure having dinner with you." He looks pointedly at my grandparents.

Nice. He might as well have said it wasn't a pleasure sharing a meal with *me*—which is fine. The feeling is mutual, especially if you ignore the dampness in my panties.

"Olive, please walk Oliver out," Grandma says, her eyes gleaming mischievously.

Wait a second. Is she setting us up?

Yep. Given the self-satisfied look she gives Grandpa, this is all part of a Machiavellian plan to get great-grandkids. I bet it goes deep. Maybe even the tentacle porn was part of it—a way to make sure I'd be nice and horny for this dinner.

But no. I mentioned this guy to her myself. The porn was prior to that.

I leap to my feet before Oliver says something nasty, like, "I can walk myself out." The problem is, in my hurry, I trip over the leg of my chair and begin to fall, flailing my arms like the inflatable Wacky Waving Tube Man.

Strong hands catch me before I can break my head open.

I smell fresh ocean surf.

Wow. That's nice.

"Be careful," Oliver says from a few inches behind me, confirming that he is indeed the one who caught me.

Anger shoots through me as I process his words. Jerkily, I twist out of his grasp. "Don't tell me what to do." My breathing is fast, and my teeth are clenching.

By Cthulhu, it looks like I'm not only triggered when someone tells me what to wear. What to do is also on the list.

Ugh. I may actually need ex-related therapy after all.

"Fine." Oliver turns his back to me. "Next time, go ahead and fall."

What a gentleman.

I proceed with the charade of walking him out, going as far as demonstratively opening the front door and holding it wide, like a doorman at a hotel.

"Thanks," he says, stepping out and stopping right next to me. He seems to mean it.

With him this close, the smell of ocean is stronger, and it must contain some sort of pheromone—either that, or someone's snuck a jellyfish into my panties.

My anger fades. Even if my name weren't what it is, I wouldn't ignore a proffered olive branch.

I push the door closed and give him an almost earnest smile. "I'm sorry if this whole thing was as transparent to you as it was to me."

The corners of his eyes crinkle. "You mean your grandmother's matchmaking?"

"Yeah. That."

He puts a hand on his chest. "I didn't notice it at all."

I moisten my suddenly dry lips, but it doesn't help. I think I'm experiencing wunderpus-related dehydration. "Grandma means well, but obviously, we're the worst match ever."

He stares hungrily at my lips. "Obviously?"

"Well, yeah." I double-check the glass portion of the door to make sure Grandma isn't snooping. "We're like two betta fishes sharing a tiny tank."

He steps forward, enveloping me in more of his sea-scented pheromones. "Is talking about small tanks allowed again?"

"See? Worst match ever." I resist the urge to tuck a strand of hair behind his ear.

He dips his head. "Whom are you trying to convince?"

I feel myself getting pulled toward him, like a tidal wave to the shore.

No. No way.

With effort, I take a step back.

He looks disappointed for a moment, then glances behind me and grins.

Turning, I catch Grandma with her nose flattened against the glass of the front door.

Ugh, I knew she would snoop.

"I should go." Oliver's hungry gaze is on my lips again.

Resisting the urge to lick said lips, I extend my hand. "Have a good night."

With a sexy smirk, he reaches out to shake on it.

By Cthulhu's dopamine. When my skin touches his callused palm, a jolt of electricity shoots up my whole body. It reminds me of the time I touched an electric eel, only it's pleasure that's coursing through my nerve endings instead of pain.

Just like with the eel, though, my heart is at risk of stopping. But unlike with the eel, my ovaries are in trouble too.

At some point, he gently pulls his hand back.

Right. It's his, so that's fair.

In a stupefied haze, I watch him stride over to his Tesla, get inside, and drive off.

It takes all of three seconds for him to park in the nearby driveway—at the house with the solar panels.

I look back at the door as if to ask my grandmother what just happened.

She's grinning like a loon, clearly of no help.

"Oh, boy," she says when I step back inside. "That was pathetic."

CHAPTER
Five

IF GRANDMA IS anything like my sisters, my best strategy is to disengage.

"How weird," I say. "Why did Oliver drive such a short distance?"

She puts her hands on her hips. "Because he came here straight from work. Nice try changing the subject."

Sneaky Grandma, slipping the job bit in. From prior conversations, I happen to know that she's strongly opposed to women dating men who don't have a job, unless "they're retired, like your grandfather."

I fake a yawn. "What time is it? I'm feeling pooped."

Grandma positions her tiny body in my way. "Nope. We're talking about that disaster of a date."

Fine. I'll unleash my second-best dealing-with-a-sister strategy—defense as offense. "A date?" I make the question sound as indignant as I can. "Who said it was okay for you to pimp me out like that?"

Grandma rolls her eyes, and it's eerie how much she resembles my sisters in this moment. "Please. I just invited a neighbor for dinner. The lady—and I'm currently using this term loosely—doth protest too much."

I groan theatrically, then remind myself to respect my elders.

Yeah. Must respect the elders, especially when it's hard to do.

"Grandma. He hates me," I say when I have my knee-jerk reactions under control. "You saw."

She pats her white locks. "What I saw was him looking at you the way your grandfather looks at me—like he wants to cover you in whipped cream and lick you all night."

How can the same image be both adorable and pukey?

"Did you smoke something as an appetizer today?" I ask. "I know they legalized medical marijuana here in Florida, but I didn't know you partied this hard."

"I didn't smoke anything," Grandma says. "I did eat some cannabis-infused maple-chipotle peanuts earlier, but that doesn't change the facts."

Wow. I was just kidding. My grandparents get high? I have a feeling my parents would be pleased.

"Oliver and I hate each other," I say firmly.

"Doubt it." She finally moves out of my way. "But even so, you can still hate-fuck him, can't you?"

I skedaddle without dignifying that last bit with a response.

———

Still, as I go through my evening routine, Grandma's idea wriggles in my brain, like a fish roundworm.

Could I hate-fuck Oliver? Should I? Would that quench my lust?

After a long deliberation, I decide that a) it's a bad idea, and more importantly b) he wouldn't want to participate anyway—no matter what Grandma thought she saw. Oh, and c) there's Betsy. If he's her man and I hate-fuck him, she'll rightfully hate me, and that's a weird spiral of hate I want no part of.

What sucks is that I'm not feeling sleepy in the slightest, which makes me dread a repeat of last night.

Well, maybe I can get ahead of the game today. I take out the tentacle dildo from the nightstand. Is it considered hate-fucking if I hate myself for picturing Oliver as I masturbate?

From the corner of my eye, I catch Beaky waving his arms.

I smile at him. "Hey, bud, did you want a cuddle?"

Beaky turns white.

Is the Tank not the center of the Universe? Does the Universe not revolve around the Tank? Do sea anemones not poop from their mouths?

Oh, that reminds me: he didn't get his cuddle last night. No wonder he's so eager for one.

Carefully, I unseal the tank.

Beaky knows what's up and swims to the surface.

I extend my hand.

He envelops it with two of his arms. It feels like a tickly kiss when he brushes his suckers against my skin.

Octopuses can touch, taste, and smell with the two-hundred-and-eighty suckers on each of their arms. The suckers are pretty sensitive too, which is why I try to only cuddle with him before bed, when I'm clean and won't introduce unpleasant chemicals into the equation. My last ex called this evening routine obscene, but I don't see the difference between this and someone's dog licking their hand.

Beaky's intelligent eyes are hypnotizing.

I grin as I recall how much he disliked said ex. At least I assume that's why he'd squirt the asshole with cold water every chance he could get.

Using two more arms, Beaky starts to pull me into the cold water of the tank.

"Sorry, bud," I say as I pull back. "As much as I wish I could, I can't live underwater."

Realizing that I'm being serious about the whole not-drowning thing, he lets me go with one of the arms, then extends it quickly toward the nightstand.

"Wait, no!" I yelp, but it's too late.

Beaky is already at the bottom of the tank, the tentacle dildo in his grasp.

"Give that back." I stick my hand into the water.

Beaky turns all black and makes himself big—an

aggression display that makes him look like a vampire's cape.

I jerk my hand away. Those same suckers that gently "kiss" my arms during cuddles have the potential to grab on hard enough to leave a bruise at best or pluck an eye out at worst.

Also—though I doubt Beaky would ever do this to me—he does have a beak that can bite and deliver venomous saliva.

"Fine. Keep it," I tell him.

This impertinence is why we make the sun rise each day, no matter how much you loathe it.

I shake my head as Beaky figures out how to turn on the vibration on the dildo, then turns a kaleidoscope of colors as he investigates this new development.

"Don't get too used to that," I say. "The battery will die eventually."

Then again, maybe I can rig up something that would charge the battery? Being waterproof, the dildo charges via a cable with a magnet on top, so all I'd need is—

I stop myself and grin. Looks like Beaky and I might've just invented a new—albeit slightly eyebrow-raising—form of octopus entertainment. I can only imagine what the folks at Octoworld would think of it, or the people at Sealand for that matter.

Then again, repurposing toys is not a new concept for me. Lots of children's and dog's toys are the bases for my inventions. However, I've never ventured so far outside the box as to think of human sex toys in that way... but I might now.

In fact, now that I think about it, fake pussies have a lot of potential. Their texture might well appeal to all cephalopods, not just octopuses.

I re-seal the tank very carefully. This lid is my proudest creation. Octopuses have no bones, so even a six-hundred-pound specimen can squeeze itself through an opening the size of a quarter. Basically, if the beak fits, the rest of the octopus will as well.

I watch Beaky have fun with the dildo, and part of me wonders if he might be using it as a human would —to masturbate.

It's possible, but unlikely, and not because Beaky is a male.

Octopus reproduction is as fascinating as it is strange. First, there's their odd plumbing. Instead of a penis, a male octopus has a specialized arm called the hectocotylus. During mating, this arm goes into one of the two siphons on a female's mantle—the orifice that's also in charge of breathing, expelling waste, and jetting out water when the octopus wants to swim or annoy my ex-boyfriend.

Secondly, there's the sexual cannibalism— commonly done by the larger females. Sometimes males get strangled during the sex act, sometimes soon after. Some males even choose to sacrifice their entire mating arm to the female in order to get away. Talk about swiping right.

And hey, if I had been an octopus and bigger than

my ex, I would've also strangled him for demeaning me and telling me what to wear—though I wouldn't have eaten him. Then again, I'm not swimming around starved all the time.

Arms wrapped around the dildo, Beaky turns off the vibration, then turns it back on again.

He then finds the pulse mode and keeps that on.

"Have fun," I say. "I'm going to sleep."

Know that this latest offering greatly pleases us, priest-ess-subject. This is what embracing Cthulhu's mighty hecto-cotylus would feel like, blessed be his wings.

First things first: I check if I can block out the morning sun from the window. Nope. The curtains are more decorative than functional. Fine. I sunblock my face and neck, then turn off the lights and get under the blanket.

Hmm. With the dildo missing, I only have one choice left—old-school diddling.

With an effort of will, I banish Oliver from my mind and slide my hand under the blanket.

Carp.

As I touch myself, images of Oliver's fingers—and Aqua-manhood—intrude at regular intervals, making the whole process feel hotter. I guess I like that I'm being a naughty, dirty girl who does what she shouldn't.

It's only after I finally come undone that I curse my traitorous imagination.

The worst part is that, despite the orgasm, I can't

sleep. The looming conversation with Davy—I mean Dr.—Jones is back at the forefront of my mind.

Grr. I should've done some physical exercise to tire myself out before heading to bed. Apparently, hate-fucking myself isn't enough.

Desperate, I start counting octopuses in my head and drift off at some point after thirteen hundred.

———

I'm groggy when I get to work the next day.

To wake myself up, I ponder the biggest challenge of my career: entertainment for starfish.

I scratch my head.

What can be fun for a creature that doesn't have blood, moves using little tube feet, and eats by pushing its stomach through its mouth?

For starters, I could make one half of the starfish tank dark, while leaving the other half exposed to light. These creatures have eyes at the ends of their arms, and I figure if you have eyes, you can find visual stimuli entertaining.

I'm halfway through my little project when someone clears her throat.

"Hey," I say to Aruba as I look up. "I was just thinking of enrichment for starfish."

Aruba wrinkles her nose. "The proper term is 'sea star.'"

I sigh. It's true that starfish aren't really fish. They don't have gills and so on. Still, I don't get the need to be such a stickler for terminology. Crayfish aren't fish either, but no one tries to call them "river crays."

"Do the dolphins look bored today?" I ask.

She shakes her head vehemently. "Mrs. Aberdeen asked me to find you. She has an urgent task for you from Dr. Jones himself."

The reverent way she says Dr. Jones makes me cringe.

"Thanks," I say. "I'll be over in a second."

With a satisfied nod, she spins on her heels and strides out.

"I'll be back," I tell the starfish and make my way to Rose's office.

––––––––

"The manatees are to be your top priority," Rose says instead of a hello when I enter her office.

"Oh?"

"Dr. Jones thinks they're on the verge of depression, and our usual enrichment doesn't seem to be working."

I picture the mercurial Dr. Jones as Davy Jones once again, stroking his octopus beard, his expression stern when he discovers the state of manatee affairs.

I smooth my hands over my khaki shorts. "What do you currently do for them?"

She hands me a printout. "It's all there. My favorite was when we stuck kale into a carved-out pumpkin and attached that to a metal tube. They loved that, as well as a tube with broccoli sticking out of it."

"Encouraging foraging is great." I skim the list. "Let me see if I can take things to another level."

"Great," she says. "That'll help you when you talk to Dr. Jones tomorrow. He's a huge manatee fan."

I chuckle. "So I should butter him up with manatee talk?"

She meets my gaze, her expression serious. "You'll need all the help you can get. Aruba just sent an email proposing we create a memorial for Flipper, which no doubt has reminded Dr. Jones of that awful business."

Carp. And I was the one who reminded Aruba about that incident by asking about octopuses.

I leap to my feet. "Okay, I'll be by the manatees if you need me."

She waves, and I make my way to the exhibit, reapplying sunblock as I go.

My phone dings.

Ah. A message from Lemon—and I can guess what she'll say.

Hey cistern, how are tits going?

Grinning, I write back:

My tits are fine, thanks for asking, but I don't like being compared to a cistern or other large objects.

The reply is instant:

Funky autoerotic asphyxiation.

I snort. My autocorrect has been acting up too, but hers seems to be going out of its way to be evil.

Did you mean 'fucking autocorrect asshole?'"

She replies with a thumbs up and adds, *I wanted to tell you that Fabulous and I will cum tonight.*

It just gets better and better.

By Fabulous, did you mean Fabio... and by cum, did you mean arrive in Florida?

Fabio is gay, so it's unlikely he'd want to cum anywhere near her, or any female.

She replies with an undecipherable string of curses directed at her autocorrect, some of which get autocorrected into gibberish.

Sounds like I'll see you when you get here.

Putting my phone away, I look around.

The manatee tank is huge, as it should be. These gentle giants weigh more than a ton and need the space.

Finding a shady spot, I watch them, increasingly fascinated. Though I'm not a shrink like Rose, these animals don't seem depressed to me, just bored. They're amusing themselves by barrel rolling and body surfing—the most adorable sight aside from my octopus changing colors.

I take my phone out and supplement what I already know about these creatures with some online research, focusing specifically on this branch of the family—the Florida manatee, or *Trichechus manatus latirostris*. They are sea mammals, of course. In fact, they're a distant cousin of elephants, which is neat.

Maybe I could try some elephant enrichment on the manatees? Elephants like to play with tires and giant balls, for example.

What else? Oh, here we go. They eat ten percent of their massive body weight in sea salad. Cool. That provides tons of opportunities to make their eating more fun—something the folks here have already discovered. Some articles refer to manatees as "sea cows"—which sounds a bit like body shaming, though maybe it's more of a reference to all the grazing they do, and to their gentle natures.

One useful factoid is that they like warm water.

Maybe I could rig up a device that would spray them with a jet of extra-warm water when they push a button? Better yet, could we build a Jacuzzi for them? Sounds pricey, but if Dr. Jones likes them so much, maybe he'll splurge?

Another useful tidbit: despite their relatively small eyes and ears, they have excellent sight and hearing. Would they like watching TV? I bet they would, especially if I come up with interesting content, like a sea-related nature program, a salad-oriented cooking show, or that "Gangnam Style" video on a loop. Again, price could be a problem. A small tablet wouldn't cut it for creatures this size. We would probably need to waterproof an eighty-five-inch TV and drop it into the tank.

Some facts about manatees are fascinating but unusable. My favorite is how they're sometimes confused for mermaids. Since I'm an aspiring mermaid myself, that makes me almost jealous.

Christopher Columbus was guilty of that mix-up—not surprising for a guy who managed to mistake North America for India. When he spotted three manatees near the Dominican Republic, he thought he saw mermaids, and described them as "not half as beautiful as they are painted." Hey, dude, poor manatees should not be judged by the unattainable beauty standards in fourteenth-century art. I mean, women in that time period would pluck their hair to get those highly desirable super-high foreheads that would nowadays send them hunting for Rogaine.

Thank goodness modern women aren't crazy enough to shave their hairline. We just shave where nature intended: armpits, legs, bikini area, fingers, and toes.

But back to manatees. Manatees have toenails on their flippers. Maybe we could get them pedicures? No, again with the beauty standards.

They're also known to be extremely dedicated moms. Hmm. Maybe that means they'd like to play with a baby manatee toy? It's possible, assuming I can find a submersible waterproof toy in the right size.

I make a note of these ideas and come up with more for the rest of the day.

———

Returning home that evening, I check the kitchen first to make sure Oliver isn't there again.

Nope. It's just the three of us eating dinner this time —and I'm not sure if I'm relieved or disappointed.

As we finish dinner, I start to preemptively worry about another sleepless night—that is, until I recall my idea to exercise in order to tire myself out.

Yeah. I've been in Florida for several days, yet still haven't gotten a chance to swim. More importantly, I haven't used my mermaid costume yet—an itch I feel like scratching even more after working with the mermaid-like manatees.

The more I think about it, the more I like this idea. The sun has set, so I'll just need a small coating of sunblock. And no one should be at the beach now, so I won't need to explain the mermaid bit.

As soon as the dinner is over, I put on my bikini swimming suit, top it with a wrap, and stuff my mermaid tail into a special carrier—a repurposed guitar case. Walking in a tail is too hardcore, even for a mermaid pro like me.

"Caper," Grandpa says sternly when I open the garage door.

"Where are you headed?"

I look down at my barely covered-up bathing suit. "The beach."

"I see," he says. "I'm going with you."

"No." I punctuate my point by vehemently shaking my head. I'm not yet ready to come out as a mermaid to my family.

He pulls out a shotgun from somewhere. "In that case, take this with you."

I blink a few times. "Grandpa, I'm going to a private beach in a private community."

He narrows his eyes. "Take it, or I'll forbid you from going."

"You can't forbid me. I'm an adult."

His bushy eyebrows snap together. "You're not acting like it."

"Because I refuse to kill people with a shotgun?"

He sighs. "What if I load it with bean bag rounds?"

I cock my head. "What?"

He removes the shells from the gun and replaces them with a different set in one quick motion. "Bean bag rounds are a special nonlethal ammo. It's what the police use during riots. They'll knock out your attacker but keep them alive. Usually."

I eye the stupid gun. "Is it legal for me to carry this?"

He thrusts the thing into my hands. "Who cares? There won't be anyone at that beach to get you in trouble."

"What's the point of a gun if there's no one there?" I mutter, but he's already gone.

With a sigh, I stash the shotgun in my mermaid tail carrier and head out. A short walk later, I'm on the beach, which is as empty as I hoped. The water is choppy tonight, but I'm a strong swimmer and there are rarely rip currents here.

Mermaid swim, here I come.

CHAPTER
Six

As OFTEN HAPPENS when I'm about to do this, I feel an excited fluttering in my stomach that reminds me of how hungry piranhas behave when you throw them a juicy piece of raw meat.

I love mermaid swims, but there are two reasons I don't do them more often. The obvious one is that not everyone understands the whole wearing-a-tail bit, and the less obvious is that for some reason, doing this makes me horny. And I mean *very* horny—almost as much as seeing Oliver the other day did. I have no idea why this is, and I'm not willing to see a therapist to find out.

I slip out of my flip-flops and carry them as the still-warm sand pleasantly squishes between my toes. Stopping far enough from the crashing surf to make sure my things don't float away, I take off the wrap and pull out the tail.

Damn. Could I be more of a weirdo? Just sliding my

legs into the waterproof fabric of the tail is an extremely sensual experience—like putting on sexy lingerie times a thousand.

Ignoring my libido, I secure my tail and debate the best way to get into the water. My options are to hop, crawl, or walk in tiny steps like someone about to poop their pants. When I took a mermaid swimming class, it was in a pool, so we crawled into the water due to safety concerns. In this case, given that the soft sand would break my fall if I lost my balance, I decide to hop, as that gets me to my destination faster.

I hop once, twice. By the fourth hop, I feel the cool wetness of the Atlantic Ocean through my tail, which is when a wave makes me trip and plop right into the water.

Giggling, I regain my equilibrium and begin swimming, using my core as I was trained, with my tail and arms pushing against the water.

Here we go. I feel weightless and free, and it's like a taste of childhood... at least if I ignore how insanely turned on I am.

Once I get enough exercise, I might pull the tail down a bit and spend a little quality time with my wunderpus. No one would be the wiser.

Wait. What is that sound?

I look toward the shore.

No one seems to be there. Still, maybe I'll save polishing my pearl for when I'm in bed. For now, I swim and swim, until my core muscles ache.

Okay. Enough. I return to the shore, moonlight illuminating my way. When the water is shallow enough, I get onto my tail and hop, but a wave knocks me over.

Fine.

I start to half-swim, half-crawl, and I'm partially out of the surf when a new wave comes, carrying *something*.

I squint, mentally cataloguing all the shark species native to Florida.

Whew.

It's not a shark. As the water recedes, I make out a surfboard with a man on it.

And not just any man.

Oliver.

Dressed in nothing but a pair of swim trunks.

CHAPTER
Seven

TIME SLOWS as I gape at every mouthwatering groove of Oliver's glistening-in-the-moonlight muscles. I imagine this is what Poseidon might look like, rising from the sea, his long, wet hair streaming down to his powerful shoulders. Or Aquaman. Yeah, definitely Aquaman. The resemblance is so strong I half expect the surfboard underneath him to turn into the Karathen.

He notices me as well, a startled look flitting over his features.

My heart rate doubles. I have no idea what to do, so I stay put, which keeps my tail hidden under the water.

"Hi," he says, gliding toward me over the surf, either to hear what I'll say or to see if my ovaries will explode at his proximity—which they might.

"Just keep swimming."

Yeah, I just blurted that. In my defense, I was already hot from the mermaid tail. With the introduction of his nearly naked gorgeousness into the equation, it's a wonder my brain is functioning enough to move my larynx.

He stops within licking distance, moonlight dancing in his eyes. His voice is low and deep. "You want me to leave?"

I shake my head, forcing my brain to function. "No. Sorry. I think I've watched *Finding Dory* one too many times."

A smirk curves his sexy lips. "I see... kelpcake."

Holy mackerel, that's a Dory reference. Now I *have* to fuck him. And not just hate-fuck him, either—not when he's a fellow *Finding Dory* enthusiast.

"So." He slides his board sideways, inching closer. Amusement glints in his eyes, along with something else. Something that reminds me of the tail I'm wearing and how it makes me feel. "How does this place compare to the beaches in New York?"

I'm so distracted by the sensations coursing through my body that it takes me a second to process his words. Once I do, my spine stiffens.

If he's back on the whole New York versus Florida thing, it might be a hate-fucking after all.

"Far Rockaway beaches are great, especially for surfing." I mean the words to come out sharp, but they're breathless instead. I run my tongue over my lips, tasting the salt of the ocean.

He stares at my lips, his nostrils flaring. "Aren't they covered in snow most of the time?"

My heartbeat intensifies, and I feel that tidal pull

toward him, just like on my grandparents' porch. My voice is even more breathless. "Snow or not, you'll find surfers there, in wetsuits when needed. Compared to them, Florida surfers are wimps."

Speaking of wetness and suits, it's a wonder my mermaid tail hasn't spontaneously slid off my body.

He leans in, his voice deepening. "Such a New Yorker."

That's it. I can't hold out any longer.

I grab the back of his head and drag him toward me.

Our mouths clash like two rogue waves. I drown in the sensations, a tiny ship in a hurricane. His lips are soft, delicious, his beard slightly rough. The smell of him is inseparable from that of the ocean, and just as intoxicating. His big, warm hands roam over my back as I slide my palm down his abs while kneading his wet hair and raking my nails over his scalp. Groaning, he deepens the kiss, his tongue dueling with mine, greedily exploring every inch of my mouth.

I've never been kissed like this. It's like I'm being devoured. Consumed. And I consume him right back, the heat inside me intensifying until I feel like the ocean around us may boil.

Growling low in his throat, he tears his lips away. His breath is harsh, his voice ragged. "What are we doing?"

Breathless, dizzy with want, I do what I've been dreaming about since I first saw him. I slide my hand into his trunks and wrap my fingers around a rock-hard and impressively thick Aqua-manhood. My voice is as hoarse as his. "Releasing frustration?"

His shaft jumps in my hold, impossibly stiffening further, and his voice drops another octave. "Do you have protection?" He pushes his trunks down, revealing an erection that even the mighty Cthulhu would be proud of.

Does a shotgun with nonlethal ammo count as protection?

Dazed, I shake my head. "I'm clean and on the pill."

My tail feels like it's suffocating my wunderpus, keeping my legs together when I want them apart. Without thinking, I begin to shimmy out of the tail.

A part of me worries that this is some sort of Machiavellian plot Oliver has concocted. Instead of convincing me to sell Beaky, maybe he decided to just get *me*. After all, married people share everything, even octopuses.

Wait. Married? What am I—

"I'm clean too," he says thickly. Then his gaze shifts to my lower body, revealed by a receding wave, and his jaw drops. "The fuck?"

Oh, shit. I had no intention of coming out as a mermaid to *him*. Only it's too late now. I raise my chin. "What? You've never seen a mermaid tail?" Finally managing to shimmy out of it, I use all of my arm strength to toss it onto the shore, just out of the waves' reach.

He copies my action with his trunks and pushes his

surfboard in the same direction, getting it out of the waves. "Why?"

"Long"—I slide my hand up and down his cock—"story. You sure you want to talk?"

His answer is another devouring kiss that steals my breath and makes the cool, wet sand under my butt feel like magma.

Smart man.

He rains hot, biting kisses over my neck and collarbone.

Did I say smart? I meant genius.

He pulls up my bikini top, and his lips travel down to my breasts, his hot, wet tongue flicking over my nipples, one after the other. I feel like I'm about to lose it. Breathing hard, I roll on top of him. The hard parts of him press into the soft parts of me, and I've never wanted something inside me so badly. My nipples could puncture steel, and there's enough blood in my clit to make it as hard as a pearl—my favorite euphemism for it.

"Ready?" I pant as I lean up so I can slide him where I need him.

"Fuck, yeah," he grunts, but then he stiffens, his eyes widening.

Carp. Did I scratch his dick? Worried, I roll off him as he begins to curse up a storm.

"What's the matter?"

He rolls onto his stomach and points at his tight ass. "It burns."

His ass *burns*? Sounds like he might need a proctologist.

Then I spot it.

A large jellyfish.

"That's a sea nettle," I say urgently. "Venomous."

"Fuck." He looks over his shoulder. "You're right."

Leaping to my feet, I rush to my mermaid tail carrier and rummage in it for something I can use to help him.

Nothing.

Well, almost nothing. There's the shotgun. I grab it and rush back.

His pained expression turns into a confused one. "Are you planning to shoot me?"

I roll my eyes. "Yeah. Figured I'd put you out of your misery." I step closer. "I want to use the barrel to push the jellyfish away before you get stung more, and to remove any tentacles if they're attached. Is that okay?"

He nods, grimacing, and I match actions to words.

"There might be nematocysts in your skin, so don't touch it," I say when I'm sure the jellyfish isn't going to harm him anymore.

"So what do I do?"

"How about we get you out of the water, in case another jellyfish turns up?" I help him crawl to the shore. "Let me take a look."

I crouch over his butt and squint. Oh, boy. His left buttock doesn't look good at all.

Unsure what to do, I blow on it carefully. "Is that better?"

He clenches his teeth. "No, but if you have a cigarette, I guess you could try blowing smoke up my ass."

I look around for his bag, but I don't see it. "Do you have a phone with you?"

"No." With a grunt, he pushes up onto his elbows. "Do you have any vinegar?"

I make sure my gun is pointing away from him to avoid the temptation to use it. "Is that a dig at my name?"

"What the fuck are you talking about?"

I narrow my eyes. "You know. Olive oil and vinegar go together."

He scowls at me. "I'm not interested in jokes or making a salad right now. I've heard vinegar can be helpful with these types of stings."

"Oh. Sorry. I don't have any vinegar. Do you?"

"Only my surfboard." He grimaces again. "I've also heard that the ammonia in urine can help. Might be an urban myth, though."

I back away. "I'm pretty sure that's a myth, but if you want to try it, I'll look away."

He clears his throat. "I can't exactly pee on my own ass."

Wait, what?

I gape at him incredulously. "You want *me* to pee on you?"

CHAPTER
Eight

"WANT IS PUTTING IT STRONGLY," Oliver growls. "I just need the pain to stop."

Carp on a cracker. My face feels red hot. On the one hand, he's clearly hurt. On the other, we're not at the golden shower stage yet.

In baseball metaphors for sex, we'd go from almost having gone to fourth base straight to tenth... on a rainy day.

"Okay," I surprise myself by saying. "But don't enjoy it."

He glares at me. "There's nothing about this to enjoy."

I inch toward him. "Good. Don't look at me when I do it, and we'll never speak of this afterward."

"Deal." He lies flat, hiding his face in his folded arms.

I approach carefully. "Plug your ears too. I don't want you to hear the tinkle."

He groans. "How about I sing out loud, to drown out the sound?"

"Yeah." I step out of my bikini bottoms and squat over his butt. "That works."

Oliver begins to sing in a low, smooth baritone, and I recognize the lyrics of my dad's favorite Led Zeppelin song, "When the Levee Breaks."

Great. I'm pretty sure this is the exact song my parents played when potty-training the six of us.

Oh, well. Let the healing begin.

Only one problem: I can't go on command like this.

I strain, but nothing comes out. I keep wondering what we'd say if someone were to walk onto the beach at this moment. Also, I'm not sure how well I can direct the flow. It's bad enough I'm going to pee on his butt, but what if some gets—

No. Must not think any stressful thoughts, or I'll never go.

I breathe deeply and listen to the surf, but that doesn't help.

I picture waterfalls, running faucets, flowing rivers...

Just keep swimming. Just keep swimming.

Finally. It begins—and luckily lands roughly where it should.

I suddenly remember Betsy, the lettuce lover. I can't believe she skipped my mind in the heat of the moment. Would Betsy pee for him like this? Would her vitamin-rich pee work better than mine?

Oliver's song grows louder, and there might be a hysterical edge to it.

On my end, I thank Cthulhu that I didn't eat any asparagus today. And stayed well hydrated. Unless... is my urine too diluted to work properly?

I guess we'll find out.

After I finish, I realize I don't have any paper. Wincing, I walk over to the ocean and clean myself with sea water. I'm feeling vaguely violated, even though it was Oliver who got peed on.

Speaking of Oliver, he's still singing.

Can't he tell I stopped?

I hurry back and pull on my bikini bottoms. "Hey. Feeling better?"

He keeps singing.

I poke him gently with a toe.

He stops singing. "You're done?"

"Yeah. I take it you don't feel any different?"

He lifts his head up. "Still feels like an acid burn."

Carp bite me. "Maybe my urine is too diluted? That or this whole thing is an urban myth, after all."

Clenching his teeth, he pushes up to all fours, and I help him get up.

Even wounded and peed upon, he looks glorious in his nudity, and though Aqua-manhood is not hard anymore, it's still pretty big.

"I'll just go home and use some vinegar," he mutters.

"Smart." I grab his trunks and hand them to him.

He grimaces as he looks at them. "I can't."

I blink. "Can't what?"

"It would hurt too much to have fabric touch it."

I nearly smack myself on the forehead with his trunks. "Of course... but what's the alternative?"

"I walk home like this."

"Naked?" I shout. Lowering my voice, I ask, "Won't you get arrested?"

He shrugs. "It's after dark, and I'll be walking from a private beach into a private community."

I blow out a breath. "Legal troubles are the last thing you need right now. How about this: you hold the trunks in the front, and I'll cover your backside with the surfboard."

He snatches the trunks. "All right. Let's go."

I pick up my wet tail and stuff it into the guitar case along with the shotgun. Hanging the case over my shoulder, I pick up the surfboard and hold it out in front of me. We head back like that, with me covering him from behind and doing my best not to stare at his firm, muscular glutes as he walks—which turns out to be challenging.

When we're close to our destination, I pray to Cthulhu and all his fellow Great Old Ones that my grandparents don't catch me walking a naked guy home. I'll never hear the end of it.

Finally, we're next to his garage door.

He turns his butt away from me and keeps his trunks up to cover himself. His tone is gruff. "Thanks for this."

I put the surfboard on the ground. "Need any help applying the vinegar?"

"I've got it from here." As if realizing the words came out too harshly, he gives me a forced smile. "You're too kind."

I grin. "For a New Yorker, you mean?"

His smile turns wry. "Sorry about all that. Now I'm going to run, if you don't mind."

Oh, right. I'm keeping him from pain relief.

I should just turn and go, but the words spill out of their own accord. "Could you text me when you're feeling better?"

Otherwise, I'm going to worry about him all night.

"Sure," he says. "What's your number?"

I tell him, and he repeats it a few times, committing it to memory. Turning away, he types a passcode into a dial by the garage door, and when the door opens, he waves and disappears inside.

Unsettled yet weirdly elated, I head home too.

CHAPTER
Nine

As I shower and go through my evening routine, I replay everything that's happened in my mind.

I almost had sex with Oliver—a head-exploding event.

I peed on him—a head-scratching event.

Net result: I'm hornier than a gaggle of male teens at a porn convention.

Well, masturbation is quickly becoming my go-to sleeping aid, so there's that. A big-enough orgasm just might silence my anxiety about tomorrow's meeting with Dr. Jones—and put to rest questions such as, "What will happen the next time I see Oliver?"

Speaking of Oliver, how is he doing?

I locate my phone and see a text from a new number.

Hi, it's Oliver. The vinegar worked. Thanks for your help today.

I save his number and reply with:

Don't mention it. Have a good night.

I feel floaty when I realize that I can text him again tomorrow—just to find out how he's feeling, of course, but if it leads to something...

Okay, I definitely need to burn off some of this sexual energy, or else I might booty-call him *tonight.* After all, there are plenty of positions where his butt isn't at risk.

Hmm. That came out kind of wrong.

Before taking care of myself, I head over to cuddle Beaky.

Huh. He's wrapped around his dildo, but the thing isn't vibrating anymore.

"If you give it back, I'll charge it for you," I say as I open the tank. "I haven't figured out how to charge it in the tank."

I'm not sure if he understands, or if he's bored with the toy by now, but he tosses it out of the tank as soon as the lid is open.

Bring life back to Scepter, priestess-subject, or feel the full might of our terrible wrath.

"I'll do it after the cuddle," I say, reaching out to him.

Beaky "kisses" me with his suckers as usual, and this time, he doesn't steal anything. At least not that I'm aware of.

"Tomorrow, I'll know if you're getting a tank upgrade," I tell him as I re-seal his tank.

I see him staring at the dildo on the floor, so I take out the charger, attach its magnets to the toy, and place it near the tank so he knows it's almost within his grasp.

The dildo begins to pulse with a blue LED light, indicating that it's charging. Beaky watches as if hypnotized, then makes one of his arms turn blue.

Okay. Now for some Me Time. I turn the lights off, but before I can remove my pajamas, the doorbell rings.

My pulse jumps.

Has Oliver recovered enough to come over and finish what we started?

Then it hits me.

Lemon said she and Fabio were coming today. Carpy carp. How could I have forgotten?

I turn the light back on, pull on a robe over my PJs, and head out of the room.

Yep. Grandma is kissing Fabio on the cheek while Grandpa is hugging Lemon.

"You should've let me pick you up," Grandpa says as he lets go of my identical sister and shakes Fabio's hand.

"I'm glad I didn't." Lemon hugs Grandma. "Our flight was delayed."

Spotting me, Fabio huffs. "Another one? Which are you?"

I roll my eyes. "Olive. You know, the one who told you she took a job in Florida?"

Grandma tsk-tsks at Fabio. "I thought you were best friends with all of my granddaughters."

Fabio theatrically runs his hand through his lush

hair. "I am, but that doesn't mean I have to keep track of *olive* them."

I groan. When not telling jokes older than my grandparents, Fabio loves making fun of our names. It was so bad in high school that I used powder-based makeup to keep my forehead matte in the hopes of avoiding "olive oil" jokes. And, at least on some level, I think I lost my virginity in order to stop the variations on "extra virgin."

"Are you guys hungry?" Grandma asks.

"We ate on the plane," Fabio says.

Grandma looks at Grandpa. "Don't we have that cheesecake left? You know how much little Lemon likes her sweets."

Grandpa grins at Fabio for some reason. "Sorry. We ate *olive* it."

Ignoring our groans, the two men high-five each other.

Lemon pouts. "I like sweets only as much as the next girl."

"Sure. Just like how Popeye's girlfriend"—Fabio nods at me—"likes octopuses as much as the next girl."

I cross my arms over my chest. "Hardy-har-har. Popeye's girlfriend, Olive Oyl. You're hilarious."

"Sorry." Fabio draws a heart in the air. "Olive you."

That does it. I pinch his bicep, making him squeal.

Grandma shakes her head. "Stop acting like children and decide who's sleeping where."

"I call dibs on the bed in the guest room," Lemon and Fabio shout in unison.

I grin like the Grinch. "So… you don't mind sharing the room with my octopus?"

"Dibs on the couch then," Fabio shouts.

Lemon's shoulders droop. "I guess I'll take the folding bed."

"Sorry," Grandpa says. "Your brilliant father somehow managed to break it while giving me an unsolicited massage the last time he and your mother visited."

Okay. There's a lot to unpack in that statement. I'm just glad Grandpa didn't shoot Dad for said massage.

"I guess the Hyman sisters are having a slumber party," Fabio says, and pointedly steps out of pinching distance. "When life gives you lemons and all that."

Lemon swats at him but misses.

"Peel better?" Fabio asks her.

Lemon groans. "Seriously?"

Ignoring her, Fabio looks at me. "Are you still doing your sunblock thing?"

I cock my head. "Don't take this as a threat, but Grandpa gave me a gun today."

Fabio puts on an innocent face. "I was just going to say that you should give some to Lemon. Without it, she peels all the time."

Lemon leaps at him, and he runs away screaming.

"I'll be in the guest room," I yell at no one in particular.

Grandma and Grandpa wish me good night, and I return to the room and get into bed.

Lemon joins me shortly. She cozies up to me on the

right side of the bed, staying as far away from Beaky's tank as she can.

"Good night," I say, turning off the light.

"Night, sis."

I sigh and punch my pillow.

So much for that orgasm.

CHAPTER
Ten

I WAKE up with the sun in my face again.

Motherfucking Sunshine State. I completely forgot to apply sunblock before bed.

Also, where is Lemon?

Leaping to my feet, I head to the bathroom to apply a triple layer of protection before dressing for work.

Today, I meet Dr. Jones.

As I leave the guest room, I hear familiar music coming from the living room, so I head there.

Grandma and Lemon are sitting in front of the TV, watching ballet. If the music is anything to go by, this is *Swan Lake*. I recognize it from that movie with Natalie Portman.

My sister Blue is lucky she's not here to see it. People pretending to be birds would surely make her brain ooze out of her ears.

The pair are eating breakfast. Grandma is munching on a bagel while Lemon is devouring cereal that looks suspiciously like chocolate chip cookies drowned in chocolate milk... all sprinkled with powdered sugar.

"Is that him?" Grandma points at a male ballet dancer on the screen.

"Yeah," Lemon says dreamily and swallows her drool. "I call him the Russian."

A *Sex and the City* reference, of course. She likes that show even more than she likes sweets—which is saying something, seeing how she's on the verge of either getting diabetes or turning into one of Santa's elves.

Grandma grunts approvingly. "I can see the appeal."

I can too. The guy has strong features and the greatest pair of legs in the history of appendages. But even better is that bulge in his tights. It almost makes me wonder if this isn't some form of porn.

Hey, I'd rather catch Grandma watching this than purple tentacles.

I clear my throat. "Good morning."

Lemon turns my way. "Hey, sleepyhead. I shook you when I woke up, but you were out cold."

Grandma smiles mischievously. "No doubt dreaming about the neighbor."

Lemon pauses the ballet. "The one who was strutting around naked last night?"

Oh, carp. "How do you know about that?"

Grandma's smile widens. "Retirees are nosy. You were seen by a lady who was walking her dog, and she told a friend, who told me."

"Chasing after a naked guy." Lemon gestures with her spoon. "You're such a Samantha."

"I wasn't chasing him, and it's not what you think." Under my breath, I mutter, "Unfortunately."

"What do we think?" Grandma asks.

"I'm starving," I say. "And can't be late for work."

"Right. Let me feed you." Grandma scurries to the kitchen, and Lemon and I follow.

When an omelet is placed in front of me, I tell them a version of last night's events that doesn't involve the mermaid tail.

Lemon stares at me, bug-eyed. "You gave him a golden shower?" Then her expression sours. "Like when Carrie was dating that politician."

Grandma gives her a stern look. "There's no kink shaming in this house."

I glower at them both. "It wasn't a kink. He was in pain."

Lemon grins. "Sure. Sure. That's what they always say. 'Oh, no, my blue balls. Oh, no, the jellyfish sting.'"

To avoid saying something unkind, I stuff my mouth with eggs and take a long minute to chew and swallow while Grandma describes Oliver to Lemon using adjectives like "scrumptious" and "panty-wetting hot."

"Why'd you wake up so early?" I ask Lemon, hoping to change the subject.

"We're going to the beach," Lemon and Grandma say in unison.

"Ah. Nice and early while the UV index is still low.

Smart." I take out my sunblock and put it on the table. "Make sure to use this. Both of you."

Lemon opens the tube and takes a sniff. "Gross. Too stinky."

Grandma and I exchange amused glances. Lemon's sense of smell is legendary in our family—it could blow dogs and pigs out of the water. Speaking of water, the creature that doesn't get enough credit for its amazing sense of smell is the shark. Lemon shark, in particular, can detect even the tiniest amount of blood in the water—a factoid I'll tease my sweet sister with at some opportune moment.

"Where is Fabio?" I ask. "And Grandpa, for that matter?"

Lemon rolls her eyes. "They went to the shooting range."

"Doesn't Fabio hate guns?" I shove the last of the omelet into my mouth.

She sighs. "Not when he's with Grandpa."

Grandpa? What on earth does that mean?

Grandma chuckles. "The boy has a little crush. Then again, can you blame him?"

Ew. I gape at them. "Hell yeah, I can blame him. It's our grandpa!"

"It's really pukey too," Lemon whispers. "I could swear terms like 'Polar Bear' and 'Daddy' were mentioned in reference to Grandpa."

I stand up. "For the love of Cthulhu, please don't explain what any of that means."

It's a miracle I don't get a speeding ticket on my way to work. On the plus side, I'm not going to be late for my meeting with Dr. Jones. However, I'm so sweaty from the heat and anxiety that I need a change of clothes.

I have a few minutes before the meeting, so I run to Rose's office and request a new uniform.

"Here." She hands me a stack. "That's five more."

Am I so sweaty she thinks I need this many?

"Thanks," I say.

"Good luck," she says, but in such a way that it makes me worry about meeting the big boss even more.

With a rushed thanks, I dash into the ladies' room and change. Then, with just a minute to spare, I knock on the door of Dr. Jones's office.

"Miss Hyman?" asks a voice muffled by the door.

"Present."

Carp, why did I say that? He's not taking attendance during homeroom.

"Please, come in."

I step inside the office, my knees slightly wobbly.

"You?" a familiar male voice exclaims. "What are you doing here?"

The light reflecting off Dr. Jones's features enters my retinas and is absorbed by the photoreceptor cells. Then an electrochemical signal goes on a merry-go-round until the vision center of my brain registers what shouldn't be true.

My mouth goes dry as my heartbeat jolts into the stratosphere.

Dr. Jones is the man I almost slept with last night.

Dr. Jones is Oliver.

CHAPTER
Eleven

HE REGARDS me with an equally shell-shocked expression.

Unlike the other times I've seen him, his long hair is gathered into a man bun, but there's no mistaking it. Or him.

Once you pee on someone's ass, you never forget their face. Or their ass.

Also, he's wearing the same outfit he had on at the dinner with my grandparents: a white polo shirt and khaki pants. Which, come to think of it, looks almost identical to my uniform, just with pants instead of shorts. The pants must be a boss thing—more dignified, albeit less practical in the Florida heat. On the plus side, they should help protect his legs from the sun. He won't need to reapply sunblock there as much.

Wait, why am I thinking about his pants?

This is a disaster.

I almost slept with the big boss.

And repeatedly called him Florida Man.

And peed on him.

Because he was hurt.

Carp. That must be why he's standing at his desk instead of sitting—that or he's just one of those people who try not to sit too much for optimal health. His desk *is* the sit-to-stand kind, which supports the latter theory.

Before I can think better of it, I blurt, "How are you feeling?"

He pinches the bridge of his nose, takes in a deep breath, and lets it out slowly. Dropping his hand, he pins me with a cool cyan stare. "I feel like the situation with the manatees is becoming dire, and I would like to hear your ideas. I have another meeting in an hour, so we'd better get to it."

Huh, okay. I see how it is. He's decided to avoid the elephant in the room by focusing on work and talking about the elephant's cousin, the manatee. That, or he loves the manatees so much all other subjects are trivial in comparison. And hey, I can relate. Out of the million concerns I have now—like whether or not I'll be allowed to keep this job—the top one is what this revelation will mean for Beaky's big tank.

Wait a sec. Beaky. This must be why he wanted to buy him—to bring him here, where he'd have a better life. I suddenly feel stupid for being mean—

"Miss Hyman." He frowns at me. "Are you going to be able to perform your duties, or—"

"Sorry." I shake my head to clear it of the residual

shock and the sneaky hormones that make me want to smooth that crease between his eyebrows with my tongue. "I was gathering my thoughts. I have so many ideas for manatee entertainment that I don't know where to start."

He arches an eyebrow. "That many?"

I bob my head. "Do you want me start with the cheapest or the most effective?"

"Effective."

Calling on every bit of my professionalism, I launch into it, starting with the TV inside the tank idea. He listens with ultra-focus and asks extremely intelligent questions—and I feel all the dumber for not realizing he was a fellow marine biologist.

In my defense, we had agreed not to talk about sea life at the dinner with my grandparents, and we didn't get a chance to talk much on the beach.

"Thank you," he says when I finish my list. "I'd like you to start implementing your ideas in order of effectiveness, starting with the TV. The situation is dire. Betsy didn't eat this morning."

I suppress a hysterical giggle. "Betsy is a manatee?"

"Well, yeah." His frown returns. "Weren't you working with them all day yesterday?"

I shrug. "I didn't learn their names. I was too busy—"

With a sigh, he hands me a credit card. "Use this to buy the TV."

As I take the card, our fingers touch, and a zing of sexual energy scrambles my synapses again. Showing no sign that he's affected, Oliver fixes his gaze on his monitor.

Carp fuck me. "Actually, there's one more thing I'd like to discuss."

He tears his gaze away from the monitor. His cyan eyes are narrowed. "If it's about last night—"

"My octopus," I blurt. "I want him here."

I can tell he doesn't want to touch on last night, and I can't blame him. I'd like to strike it from the record also, but sadly, I don't have a time machine.

He checks his watch. "My next meeting is—"

"You saw his current tank," I say with increased urgency. "You alluded to it yourself. He needs a much bigger one."

He sighs. "The issue isn't so simple."

"Why not?"

He drums his fingers on his desk. "For starters, you just called him *your* octopus. We don't allow pets here."

I see where he's going with this. My chest sinks, but I make myself say it. "If it's the only way to get him a bigger tank, he can be yours."

"Sealand would own him, not me."

"Isn't that the same thing?"

He shakes his head. "Sealand is a corporation—a legal and tax entity that isn't me. And that's good. If something were to happen to me, Sealand would go on, and your octopus would continue to have a home."

My heart squeezes at the idea that something could happen to Oliver. And that I'm going to be separated from Beaky. But this is what's best for him.

"Okay," I say. "Sealand would own him."

"Which also means he'd live here permanently, regardless of your job status."

I realize I've been standing all this time and my legs are tired. I walk over to the chair in front of his desk and take a seat. "Thanks for clarifying," I say, with a good dose of bitterness in my voice. "I understand. Beaky won't be mine anymore."

Is that a glint of kindness in his eyes? "We'll take good care of him, I promise."

I figure now isn't a good time to remind him what happened to the last octopus under Sealand's care, so I say, "I'll design the lid for his tank. The last thing I want is for him to escape and get hurt."

"Great idea. Make that a priority after helping the manatees."

I stand up. "Thanks."

His gaze warms a fraction. "Thank *you* for taking the manatee situation so seriously."

Was I? I was just doing my job. I do like this look in his eyes, though. It's so much better than the cool, distant big-boss mask he's been wearing throughout most of this meeting.

There's a knock on the door.

Must be his next appointment.

"Bye," I say.

"Bye," he replies, his expression unreadable again.

Tearing my gaze away from his delectable face, I leave the office.

CHAPTER
Twelve

AN UNFAMILIAR MAN is waiting outside, and I tell him that Dr. Jones is ready to see him.

Before I can process what has just happened, I bump into Rose.

"How did your meeting go?" she asks.

I tell her about Beaky and the credit card.

"You should take Dex with you when you go to the electronics store," she says. "A large TV is too heavy for you to carry."

What she seems to say without saying it is: "If his majesty Dr. Jones wants it done, do it *now.*"

Fine. A little trip just might keep me from worrying about my upcoming separation from Beaky—and freaking out about the fact that Oliver is Dr. Jones.

I thank her and walk over to Otteraction, where I explain my need for a shopping trip to my otteresque colleague.

Dex chuckles. "TV for sea cows? Now I've heard everything."

I decide not to correct his use of the c-word. "Will you help me?"

"Sure. We can take the company truck. There's a shopping plaza nearby."

————

A member of the Geek Squad helps us choose the TV.

"It's designed for the outdoors and has IP66 waterproofing," he says about one sturdy-looking model.

"That's a good start," I say. "How much is it?"

The price he quotes is higher than it would be for a regular TV this size, but the waterproofing is worth it. Plus, it's not my money I'm spending.

"Throw in waterproof speakers that'll work inside a pool, and we'll take it," I say.

He has to clear it with his manager, but we get a pretty good deal in the end, considering I would've bought the speakers anyway.

"Can you load it into our truck?" I ask when the transaction is done.

No need for Dex and me to overexert ourselves unnecessarily.

The Geek Squad guys help us out, and then Dex and I set out to the hardware store, where I purchase sealant, fiber glass resin, tubes to encase wires in, and a bunch of other components that will allow me to waterproof the TV and the speakers further. I also get everything I'll need to mount the TV inside the tank and to adjust its viewing angle as needed, plus a few cheap things to help me implement some of my other, simpler ideas, including a bunch of large brushes for a scratching post.

As Dex drives us back, I psych myself up to ask something that's been on my mind ever since I learned that Oliver is the big boss.

"Dex," I say as casually as I can, "how strict is the HR policy on dating?"

"Insanely strict." He turns his weasely eyes from the road and gives me a once-over. "As tempting as it would be, I wouldn't dare risk it."

I roll my eyes. "Dude. I wasn't coming on to you. I was just wondering, in general."

He looks like an otter whose crawfish has just run away. "Batting for the other team? Aruba *is* hot... Unless you like them older, in which case R—"

"Just stop," I say. "I've got a feeling you're breaking HR policies right now."

Speaking of HR policies, how many did I break when I peed on the big boss man?

"Sorry," Dex says, returning his full attention to the road. "I like my job, so I don't even think about this stuff. The policy came all the way from the top."

I arch an eyebrow. "From Dr. Jones himself?"

Dex nods solemnly. "Rumor has it, he founded Sealand with his girlfriend. When they broke up, the place nearly went under—and he's been touchy when it comes to work relationships ever since."

"Huh," is the most intelligent thing I can come up with.

Does that explain how strangely he acted when he realized I work for him?

Then again, *did* he act all that strange?

Before Dex can sniff out why I am asking all this, I steer the conversation to my ideas for otter enrichment. Eventually, we run out of otter-related things to discuss, so I turn my attention to the ocean in the distance and let disappointment wash over me.

Nothing can happen between me and Oliver.

The reasons are countless, and many have nothing to do with today's revelation. For instance, the mere fact that I'm drawn to him is proof that he's probably an asshole of the first order.

As in, a restraining order is probably in my future.

No, thanks. Been there, fed that fish. It's probably a good thing Oliver has turned out to be my boss. Between the HR policy and his past, any hanky-panky would lead to me losing this job and access to Beaky along with it.

We turn into Sealand's entrance, Dex parks the van, and we lift the TV out of the truck together.

Wow. This thing is heavy. Rose was right to insist I bring a helper.

Besides the weight, there's another issue. Our current positioning has put our faces way too close together—uncomfortably so, especially considering our HR policy chat.

Oh, well. I do my best not to strain my back and keep my gaze away from his otterly eyes.

"Put that down," a familiar deep voice growls behind me.

We set the TV on the ground, almost dropping the damn thing in the process.

I turn.

Yep.

It's Oliver. For some reason, he's looking at Dex as if the poor dude were an Alaskan otter and Oliver a killer whale—the only predator that protected species has to worry about.

Did one of Dex's charges get into trouble while we were away?

Oliver's voice remains growly. "What is this?"

"I was j-just helping with the TV," Dex says with a slight stutter.

Oliver glares at him. "Then you should carry it yourself."

"Hey!" I narrow my eyes at Oliver. "I'm not some weak damsel."

It's my turn to be on the receiving end of his glare. "You should've arranged for the store to deliver this."

I straighten my spine. "You said Betsy's situation was dire, so I figured you'd appreciate the haste."

His nostrils flare before he turns back to Dex. "Get back to your post."

Dex doesn't need to be told twice. In an eyeblink, he's gone.

Without saying another word, Oliver stalks over to

the TV and picks it up by himself, making it look effortless.

I know I should be angry, but I can't deny the acceleration of my pulse as I watch his back muscles flexing in his shirt. Grr. Clearly, it's some vestigial cavewoman instinct that appreciates his strength, an instinct that's as helpful in the modern world as a palate for greasy foods and sweets.

Swallowing my drool, I follow him until we reach the manatees. Then Oliver carefully sets the TV down and turns toward me. "When you're ready to lower this into the tank, come get me."

And just like that, he stalks off.

I stare after him, feeling oddly unsettled. What was that? Not jealousy, surely? My ex was a jealous asshole, so I'm intimately familiar with that character flaw. But Oliver—Dr. Jones—has no reason to act this way. We're nothing to each other. And even if we were, nothing was going on with Dex.

Maybe he thought I'd hurt my back and sue Sealand?

Needing a second to gather my wits, I reapply my sunblock. It's been a whole hour, so it's an emergency.

Once I'm safe from the lethal rays, I examine the plaque with the manatees' names to figure out which one I was jealous of.

It doesn't take me long to locate Betsy—a small and relatively lean specimen of her plump species.

I study the plaque. Betsy was born in a seaquarium in Miami—a fairly rare event—which means she's not a candidate for release into the wild. I bet that's part of the reason why Oliver is so attached to her. She's resided here for most of her life and will continue to do so for many years to come. She's in her teens, and these animals can live up to sixty-five years.

"I'll make sure you're not bored here," I tell her.

She gives me a grumpy look. *Great, thanks, but I'd be much happier if you kept your grubby flippers away from my human. I'm more of a mermaid than you can ever hope to be—and no pathetic fake tail will ever change that. Oh, and even on my current diet, I have curves that you can only dream of.*

With a snort, I get to work. I further waterproof the TV and the speakers, which takes so long that I have to break for lunch midway through. When I'm done, I text Oliver that I need help getting the TV into the tank. While I wait, I install the speakers. They're light, so I hope Oliver won't throw a hissy fit because I lifted them with my puny feminine muscles.

When the last speaker is in, Oliver is still nowhere to be found.

Fine. I attach part of the mount to the TV so there's less to do when the big boss deigns to show up. When I can't make any more progress on the mounting, I text him again:

Look, if you're busy, I'll ask Dex for help.

Maybe that'll rush him a bit? For now, I set up the TV with some initial content: a nature show about the Sargasso Sea. Unlike other seas, this one has no land boundaries and is instead located inside an ocean gyre, which is a system of rotating currents. My hope is that the manatees will enjoy watching the large quantities of *Sargassum*—a type of seaweed—that the Sargasso Sea is known for. After all, it's like an all-you-can eat seaweed buffet and should be as fun for Betsy and the gang as *Charlie and the Chocolate Factory* is for Lemon.

A sound startles me, and I spin around to confront Oliver's yummy face.

No. He's the boss. His face and other parts are off limits.

"Thanks for making the time," I say. Maybe snarking at the boss is a bad idea, but it's hard to resist.

He picks up the TV. "Where do you want it?"

Huh. No snarking back.

I walk him through how to attach everything before he submerges the TV in the tank.

"They're watching us in fascination," Oliver whispers.

I check, and indeed, the manatees' eyes are trained on us. "If they like to watch humans do this sort of thing, we could put on HGTV for them."

He chuckles, then catches himself and makes his face stern again. "What now?"

In reply, I turn the TV on and start the Sargasso Sea show.

Betsy is the first to swim over to check out the new development, and the other manatees swim after her with curious expressions on their whiskered faces.

We wait a few minutes to be sure, and then I call it. "They're totally watching it."

"Yeah," Oliver says reverently. "Great job, Olive."

Wow. Piranhas are having a carnivorous feast in my belly, and I can't help but grin. "Thank me if they come out of their funk."

He nods. "The feeding is in a few hours. Let's see how it goes."

"Okay," I say. "In the meantime, I got the hardware to make more goodies for them, so I might as well get to it."

He looks at his watch. "I've got another meeting."

"Thanks for the help," I say, then worry he might think I'm snarking again, even though I mean it this time.

With a wave, he leaves.

Grr. I can't believe I liked it more when he was confrontational.

Whatever.

I get the brushes I bought earlier and attach them to some aluminum planks to create a scratching post for the manatees. Then I put together a few more things, losing track of time in the process. When I look up, Aruba, Dex, Rose, Oliver, and a few people whose names I haven't memorized are there, all throwing lettuce to the manatees.

At first, Betsy and the others don't even notice the food, thanks to the TV. Then they tear their gazes away and begin munching with great enthusiasm.

Did the nature show stimulate their appetites, or is it simply a matter of their being in a better mood?

"Wow," Aruba says grudgingly. "Amazing results. And so soon."

Rose puffs up. "My hiring skills never fail."

Dex turns my way. "Can you do this for the otters?"

"The dolphins first," Aruba says.

Oliver turns away from the manatees. "Everyone will get their turn, but for now, Olive will focus on the manatees and the octopus that will be joining us."

He's talking about Beaky's move like it's a done deal. I know I should be grateful, but all I feel is separation anxiety.

"An octopus?" Aruba's voice sounds like the whistles and clicks of a horny dolphin. "Why?"

Rose's expression turns stern. "Because it's for Dr. Jones to decide. Not you."

Oliver levels a cool gaze at Aruba. "Is there a problem?"

She blanches. "Not if this one stays in its tank."

"I'll make sure of that," I say. "In fact, if it's okay, I'd like to start on that project."

Oliver nods imperiously at me. "Rose, can you show Olive the tank?"

"Come." Rose grabs me by the elbow and drags me into a nearby building.

"This is it." She points at a humongous tank that occupies almost all the space in the large room. "What do you think?"

I whistle. "I bet I could live there myself and be happy as a clam."

Rose grins. "It's got temperature controls and all the bells and whistles."

"Wow." I smile, but my heart aches. Parting with Beaky will be hard.

Rose puts a hand on my shoulder. She's clearly not just a fish shrink; she knows a thing or two about how to cheer up a human as well. "Your octopus will be happy here, I'm sure."

"I know." I take in a breath. "That's why I'm doing this. Now I just need to octopus-proof this thing, so he doesn't run off to feed the dolphins."

"I'll leave you to it," Rose says.

I wave her goodbye and examine the tank.

It's a wonder the previous octopus took so long to escape. Security holes—literal holes—are all over the lid.

I square my shoulders.

I'm not going home until I Beaky-proof this thing.

CHAPTER

Thirteen

IT TAKES ME HOURS. I have to rent welding equipment and make three trips to the hardware store, but eventually, I deem the tank octopus-safe.

After washing the grime from my hands, I check the time on my phone.

Carp. It's past my bedtime—and Lemon, Fabio, and my grandparents have been texting me because I didn't show up for dinner.

I let them all know I'm headed back and hop into my car.

When I pull into the driveway of my grandparents' house, the lights are off, which probably means everyone is asleep. I should've grabbed a sandwich on the way. I'm hungry.

Turns out, not everyone is asleep. Grandpa is waiting for me in the garage, an obligatory shotgun in his strong hands.

"Don't shoot," I say with a grin.

His bushy eyebrows gather in the middle of his forehead. "Caper, do you know what time it is?"

I explain that I had to work late—new job and all that.

"This isn't New York," Grandpa says. "People who work more than a nine-to-five here make everyone else look bad."

I yawn. "I'll take that into consideration."

He opens the door into the house for me, and I tiptoe into the kitchen to raid the fridge for leftovers.

Lemon is snoring when I sneak into the bedroom. Using my phone as a flashlight, I pet Beaky, give him back the now-charged dildo, and throw in some food.

"Soon, you'll have a tank that will make all the other octopuses jealous," I whisper.

Rejoice, faithful priestess-subject, for you have avoided our wrath. Now that we're reunited with the Scepter, we'll allow the world to keep rotating around the Tank. Keep this up and remember: when Cthulhu awakens, the devout will be devoured first.

"Olive?" Lemon says in a sleepy voice. "Is that you?"

"Sorry if I woke you," I whisper back. "Now hush. I'm going to bed."

She doesn't reply, so I smother my face in sunblock and crawl under the covers.

Another day, another masturbation session skipped.

If this continues, my ovaries might turn blue the next time I see Oliver.

113

———

When I wake up, Lemon isn't in the bed.

I get ready and leave the guest room. I find Lemon and Grandma in the living room, watching ballet again, only this time Grandpa and Fabio are here as well.

I'm not sure which ballet this is. *The Sleeping Beauty*, perhaps? The reason it's on is clear, though. Lemon's crush, the Russian, appears on the stage, grabs a ballerina, and tosses her in the air as effortlessly as regular people do with babies.

"As tragic as it is, that guy is *not* gay," Fabio says, staring at Lemon's obsession with unabashed appreciation.

Lemon looks like she might drown in excitement. "You sure?"

Fabio examines his nails. "Sour sweetie, my gaydar is as accurate as a screw gauge."

"That's one lucky man," Grandpa mutters as he watches the Russian practically juggle ballerinas. "Being surrounded by so many gorgeous women."

Lemon frowns, and Grandma lifts an eyebrow as she turns to her husband.

"I'm not saying I'm not happy with the wonderful woman I have," Grandpa says hastily. "I was just—"

"Olive!" Lemon exclaims, spotting me. "What time did you get home last night?"

"Why don't we talk as we eat breakfast?" Grandma says.

I smile at everyone. "Breakfast sounds great."

"Give me a minute," Grandma says, and rushes away.

I take her seat and look from Fabio to Lemon. "What are you guys doing today?"

"Ziggy and I are going fishing," Fabio says, eyeing Grandpa adoringly.

I frown—in part because I don't like fish getting slaughtered for sport, and in part because of "Polar Bear" and "Daddy."

"Don't worry," Grandpa says. "We'll do catch and release."

"That doesn't make *me* feel any better," Lemon mutters.

Me neither. Grandpa is clearly enjoying the grandson he never had, but I don't want to think about what Fabio is getting out of this arrangement.

The doorbell rings.

"I'll get it." Grandpa heads over to the front door.

In a few seconds, he comes back, but he's not alone.

Oliver steps into the room, dressed in his Sealand uniform of white polo shirt and khakis. At least I think that's what's happening. It's possible my masturbation abstinence is causing me to have wet dreams, and this is the start of a very weird one, considering friends and family are around.

Fabio and Lemon gape at my boss like they've never seen a hot man before, while my body goes haywire, my skin flushing hot and my lungs constricting until I can only gulp in shallow breaths. It takes all of my willpower not to drool—though what liquid I manage to suppress in my mouth seems to come out in my panties.

"Hi, Oliver," Grandma says over her shoulder from the stove. "You're just in time for breakfast."

Oliver shakes his head. "Thank you, but I just came to help Olive transport Beaky to his new home. I didn't mean to intrude on a family event."

That explains a lot—and I'm not sure how I should feel about it. I don't know if he's being kind or making sure I don't back out of our agreement.

"Nonsense," Grandpa says. "Join, or you'll offend us."

A rueful smile twists Oliver's lips. "The last thing I want is to offend my neighbors."

"Then it's settled," Grandma says. "Do you want oats, omelet, or pancakes?"

"Oats would be great," Oliver says. "Thank you."

Grandma poses the same question to everyone else, and I answer last, going for pancakes, with one-tenth of the syrup Lemon asks for on hers.

"So," Fabio says petulantly. "Is *anyone* going to introduce us?"

Grandpa smacks his forehead. "Where are my manners? This is Oliver, Olive's boyfriend."

"No, he's not," I say, startled, just as Oliver says, "I'm not."

Hey, he doesn't need to deny it so vehemently.

Pretending he didn't hear, Grandpa says, "Oliver,

this is Fabio, Olive's childhood friend. And as you can tell, Lemon"—he nods at my sister—"is one of Olive's many identical siblings."

Fabio extends his hand, and Oliver shakes it.

"Did you even know which was Olive and which was Lemon?" Fabio whispers conspiratorially.

Oliver glances at me. "I can tell."

The stupid piranhas in my belly need to chill.

"Sit, folks," Grandma says.

We obey, and she brings out the food for everyone else before joining us with a bowl of oats for herself.

I pay attention to Oliver as he sits down to see if the jellyfish sting makes him wince.

Nope. He must be completely recovered.

"So, Oliver," Grandpa says when we start eating, "you mentioned your two brothers before. What do they do?"

"And is either of them gay?" Fabio whispers loudly.

Oliver hovers his spoon near his lips. "They're both straight, sorry. One is a NASCAR driver, and the other is a surfing instructor... for dogs."

I snort. "How very Floridian."

Oliver doesn't show that he's heard me. "What about your family? What do the Hyman sisters do?"

"Our sister Blue is a spy of sorts," Lemon says excitedly, then proceeds to tell him about the others—no doubt purposefully skipping herself. At the end, she says, "And you probably know that your not-girlfriend is a marine biologist. She just started a new job at some aquarium nearby."

Oliver shoots me a confused glance. He's probably wondering why I haven't told anyone that I work for him. The truth is, I haven't had the chance. Maybe if I had, my grandparents wouldn't have invited him to stay for breakfast.

"Speaking of jobs," Fabio says to me. "Did you have any luck with Octoworld?"

Oliver arches an eyebrow. "Octoworld?"

I make a cutting-throat gesture, but Lemon doesn't notice it.

"Yeah, it's all she talks about," she says. "She took her current job as a stepping stone, but what she really wants to do is work with all those octopuses."

No. Shut up. He already has plenty of reasons to fire me. Why give him more?

"I'm perfectly happy with my new job," I say a little too quickly, and a touch defensively.

"You are?" Lemon pours about a cup more of syrup onto her pancakes. "Do they have octopuses?"

Seriously, why can't she get how much I want her to shut up? I'm not asking for any spooky "twin telepathy" here—just read the horror on my face.

"Sealand *is* getting an octopus," Oliver says, his expression indecipherable. "So maybe that will keep Olive happy?"

"It will," I say firmly.

"Just one?" Lemon shakes her head. "I thought it would take a thousand." She turns to me. "What about your girl crush, Ezra Shelby? She still owns Octoworld, right?"

"Ezra Shelby," Oliver repeats slowly.

"I think that's the name," Lemon says. "She's that—"

"Oh, I know her," Oliver says. "I just—"

"Oliver owns Sealand," I blurt. "They probably hang out on the weekends."

Lemon turns pale and finally stops talking.

"Wait," Fabio says. "Your boyfriend is your boss?"

I shoot Grandpa a squinty glare. "Oliver is not my boyfriend."

"We're colleagues," Oliver says.

For now. If this conversation continues for much longer, I'll be unemployed for sure.

"What a small world," Grandma says. "One night, you walk him home naked; the next, you work for him."

Seriously, why? Why? Next thing you know, Lemon will say something like, "Wait, so he's the one you gave a golden shower to?"

In a desperate attempt to switch topics once and for all, I rattle out, "You know, guys, Oliver is a native Floridian, so he might have some fun ideas for your vacation."

"It's true," Oliver says. "Born and raised."

I guess he's as eager as I am to stop talking about that naked walk of shame.

Lemon wrinkles her nose like there's a bad smell—and with her eerie olfactory powers, she may well have just detected Tofu farting inside Oliver's house. "I thought the word 'beach' encapsulated all the fun to be had here."

Oh, right. Lemon is a much bigger New York snob than I could ever hope to be. I think it might be a side effect of watching too much *Sex and The City.*

"The beaches here are great," Oliver says. "But there's a ton more to do besides that—especially if you're willing to drive a few hours."

Lemon's eye roll is subtle, but I can tell it's there thanks to years of experience with faces just like hers. "I'm not interested in fishing or going to a gun range," she says.

Oliver clenches his jaw. People dissing Florida is his pet peeve, clearly. But hey, at least he's not mad at me anymore. Hopefully. Then again, being mad at Lemon could condition him to be feel angry toward someone with my face, so maybe I should nudge Fabio into pissing off Oliver instead?

"What about Disney World?" Oliver asks. "People bring their families from around the globe to see it."

Lemon scratches her chin. "I didn't think of that one."

"You could visit the Everglades," Oliver says. "And Universal Studios, the Kennedy Space Center, Dry Tortugas National Park, the Salvador Dali Museum, St. Augustine's Historic District, Legoland—I could go on all day."

"Hmm." Lemon's nose returns to normal. "Which are closest?"

Looking triumphant, Oliver gives her and Fabio an itinerary that a travel agent would be proud of.

My phone blares, and everyone looks at me.

"Sorry," I say. "I set an alarm to remind me to go to work."

Oliver puts down his spoon. "Right. We both had better go."

I rise to my feet. "Let's go get Beaky."

Oliver joins me, and as we head into the guest room, I hear snickers and innuendo from my "friend" and "supportive family."

As we step into the room, I realize they had a good reason for teasing. I suddenly feel extremely aware of the bed in front of us—that is, before I start cursing myself for not making it this morning.

Hey, at least there aren't any unmentionables lying around... unless you count the tentacle dildo Beaky is clutching in his arms—the exact thing Oliver is staring at with a bemused expression.

"Inventive," he says.

"Don't be a slippery dick," I blurt.

Carp. Though it's just the name of a fish, "slippery dick" could still be perceived as an insult and is definitely not something you should say to your boss.

To my relief, the corners of Oliver's eyes crinkle. "Why does giving you compliments make me a member of the *Halichoeres bivittatus* species?"

I grin. "Only a fellow marine biologist would reply with that."

His eyes gleam. "I'm just glad you didn't call me a protogynous hermaphrodite."

Shaking my head, I become hyperaware of the nearby bed again. Oliver is talking reproduction now—

slippery dick reproduction, but still. Protogynous hermaphrodite fish start their lives as females but become males later in life, when there's a reproductive need. If I were a slippery dick, and if horniness could bring about that sex change, I'd be sprouting a dick right about now.

"When they annoy me, I call my brothers slime-heads," Oliver says.

I nod approvingly. "*Hoplostethus atlanticus*. Also goes by orange roughy—but that isn't as fun of a name to call a brother, unless he's into self-tanning."

Oliver frowns. "Orange roughy is just a rebrand, so it sounds more appetizing when it's served in restaurants. Never mind that this fish can live for hundreds of years. That kind of rebranding is how gizzard fish became whitefish, hog turned into king mackerel, toothfish is suddenly Chilean sea bass, mudbug changed to crawfish, goosefish transformed into monkfish, and worse of all, dolphinfish became mahi-mahi."

I cock my head. "You don't eat sea creatures, do you?"

He sighs. "What gave it away?"

"I'm not making fun; I don't eat them either. 'Fish are friends, not food.'"

He steps into my personal space and locks eyes with me. "I couldn't agree more… *kelpcake*."

By Cthulhu's fallopian tubes, I'm getting pulled into Oliver's orbit again—just like on the porch the other day, and at the beach.

The same unholy magic seems to be overtaking him as well. He starts to dip his head, his eyes hooded.

Holy pollock.

If history is any predictor of the future, we're about to kiss.

CHAPTER
Fourteen

I SWALLOW AUDIBLY.

With that bed nearby, there can only be one outcome if we kiss—and it would mean the end of my career. Not to mention, my hopes for Beaky's new home.

As if he were psychic—and hey, you never know—Beaky turns on his vibrator.

The sound jolts both of us.

Oliver draws back and clears his throat. "Do you plan to give him that toy when he's in his new tank?"

I back up as well. "Would you mind?"

"No," he says. "Most people won't even realize what it is. Probably."

Back to the business at hand. Okay. I take the remote control and set the tank into motion.

Beaky turns an excited shade of red.

Yes. Yes. The almighty Cthulhu wills Leonardo—the

tortoise on whom the Tank rests—to come into celestial motion once again.

As the tank rolls, Oliver walks next to it in silence—no doubt thinking up the most politic way to fire me.

We reach the kitchen, and by the time Grandpa peers into the tank, Beaky has already turned into a rock.

I feel an ache in my chest. This is the last prank Beaky will ever play on Grandpa... unless Grandpa visits him at Sealand.

Feeling crabby, I pointedly ignore Lemon and Grandma's libidinous eyebrow waggles.

"He's really leaving?" Fabio asks, eyeing the seemingly empty tank.

I nod.

"Maybe I'll finally be able to tell a few octopus jokes without fearing for my life," he says.

I narrow my eyes at Fabio, but he's already at it. "How do you make an octopus laugh?"

I roll my eyes. I heard this one in first grade.

"How?" Lemon asks theatrically.

"You give him ten tickles."

Did Oliver just groan?

"They don't have tentacles," Grandma says. "Those are arms."

Wow, she was paying attention in class.

Grandpa chuckles. "Octopuses are smart, being so well armed."

That's what happens when Grandpa spends too much time with Fabio.

"What do you call a gathering of octopuses?" Fabio asks next.

"They're antisocial, so there isn't a name for that," Oliver says. "Though I've heard the term 'shoal' used."

"Wrong," Fabio says. "The correct answer is: octoposse."

Har-har. That sounds like the nickname they call me behind my back: Octopussy.

"We're going to be late for work," I say.

"Who was Oedipus?" Fabio asks.

"Who?" Grandma asks, clearly intrigued.

"An octopus who slept with his own mother."

"That doesn't work," I say to hide a reluctant chuckle. Somehow, I haven't heard that one. "Having children is one of the last things a female octopus does in her life. Her son wouldn't reach maturity in time."

Fabio shakes his head. "Leave it to Olive to turn perfectly innocent incest into necrophilia."

Is Grandma going to lecture him on kink shaming?

Nope.

Grandpa laughs disproportionately loudly, then says, "This boy always krakens me up."

With that, they high-five each other, and I groan.

"Ready?" I ask Oliver before this can devolve further.

He nods very enthusiastically, so I roll the tank into the garage while Oliver says goodbye, lying through his teeth by claiming that "it was very nice to meet everyone."

In the driveway is the Sealand van Dex drove yesterday.

Was it thoughtful or Machiavellian of Oliver to bring it first thing?

"One sec," he says and sets up the ramp in the back of the van.

"Thanks." I guide the tank up the ramp and go inside to secure it.

Oliver walks up the ramp. "All set?"

I nod. "Drive slowly, please."

"Of course. Come."

I climb out of the back of the van, and Oliver opens the passenger door for me.

"Thanks," I say as I get inside.

He joins me and begins driving slowly, as I asked.

We ride in silence for a few seconds, which is made that much more uncomfortable for me by an overpowering awareness of his ocean surf smell, his strong hands gripping the wheel, his—

"So," I say, desperate to distract myself before I jump him. "Why manatees?"

He purses his lips, which makes me want to nibble on them. "This is Florida, so it was either that or gators." He smiles, showing off white teeth. "Manatees are an endangered species, and I've always been into conservationism, so it was meant to be." He glances at me. "Why octopuses?"

"I honestly don't know. I've loved them for as long as I can remember. My parents claim I saw a picture of one in a coloring book and fell in love. They also claim it was my first word—but I'm skeptical."

He stops at a red light. "I don't find it all that hard to believe."

"What about Sealand?" I ask.

He grips the wheel tighter. "What about it?"

Oh, right. Dex mentioned there was an ex-girl-friend-related mess there, so I have to tread lightly.

"What made you want to provide a home for sea creatures?" I ask. "Is that because of your interest in manatees?"

He shakes his head. "The manatees came later. I think it all started when I was just a kid. Mom brought home a live lobster, but I didn't let her cook it. At first, I kept the lobster in the bathtub, and then I got her an aquarium."

I grin. "I don't find it all that hard to believe."

"Clawdia is actually still around," he says. "You can say hi to her at the Crustacean Station."

Makes sense. When unmolested, an American lobster can live up to a hundred-and-forty years.

Speaking of molestation—time to see if I still have my job after almost doing that to my boss. "What's the enrichment situation at the Crustacean Station?" I ask. "Need any help?"

He turns onto the road that leads into the Sealand parking lot. "They're not a priority, but when you get the chance, please have a look. Currently, we're copying what other aquariums do, but I'm not sure everyone appreciates just how smart these animals are."

He sneaks a glance at me. "I have a feeling they'll benefit from your unique approach. That goes for all my charges."

Piranha massacre is in full swing in my belly—and not just because he makes it sound like I'm not getting fired.

Well, not yet anyway. If I act on my strong urge to lick my boss, that might change.

He parks, and I get Beaky's tank out.

I half expect Oliver to leave, but he insists on coming with us to "see Beaky settled."

"I had an idea I wanted to run by you," I say as we start walking.

He gathers his loose hair into the man bun, a gesture that shouldn't be arousing but is. The muscles in his arms flex as he secures the bun with a thin black scrunchie. "What's up?"

"I was thinking I'd leave this mobile tank here so Beaky can go on walks, the way he's done while living with me."

He nods. "If he likes it, I don't see why not."

Whew. Maybe having Beaky here won't be so bad for me. It's obviously a huge upgrade for Beaky himself.

Still—and I know I'm being shellfish—I will miss seeing him when I wake up in the morning.

"It's okay if you want to spend extra time with him," Oliver says softly, as though reading my mind.

I turn his way. "On company time?"

He smiles. "Keeping Beaky happy and entertained is

as much your job as keeping lobsters and manatees content. Seeing how Beaky is about to get moved into a new place, he'll be stressed—so he'll need extra attention."

I dart a glance at Beaky and his excited red color. Somehow, I get the feeling that once he gets into his huge new home, his three hearts will find a way to handle the separation much better than my single one.

"Thanks," I tell Oliver as we step into the building that houses Beaky's new digs.

"See that?" I say to the mobile tank. "That's all yours."

Beaky turns white.

We are awed, priestess-subject. The Tank is the world, but this New Tank is a whole universe. Praise Cthulhu, the multiverse theory might've been right all along, which means Leonardo might not be the only tortoise carrying a Tank on his back. There might be more, like Raphael, Donatello, and Michelangelo. Our nine brains are blown. Everything doesn't just revolve around a single Tank, but two or three, or four. Given the gravity of this achievement, by the power vested in us by Cthulhu himself, we promote priestess-subject to High Priestess... and we shall be God Emperor of the Tanks. With an "s" at the end, as in plural.

Oliver watches in fascination as I show him the safety features that I implemented last night. Next, I unseal the mobile tank and move Hulk and the other critters over to the new place before tackling the VIP himself.

As soon as I secure him inside the big tank, Beaky

begins eagerly exploring his new habitat. If he's stressed, I don't see it.

"About your work last night," Oliver says, pulling me out of my octopus observation. "I understand why you stayed late, but going forward, please work reasonable hours."

That sounds like he cares about my wellbeing. That, or Beaky's transfer has scrambled my brain too much to think clearly.

"Isn't it better for you if I work overtime for free?" I ask.

His cyan eyes gleam softly, making my breath catch and my core tingle. "I don't want you to burn out. You have too much important work still to do."

"Deal," I manage to say. "I won't work too late. What else? Do you want me to do fewer chores at my grandparents' house?"

Which reminds me… I should at least take out the garbage for them or something.

His phone rings. He tears his gaze away from me and checks the screen. "I have a meeting. Got to go."

And just like that, I'm left alone with Beaky.

———

Since my boss said it was okay, I spend half the day with Beaky and come up with a dozen ideas for puzzles I can stick into his new tank, some of which are only possible given the bigger space.

Afterward, I revisit the manatees and implement a

few more of my ideas before testing out some TV content to see if they'll enjoy something aside from seaweed-related documentaries.

Rose comes over just as *Aquaman* appears on the screen inside the tanks.

"Their appetites are much better," she says after we greet each other. "Showing them Jason Momoa might be overkill at this point."

I grin. Rose's HR hat isn't on, that's for sure. "There's a lot of water in that movie, so—"

"Oh, I trust you." Rose hands me a bundle of clothing—beige and blue this time. "You'll have to wear this tomorrow."

My good mood vanishes. My ex really messed me up when it comes to people telling me what to wear.

"I know how you feel," Rose says. "I hate doing the tours, but we all have to chip in."

I frown. "Tours?"

She looks at me with a confused expression. "We didn't tell you about the tours?"

I shake my head.

"Well," she says. "It's exactly what it sounds like. A group comes to Sealand, and you walk them around, show them everything. Tomorrow is your first one."

"What do I tell them?"

She gestures north. "Aruba is about to do her tour, so why don't you shadow her."

Great. That poor group is about to get a load of TMI about dolphins.

"I'll go do that," I say.

"Good luck," Rose says.

When I walk over to the crowd gathered around Aruba, I gape at four individuals uncomprehendingly: Fabio, Lemon, Grandma, and Grandpa.

"Surprise," Lemon says when they spot me. "We decided to check out your place of work."

"Miss Hyman," Aruba exclaims at me before looking adoringly at Fabio. "Do you know these people?"

Gee, someone with a face just like mine wasn't a good enough clue? Also, should I tell her that Fabio is even less sexually interested in her than one of her dolphins would be? Nah. That would not be appropriate work conversation, right?

As I introduce Aruba to my family quartet, it becomes clearer that she really just wanted to learn Fabio's name. She repeats it with relish and asks him if he's related to *that* Fabio.

"Fabio is my first name," he says. "And his. Why would we be related?"

I'm not defending Aruba, but there is some resemblance, considering my friend's angular facial features and longish hair—though it's not nearly as long as Oliver's. Or the original Fabio's. Not to mention, our Fabio wouldn't be caught dead holding a woman on the cover of a romance novel.

Aruba giggles coquettishly. "You're so funny."

Oh, no. I hope he doesn't take that as an excuse to make jokes.

To my relief, he doesn't. He must've picked up on Aruba's attraction to him and wants this tour to end as soon as possible. An excited vagina—or any vagina—is Fabio's worst nightmare. He likes to brag that he was a C-section baby and thus managed to avoid a vagina even when he was born.

The tour starts.

As I suspected, out of her ten facts about sea creatures, nine are about dolphins.

"Adorable," Fabio says when we reach Otteraction. "Too bad you don't have any wolves or twinks."

Aruba sidles up so close to him I half expect her to sniff him.

"Wait until you see the dolphins," she says seductively.

Can't she see that his comment was about Dex, not the otters?

The tour continues, and I notice Aruba doesn't bother showing Beaky to anyone. Though, in her defense, he just arrived today, so she might not know he's here.

"And now, the best part," Aruba says as we reach the dolphins. Speaking faster than a sailfish swims, she showers everyone with factoids such as "the Navy trains dolphins to clear underwater mines," and "Amazon river dolphins are pink," and "dolphins never drink water—seawater would make them sick, like it would us," and last but not least, "they can blow air from their blowholes at a hundred miles per hour."

I guess we're allowed to say "blowhole" on the tour. Good to know.

"Do you have killer whales?" Fabio asks.

What is he thinking? Aruba looks like she might rub up against him at any second.

"We don't." She licks her lips disturbingly. "But did you know they're actually dolphins?"

It's true. Orcas are the biggest members of the dolphin family, and unlike their "look at me, I'm cute" smaller brethren, they don't pretend to be anything but the killing machines that they are.

The tour continues, but even when we reach the manatees, Aruba explains everything in dolphin terms, including that "manatees are water mammals, like dolphins," and "they sleep with half a brain at a time, like dolphins, and for the same reasons—they need to breathe and would drown if they were unconscious while sleeping." She concludes everything with, "Unlike dolphins, manatees don't use echolocation and are herbivores."

Manatees don't kill their newborns either, the way her precious dolphins do. Also, manatees don't practice "aggressive herding," which is when males corner females and don't let them leave until they mate. This activity sounds pretty rapey to my human ears, and all the claims humans make about dolphins sexually attacking them do not help matters. #MeTuna.

I keep my thoughts to myself, however, and mentally prep the script I'll use when I do this tomorrow. It will have a lot less dolphin trivia, that's for sure.

After the tour, I grab lunch with my family, where I dodge questions about Oliver for most of the meal. Toward the end, Fabio and Lemon inform me that they won't be home tonight. They're going on a trip to Orlando and will be sleeping over there in a hotel.

When the lunch is over, I resume my Sealand duties until closing, then head home in an Uber and have dinner with my grandparents. They confirm that tomorrow is garbage collection day, so I decide to be useful and take out the garbage before heading to bed.

Opening the garage door, I wheel the heavy bin down the driveway, making sure to secure the lid with a special tie—because raccoons. I'm about to turn and head back up to the house when a bark makes me jump.

Startled, I turn and lock eyes with none other than my boss and his wiener.

CHAPTER
Fifteen

"HEY," I blurt, as unprofessional as can be. Hungrily, I take in his appearance: the same sleeveless tank as the first time I saw him, cargo shorts, long hair loose and tousled in a way that makes me think of sex. Of course, everything about Oliver makes me think of sex.

"Hello," he says, much more formally. His dog doesn't give a flying carp about his boss's tone, though. Tofu's tail looks like a Slim Jim, and he wags it so fast it's a wonder his butt doesn't take flight.

A reluctant smile curves Oliver's lips. "He likes you."

I crouch and pet Tofu's head as he frantically tries to lick me. "For someone named after a tasteless food, he's got great taste."

Oliver scoffs. "Tasteless? You've clearly never tried my sweet-and-sour tofu."

I blink up at him. "You eat tofu?" More importantly, why is my mouth filling with saliva all of a sudden?

His smile widens. "My dog's name didn't clue you in?"

Realizing that my crouched position puts my face right at his Aqua-manhood, I fix my gaze on the dog. "My octopus's name is Beaky, but I don't eat beaks."

"Good to know," he says. "I do eat tofu, all the time."

Having a conversation with his dick is too distracting, so I rise to my feet, which causes Tofu to whine in disappointment. "Are you a vegetarian?" I ask, lowering my hand to let Tofu lick it.

I thought Oliver was just avoiding seafood, like me —a way of eating that doesn't actually have a special term... unless it's reverse pescatarianism?

"I'm vegan," he says. "I don't eat dairy, eggs, or meat."

Wow. How did he manage to not mention this before? As one of Fabio's jokes goes: "How do you know if someone is vegan? They'll tell you the moment you meet them."

Biting my lip, I run my gaze over Oliver's well-defined muscles. "You don't look vegan."

He lifts his eyebrows. "Why not?

Carp. "You just look like you eat a lot of meat," I say lamely.

Great going. Next, I'll be talking about his man meat.

Oliver sighs. "Every time someone meets a vegan, they turn into a nutritionist. If I had a dollar for every time someone asked me where I get my protein from, I'd be a millionaire."

"But... where *do* you get it from?" I'm only half kidding.

He rolls his eyes. "Where do gorillas get theirs?"

"Gorillas?" I look at Tofu in case he has the answer. He doesn't.

"Gorillas are muscular herbivores with DNA very similar to that of humans."

I grin. "Are you calling yourself a gorilla?"

"I'm saying that plant foods have a lot more protein than most people realize."

"Fair enough. Have you always been vegan, or did you catch it recently?"

"Switched a few years ago."

"Why?" I ask. "Are you trying to get psychic powers, like that guy from *Scott Pilgrim vs. The World?*"

He cocks his head. "You sure you want to know? I don't want to sound preachy."

"Tell me."

He fixes me with a level stare. "The meat and dairy industries are bad for the environment."

Oh. I thought there'd be a story, like that lobster tale of his. "That's some serious commitment to the environment. The solar panels, and now this."

He shrugs. "My impact may be tiny, but every little bit helps."

I look down at Tofu. "Are vegans allowed to consort with hot dogs?"

"Only if they're tofu hot dogs." He grins at his little companion.

Why am I feeling so swoony?

Danger. Danger. This is my boss.

I clear my throat. "I'd better let you guys get back to your walk."

I turn to leave, but Oliver says, "Wait." As if afraid his words aren't enough, he touches my elbow, and my entire body jolts from the impact of his touch. My breath catches and heat streaks through my veins as I turn to face him, my heart hammering madly in my chest.

"What?" I manage to ask in a semi-steady voice.

His eyes gleam in the rapidly darkening twilight. "Can I ask you for a favor?"

"What's up?"

Is it wrong that I hope he wants a sexual favor? And is it a favor if I want it too? We'll just have to make sure not to do it right here on the street, or else our nosy neighbors will be all over us. The good news is that Lemon isn't in the guest room tonight, and there's always his house. It's just that—

"Tofu counts people," Oliver says, dumping cold water on my overactive libido.

Trying to hide my disappointment, I peer at the cute little wiener. "He what?"

"That's what I call it. He makes a mental note of how many people are walking him, and if that number decreases, he gets very upset." At my still-confused expression, Oliver explains, "Last week, my brothers were here, and the three of us went with Tofu for a walk. One of them left, and Tofu noticed his human count was off. He started whining and eventually refused to walk. I had to carry him back home."

"You think Tofu counts me as one of his humans?" The better question is: is Oliver making up this unlikely story to spend more time with me?

"Yeah," he says. "The day we first met, after we parted, he got upset because he'd counted you."

Hmm. Tofu did give me a sad look that day.

"So... you want me to walk with you guys?"

Oliver nods. "I would appreciate it."

"Okay," I say casually, as if my pulse isn't going bananas from excitement. "I'll suffer your company a bit longer, for Tofu."

Oliver flashes me a smile. "Tofu appreciates your sacrifice."

We begin walking, and I notice Tofu looking back periodically, clearly making sure his human count is up to date.

"So, do your parents live in this community?" I ask.

Oliver shakes his head. "When they retired, they moved to the Keys."

I chuckle. "I guess when a Floridian wants someplace warmer, it's either that or Death Valley, California."

Tofu tries to sniff what looks like deer poo, so Oliver pulls on his leash. "I think my folks moved to the Keys for the clothing-optional beaches—and those aren't as abundant in Death Valley."

I snort. "Never tell *my* parents about those nudist beaches, or else they'll move to the Keys too."

What am I saying? He'll never—and I mean never, ever—meet my parents.

Oliver grins. "Where do your folks live now?"

"They have a farm in upstate New York."

He asks about the farm, and I tell him about all the exotic animals my folks have rescued over the years, including a pink fairy armadillo and dik-diks.

He lifts his eyebrows. "Dik-diks?"

"Tiny antelopes. Want to see a dik-dik pic?"

Chuckling, he agrees, so I pull out my phone and show him a picture. "That's Bean and Buzz."

"Very cute," he says. "Which is which?"

"Buzz is the horny one—in every sense of the word."

His eyes crinkle in the corners. "You must've gotten your love of animals from your parents."

"I never thought about it, but you might be right."

As I speak, looking up at his face, I feel us getting pulled toward each other again. My breathing picks up, my skin prickling with heat, and it's all I can do not to sway toward him.

Oliver looks to be fighting a similar battle within himself—but then Tofu saves the day by farting. Loudly. Then, in case that wasn't enough, he goes number two.

Hey, that's better than a cold shower.

Oliver bends down and picks up the deed with a bag, making me recall the wise words of Jerry Seinfeld: "Dogs are the leaders of the planet. If you see two life forms, one of them's making a poop, the other one's carrying it for him, who would you assume is in charge?"

"This right here is why octopuses should replace dogs as man's best friend," I say when Oliver resumes walking, poop in tow.

He shrugs. "Keeps me humble."

"Good point. Maybe the world would be a better place if more men were humiliated by their wieners."

He laughs. "Well, now that Tofu has accomplished what we set out to do, we'd better head home."

I agree and we turn back.

"I heard you're doing a tour tomorrow," he says.

I nod. "I'm a little freaked out about it, actually. Mind telling me what you think about this script I've come up with?"

"Not at all. Go for it."

As I tell him what I plan to say and in what order I'll show the exhibits, we reach my grandparents' house.

"That's perfect," Oliver says. "Great job."

My chest goes all floaty, and the piranhas in my belly go at it again.

"I guess this is goodbye," I say, swallowing as I stare up at him, at his full, soft lips quirked in that warm, approving smile. I want to touch them with my finger, then lick said finger, then use my own lips to—

No. Must fight the pull.

"Yeah." His gaze is similarly glued to my mouth. "Good luck tomorrow."

A blinding beam from a flashlight hits my eyes.

"Caper, is someone bothering you?" Grandpa shouts from the front door.

"No!" I yell back. "I'm just talking to Oliver."

Grandpa comes closer, and I realize he's got a shotgun as well.

"This is my cue to go," Oliver says, warily eyeing the weapon.

I flash him a rueful grin. "Good night."

"Later, kelpcake." Oliver picks up Tofu and strides toward his house.

I hurry toward an apologetic-looking Grandpa.

"I didn't mean to scare your boyfriend away," he says. "We just got a message from Blue and—"

I freeze in place. "What message?"

"You'd better speak to her yourself."

"Fine." I rush back inside and locate my phone.

I have two missed videocalls and a text from Blue:

Brett bought a ticket to Florida. His flight is tomorrow, and the airport is too close to Palm Pilot for my liking.

Fuck. Brett is my horrible ex, and Palm Pilot is what Blue calls Palm Islet, the town I'm in.

Hoping against hope that I've misunderstood something, I videocall my sister back.

"Hey," she says. "Did you get my text?"

"Yeah. How do you know he's flying here?"

She avoids looking at the camera. "I've been keeping tabs on him ever since I filed that restraining order on your behalf."

If she thinks I'm mad about the meddling, she's wrong. The asshole mistook Blue for me while drunk and physically assaulted her. Fortunately, it ended with him getting his ass kicked and in trouble with the law. That he turned violent wasn't a huge surprise for me. When we were together, the abuse was psychological, but by the time I left him, I'd suspected he was capable of much worse.

"Will you know if he breaks the restraining order?" I whisper.

She nods, eyes glinting. "Forget one hundred feet. If he so much as gets within ten miles of you, I'll let you know immediately."

"Thanks." I hang up the phone, tell Grandpa I've spoken with Blue, and head into the guest room.

I'm not sure if it's the news about my ex or the lack of Beaky in the room, but I have trouble sleeping again.

CHAPTER
Sixteen

AFTER A RESTLESS NIGHT, I wake up late and have to hurry so I'm not tardy for the tour.

Midway to Sealand, I realize I left my phone at home.

Higgins' eye pearlymussel! If I go back now, I'd definitely let the visitors down, and there could be job consequences. Instead of turning back, I floor the gas.

When I get to the meeting spot, the tour guests are already waiting for me, looking impatient.

"Hi, folks," I say as cheerfully as I can. "Sorry for the slight delay. Let's head over to our octopus. He just joined Sealand yesterday, so you'll be the first group to see him."

Beaky's newness causes some of the faces to perk up, which is what I hoped for.

"Where are you all from?" I ask as we walk. Everyone takes turns answering, and they warm up to me even more, proving once again how much people love talking about themselves.

When we enter Beaky's habitat, he looks excited to see me—at least that's how I interpret his bright red coloring and splayed arms.

Are these worshippers here to honor us, High Priestess, or are they entertainment?

"What a creepy creature," says a lady holding a tiny Yorkshire terrier in her hands.

"Yeah," mutters her boyfriend. "Ugly fucker."

She fans herself theatrically. "It wants to eat Nacho."

"No, he doesn't," I lie. If little Nacho were to take a dip in the tank, he would end up in Beaky's beak in three heartbeats.

"I know these things," she says. "I'm a pet psychic."

Oh, right. During the introductions, she said she and her boyfriend were from Cassadaga, Florida, which is "the psychic capital of the world."

Beaky looks from the dog to its owner.

Heathen. Only the mighty Cthulhu has psychic powers, not a mere meat sack like you. If you could really read our minds, you'd throw that tasty morsel into the Tank and bow to us in supplication.

I force myself to smile at the Cassadaga couple and segue into my spiel with, "Your powers must be very strong. An octopus has nine minds to read."

Everyone except the psychic lady and her boyfriend chuckles, and I talk about octopuses until I see some eyes glazing over.

"The otters are next," I say, and this is greeted with enthusiasm.

When we get to Otteraction, Dex is there, eating tacos for lunch. As I start the tour speech, he stays respectfully silent, allowing me to drive the narrative.

"Otters are so cute," the psychic lady says when I ask if anyone has any questions. She puts a finger to her temple à la Professor X. "They're sending me their thoughts." Her voice sounds higher pitched as she announces, "'We want to play with Nacho.'"

"I'm afraid they're much more likely to eat Nacho than to play with him," I say.

"But Nacho wants to play with *them*," she says.

Dex clears his throat. "Please keep your dog away from the otters. They're predators and will eat whatever they can overpower, including beavers, raccoons, snapping turtles, snakes, and even small gators. Nacho to them would be as this taco is to me." He crunches into his taco, and the psychic lady pales.

"How about we go visit the dolphins?" I say quickly.

I'm slightly annoyed at how well that dodge works. At the word "dolphins," everyone's eyes light up excitedly, even Nacho's.

Aruba isn't there when we get to the dolphin pool, thank Cthulhu.

I start by introducing the dolphins, and when I get to Hopper—Aruba's favorite—he leaps out of the water to everyone's delight.

I hate to admit it, but dolphins make my job as a

tour guide very easy. My lecture is going over really well... that is, until there's a loud bark, followed by a splash.

"Help," the psychic lady shouts. "Nacho jumped into the pool!"

CHAPTER
Seventeen

RAM CICHLID FUCKER. The dog is totally swimming with the dolphins—and if someone doesn't do something, he might soon be sleeping with the fishes.

Before I can make a move, the psychic's boyfriend leaps into the pool.

Why, Cthulhu, why? Now tomorrow's headline will be: "Florida man cuts open dolphin's stomach to retrieve deceased dog"—and it will be on my watch.

Hopper chirps loudly and swims in the dog's direction.

"He wants to eat Nacho," the psychic lady shouts hysterically.

"They're well fed," I say, hoping I'm right. "I doubt they—"

My point is rendered moot as the guy grabs the dog and hands him over to his girlfriend.

Whew. Tragedy averted.

Or maybe not.

As the boyfriend swims for the ladder leading out of the pool, Hopper torpedoes forward and grabs him by his pants.

Seriously, Cthulhu?

"She smells dick in the water," the psychic shouts. "Stay away from my man!"

Isn't it sharks and blood? In any case, I'm afraid she's not too far from the truth, and the headline I'm dreading becomes: "Dolphin humps Florida man during Sealand tour"—an even worse thing to happen on my watch.

"It's okay! Hopper just wants his belt," Aruba shouts. She must've just come back from lunch.

The belt, freed from the pants by the dolphin, sinks to the floor, but the dolphin resumes tugging on the pants. The pants and the tighty-whities the poor guy is wearing slip off, exposing his pale, pimply butt.

Oh, carp.

Is the dolphin about to get sexually aggressive?

Seems like it. Hopper doesn't dive for the belt. He clearly still wants something from the human.

"She has a dick!" the psychic shouts, pointing frantically toward Hopper.

Cthulhu help us. That huge thing she's pointing at is definitely the dolphin's penis. Female dolphins have truly labyrinthian reproductive tracts, so the males have what's called a "prehensile penis." Highly dexterous, it can swivel, grab, and grope like a human hand. Relatedly, dolphins copulate for pleasure (like humans) and can ejaculate multiple times per hour (unlike all but a few very lucky humans).

What do I do?

Maybe Aruba can get one of the female dolphins to take one for the team? Or a male one? They do that sometimes.

My frantic gaze falls on a flotation device, and I grab it.

"Here." I toss it to the guy, who's flailing in panic next to the frisky dolphin. "Grab on and don't let him drag you under."

"Hopper would never do that," Aruba exclaims and blows angrily into her whistle.

Two things happen simultaneously. The guy grabs the device and kicks frantically toward the ladder, and Hopper swims toward Aruba, distracted from whatever he was about to do by the promise of a treat.

Moving like a ninja, Aruba tosses Hopper a fish as I help the shaking guy out of the pool.

Hopper, eating his fish, looks as happy as a geoduck clam. I guess he was hungry. Nacho got lucky. So did the psychic's poor boyfriend. Given what could've happened, the dolphin should be renamed Humper—but I keep this to myself, or else Aruba might throw me to him instead of the next fish.

"We're leaving," the psychic lady states indignantly. "And never coming back."

Aruba and I exchange glances in rare-for-us agreement. "Good riddance," she mutters under her breath.

I resume the tour, and things are blessedly

uneventful until we get to the manatees, which is when Oliver joins us.

Carp. Is he here to fire me over the dolphin debacle? It wasn't my fault, but—

"Don't mind me," Oliver says to the crowd. "I just want to hear this part of the tour."

Oh, he wants to hear me talk about the manatees. Makes sense.

I go into it. His eyes light up and stay lit the whole time, though the same can't be said for the rest of the people on the tour.

In their defense, no manatee fact can top what they just saw at the dolphin exhibit.

"Amazing job," Oliver says when I'm done. He does a slow clap.

The rest of the people echo his ovation, but probably out of social pressure.

I bow anyway. "That's the end of the tour, folks. Thank you so much for visiting Sealand."

Everyone disperses as Oliver walks over and smiles at me. "I meant it. You did an amazing job."

With that, he strides away, leaving me with a ruptured ovary.

I look at Betsy, whose gaze is a lot less grumpy than it was the last time I checked on her.

Fine. If you want him so much, he's yours. My new crush is Jason Momoa.

My stomach is rumbling, so I get some lunch. Then I work by the manatee exhibit in the hopes of bumping into Oliver again, but he never shows.

Oh, well. Maybe this is for the best.

He's still my boss.

At five p.m. sharp, I head home.

After parking the car, I walk down the driveway to bring in the now-empty garbage bin. As I wheel it toward the garage, I realize I've made a strategic mistake. If I'd waited to do this until the time I met Oliver last night, I could've "bumped into him," and Tofu would've "counted me," and we would've had another stroll together.

Again, oh well. And again, maybe for the best.

A rustling of nearby bushes catches my attention.

This is Florida, so it could be a wild boar, a snake, a raccoon, or a gator.

When the actual source of the sound reveals itself, my pulse leaps and I freeze in place.

This is so much worse than any wild animal.

It's my ex-boyfriend, Brett.

CHAPTER
Eighteen

A HURRICANE of unpleasant emotions makes landfall at the sight of his dreaded face.

We dated for four months, three of which were pretty good, but then he got possessive and controlling —which, to my shame, wasn't why I broke up with him. The last straw was when I caught him cheating.

"Hi, baby," he drawls, running his hand through his short dark hair.

Ugh. I can't believe I ever found him attractive. Knowing what I know now, he reminds me of a sickly oyster toadfish.

"'Hi, baby?'" I glare at him. "You attack my sister, violate your restraining order, and you 'hi, baby' me?"

His nostrils flare. "I just want to talk."

"There's nothing for us to talk about."

He advances on me, and I can smell alcohol on his breath.

Not good. When he attacked Blue, she said he was drunk.

"Can't we just talk?" he says, and now that I know what to look for, his speech sounds slurred.

My heartbeat skyrockets further, and I wish I'd taken Grandpa's advice about carrying a gun. "Please, Brett. I want you to leave."

He leans in. "I'm not going anywhere until you hear me out."

I back away. "If you don't leave now, you'll get into more trouble."

He narrows his eyes at me. "Are you threatening me?"

I take another step back. "Aren't you breaking your bail conditions by being here?"

He advances on me again.

Okay, I guess I'm going to flee.

I turn—just in time to see a Tesla come to a tire-screeching stop a couple of feet away.

I blink as Oliver leaps out of the vehicle.

Before I can wonder how and why he's here, he's already between me and Brett.

"Who the fuck are you?" Brett asks nastily.

Oliver balls his hands into fists. "You have three seconds to leave. One."

"Fuck you." Brett takes a threatening step toward Oliver.

Doesn't he see the murderous glint in Oliver's eyes?

If you murder someone, are you still a vegan? Probably, so long as you don't cannibalize the body afterward. Besides, Oliver is vegan for environmental reasons, so he might kill Brett and tell himself he shrank his carbon footprint.

"Two," Oliver growls.

Brett sneers.

Idiot. Can't he see that Oliver is more muscular? I used to think Brett had a nice body, being tall and lean, but Oliver makes him look like a slithering eel.

Two things happen at once.

Oliver says, "Three," and Brett swings a fist.

A spike of adrenaline makes me gasp.

Oliver sidesteps Brett's strike and smashes a fist into Brett's nose.

Brett grunts, stumbling back. Blood gushes out of his nose, but he still looks ready to charge. What a carping idiot. That, or he's really, really stupid while drunk.

I don't know what to do, but then a distant wail reaches my hearing.

A police siren?

It must be, and it makes me worry about Oliver getting in trouble with the law. I'm no lawyer, but in high school, both parties involved in a fight would get detention, so I figure the same might be true for adults.

Clutching his nose, Brett turns on his heel and breaks into a run.

Whew. He must've heard the siren too—or finally understood he was about to get his ass kicked, again.

I rush to Oliver's side and look him over. "Are you okay?"

Apart from looking much too delicious, nothing seems wrong with him.

He grips my shoulders, his cyan gaze roaming over my body. "Did he hurt you?"

"No, no. What are you doing here? How did you—"

Oliver's phone rings. "I'm sorry," he says and releases me to pick it up.

A phone call at a time like this? Who—

"Hi, Blue," Oliver says.

Blue? As in my sister?

"Yes, I got here just in time, but the asshole ran away before the police arrived."

I gape at Oliver as he hangs up the phone.

"Your sister was looking for you, but couldn't reach you," he says, confirming my budding suspicion.

"Oh, yeah," I mutter. "I forgot my phone at home today."

"She figured that out quickly," he says. "Called Sealand to get in touch with you. Since you'd already left, I asked if I could help, and she told me that your ex is a dangerous stalker and that she tracked him to your grandparents' house. Sorry I couldn't get here faster."

I rub my temples. "You got here in time. I don't know how to thank you."

Before he can reply, a car with blaring sirens pulls over next to the driveway, the word "Sheriff" written on the side.

The sheriffs (or is it deputies or officers?) come out with guns ready.

"He ran that way." I point north. "I'm not sure you'll be able to catch him."

They holster their guns. "A car is waiting by each of the community exits," one of the cops says. "We'll get him."

I blink at him. "I didn't realize you guys had so much manpower, given the size of the town and the low crime rate and all."

The cop shrugs. "Some bigwig in New York called in a favor with the Sheriff. Apparently, a dangerous fugitive was spotted here." He shows me a picture of Brett. "This is the guy, right?"

"Yep, that's who ran away," I say, wondering which bigwig he's talking about. Did Blue pull some strings, or is *she* the bigwig?

Another car pulls up, and my grandparents leap out of it, Grandpa predictably holding a shotgun.

"Sir, I'm going to ask you to put that away," the cop says to Grandpa.

Grandpa does as he's told, and then he and Grandma pepper everyone with a million questions.

"I'll be right back," I say. "I need to check my phone."

Leaving them all talking, I go into the house.

When I locate my phone, I see a million messages. Most are from Blue, but some are from Lemon (Blue tried to reach me via her) and Mom (for the same reason).

I call everyone and tell them all is well.

When I come back out, the police car is gone, and

Grandma and Grandpa are thanking Oliver for his help.

"I'm very sorry, Caper," Grandpa says when he spots me. "We were at our dance lesson with the phones turned off, so we didn't realize Blue had called looking for you."

Grandma tugs on his sleeve. "We should go."

"Go?" Grandpa looks at her as if she's grown eyes on the top of her head, like a spotcheck stargazer.

Grandma darts a pointed glance at Oliver. "We have that cartoon we wanted to watch, remember?"

Is she about to talk about tentacle porn in front of my boss?

Grandpa nods theatrically. "Right. Right. The hentai. Let's go." He looks at me and Oliver. "Have fun, you kids."

Oliver's eyes crinkle as he watches them leave, but when he turns back to look at me, his expression is serious. "How are you doing?" he asks quietly.

I sigh. "I'm kind of numb, to be honest."

He looks in the direction Brett ran before turning back to face me. "Want to talk about it?"

I avoid his gaze. "That was my ex."

He waits patiently, and for some bizarre reason, I find myself telling him the full ugly story—how I met Brett at my last job, how things started well but quickly took a turn for the worse, culminating with the cheating incident. What I don't mention are the bits where Brett would tell me what to do and even what to wear—and that I'd listen to him, like a chump. Sometimes, I wish I could get into a time machine, go back in time, and kick Brett in the balls instead of letting him control me.

"When I left him, he didn't let me take Beaky with me, and he hated Beaky before that," I say in conclusion.

Oliver's hands clench and unclench at his sides. "I should've punched that fucker in the nuts."

Huh. Great minds think alike.

"I'm so sorry you had to go through that," he continues, his voice tight.

"Hey, it wasn't your fault," I say. Carefully, I ask, "What about you? What was your worst relationship?"

I know a little about his dating history thanks to Dex's gossip, but I want to hear it from the source's beautiful mouth.

For a second, I think he'll remember that he's my employer and his love life isn't any of my business, but to my surprise, he says, "Her name was—I mean is—Brooke." He sighs. "We dated for a year before I talked her into starting Sealand with me. It took a lot of work to get it off the ground, and as time went on, she grew to resent how dedicated I was to the place, and how I didn't have as much time for her." His features tighten further. "To get back at me, she slept with a key scientist, almost causing the entire venture to fall apart."

The pain in his eyes makes my heart feel like an octopus trying to escape though a tiny hole. "That sucks," I say softly. "Your ex sounds like a cookiecutter shark."

He clasps my hand, his fingers warm around mine. His eyes are earnest on my face. "And yours is like a pirate perch."

Warmth spreads through me as I squeeze his hand. "A gilt-head bream."

The barest hint of a smile touches his eyes. "A bloater?"

"No. The Hawaiian state fish—though I can't pronounce it."

"Humuhumunukunukuāpua'a," he says effortlessly.

"Wow." I gape at him. "You're *really* good with your tongue."

His gaze heats up, and his fingers tighten further around mine. "You have no idea what things I can do with my tongue."

Holy carp. I'm picturing his tongue on my pearl, and my fallopian tubes have turned into an octopus.

My heart hammers madly, and before I can think better of it, I blurt, "Show me."

His eyes flare, the cyan darkening to the color of a storm-racked ocean, and without further ado, he pulls me to him, claiming my mouth in a kiss as scorching as a submarine volcano.

I push against him, my soft parts molding against his hardness. His lips are as soft and delicious as I remember, his tongue stroking hungrily over every sensitive surface in my mouth, his big hands roaming over my back, my hips, my ass. I can feel myself dissolving, melting into him, and the world around us disappears.

Almost.

I think I hear a car pull over nearby. That, or the feverish heat inside me is making me hallucinate.

Oliver tears his lips away, breathing heavily as he gazes over my shoulder in frustration.

Carp.

The cursed car is real, and a sheepish-looking Lemon emerges from it, followed by an unrepentant Fabio.

"Why did you stop?" Fabio asks as the cab drives away. "Continue face-suck—"

Lemon punches Fabio in the shoulder, and he yelps in pain.

"Boundaries," she says sagely.

Fabio narrows his eyes at her. "Punch me again, and I'll—"

"I have to go," Oliver says, backing away.

I touch my swollen lips, my hand unsteady. "I'll see you tomorrow?"

He doesn't answer because he's already gone.

Grr.

I kissed my boss. This time knowing that he's my boss.

What was I thinking?

But he kissed me back.

What was *he* thinking?

I blame the adrenaline and the vestigial instincts from those horny cavewomen ancestors of mine. Seeing Oliver fight for me was a huge turn-on, even though it shouldn't have been.

"Sorry about the cockblock," Lemon says, wincing.

I blow out a breath. "You probably saved my job."

Fabio rolls his eyes. "How?"

"I still work for him, and he's got a thing about dating coworkers."

Fabio is about to argue, but my phone rings. "It's Blue," I tell them as I pick up.

"The cops didn't catch the fucker," Blue rattles out without a hello.

"They didn't?" I look around, in case Brett is about to leap out of the bushes again.

"No, but I'm pretty sure he's not in your community anymore."

I frown. "Pretty sure?"

Blue sighs. "He ditched his phone a few miles away from your location. Must've realized that's how I've been keeping track of him."

I squeeze my phone a bit too hard. "You can't track him anymore?"

She scoffs. "For now. Don't worry, I'll find a way."

I exhale a breath I didn't realize I was holding. If the NSA could find Brett, so can Blue. My sister is like Big Brother—always watching.

"Stay in touch," I say. "I have to go deal with Lemon and Fabio."

"Later," Blue says.

I hang up as Fabio arches an eyebrow. "Deal with us?"

With a harrumph, I drag him and Lemon inside—

just in case Brett was clever enough to have fooled Blue, as hard as that is to imagine.

Over dinner, I update them on everything, and they tell me about their plans for tomorrow—a trip to Miami, where they'll stay until the day after tomorrow.

When I get to bed, all I can think about is Oliver and that kiss. Since Lemon is around, I don't take care of the building sexual pressure—which is for the best. Probably.

A single question swirls through my mind as I drift off.

What happens when I see Oliver at work tomorrow?

CHAPTER
Nineteen

I WORK at the manatee exhibit for most of the next day, and it pays off around four p.m., when I bump into Oliver "by accident."

"Hi," he says when he spots me.

He's looking as mouthwatering as always, but there's a tension in his shoulders and a guardedness to his expression. What's worse, he's not rushing over to kiss me—something a part of me really hoped would happen today.

"Hi yourself," I say, with all the casualness I can manage. "Here to visit Betsy?"

He nods and glances at my curvy rival. "She's been doing so much better, thanks to you."

I grin. "Maybe you can stop fussing over her now and pay attention to some other animals?"

"Great idea," he says. "I'll go check on the otters."

He turns and strides away. I stare after him, unsure

if I should be upset or relieved that he's keeping things professional.

————

As I drive home, I ponder how he'd act if we were to meet outside of work.

Would he kiss me then?

Too bad today isn't garbage day, or else I could put the bins out while he's walking Tofu—assuming I could get the timing right.

To make sure I don't miss him when it *is* garbage day, I set an alarm on my phone.

I'm totally not a stalker. I pinky swear.

Here's an idea, though: maybe I should get the mail instead?

When I pull into my grandparents' driveway, there's an unfamiliar car parked there, in addition to another one that makes my heartbeat speed up.

A Tesla.

His Tesla.

My grandparents invited him for another dinner?

I park and rush into the living room, only to come to a screeching halt.

I was right about Oliver being here, but I forgot to wonder who the other car belonged to, and now that I know, it's a disaster of blue-whale proportions.

My parents are here.

Yeah, my parents.

But it gets worse.

For some reason, Dad is massaging Oliver's earlobe.

But it gets worse.

Dad's thin ponytail has somehow gotten wrapped around Oliver's throat, like a silver eel.

But it gets worse.

Mom is staring at my boss with undisguised lust, and if she licked his free earlobe, I wouldn't be surprised in the slightest.

"Mom, Dad, what are you doing here?" My question comes out as a shriek.

Grandpa flashes Dad a grumpy look. "Someone got sick of the Hymans and came here. Happens every vacation."

Hey, at least he's not pulling his gun on Dad, like he did on Thanksgiving.

Mom narrows her eyes at her father. "We came to see Olive's boyfriend."

"He's not my boyfriend," I exclaim, sheepishly meeting Oliver's gaze.

His expression is unreadable.

Carp. Is he mad?

"Why not?" Dad asks without releasing Oliver's earlobe. "Love is lovely. All you need is—"

"Oliver is my boss," I say. "Now, can you please stop touching him?"

Dad reluctantly releases Oliver's earlobe. "The ear is a microsystem that represents the whole body."

"It does?" I don't dare ask which dangling body part

of Oliver's anatomy he thought he was fondling when massaging the earlobe.

"Yes," Dad says. "Oliver mentioned he had a headache, so I offered to trigger the release of some endorphins."

I guess it could've been worse. Blowjobs can also release endorphins.

Sighing, I ask, "Oliver, would you like a Tylenol?"

"No, thank you," Oliver says. "I'm feeling much better now."

Dad gives me a triumphant look. "See? Auriculotherapy really works."

Grandpa pretends to sneeze the words "snake oil."

Dad pulls his ponytail away from Oliver's throat. "We also came to make sure the business with Brett hasn't upset our little one's equilibrium."

Mom tears her lustful gaze away from Oliver and nods enthusiastically. "That boy is going to get karmic justice one of these days, just you wait."

Grr. Blue shouldn't have called them. They worry enough about me as is.

"Olive, why don't you sit?" Grandma gestures at a chair right next to Oliver. "The food is getting cold."

I sit down as everyone grabs something from the table.

Now that I know Oliver is vegan, his choices make more sense. He goes for the roasted peanuts appetizer, the mashed yams with herbs, and some dish I don't recognize with a lot of sauce.

Copying Oliver, I try the unfamiliar dish and accidentally moan in pleasure. "Grandma, what is this?"

Grandma grins at Oliver. "You want to tell her what you brought?"

Oliver nods. "That's sweet-and-sour tofu."

Mom elbows Dad and very loudly whispers, "He can cook too. Add in regular orgasms, and he'd be the perfect man."

Is it too much to hope Oliver didn't hear that?

Nope. He must have—that smirk is telling.

I taste the peanuts. Yum. A hint of maple and a bit of chipotle heat.

Oliver tries them as well, as do my parents.

"Nice peanuts," Dad says. "They remind me of the Reese's Pieces brownies we sometimes make at the farm."

"What peanuts?" Grandma asks. When she spots the plate in question, her eyes widen, and she exchanges a meaningful glance with Grandpa. Moving with startling sprightliness for her age, she snatches the plate before anyone can get more. "Those might not be that fresh. I shouldn't have put them out."

Weird, but oh well.

"So, Oliver," Mom says. "Has our daughter told you that Harry and I rescue animals, just like you?"

"Yes, Crystal, she did," Oliver says. "I'm actually very curious about your farm."

Mom starts telling him all about their creatures while I digest the fact that Oliver and my parents are on a first-name basis. He didn't blink when she said

"Harry," and he called her "Crystal." What else did they talk about before I arrived? I wonder if Oliver kept a poker face as they introduced themselves. Crystal Hyman sounds like a virginal membrane that could cut someone during a deflowering, while Harry Hyman is basically the maidenhead of a gorilla.

"Do you do tours?" Oliver asks. "Or do you raise funds in other ways to support the animals?"

Carp. I know what's coming.

"We have jobs," Dad says. "I'm a penetration tester by day... and often by night."

Did Grandpa just reach for his gun?

Oliver arches an eyebrow. "A penetration tester?"

Dad grins. "It involves penetrating computer systems."

"By day," Mom says. "By night, it's me."

If Grandpa *is* going for the gun, can I ask him to put me out of my misery?

Oliver's poker face deserves at least an Oscar nomination. "What about you?" he asks my mom. "Are you also in the computer field?"

"No," she says. "I'm a chick sexer."

Grandpa sighs.

"Doesn't that sound like a fun hobby?" Dad asks.

Grandpa grits his teeth and is about to say something (or shoot someone) when Grandma puts a hand on his shoulder.

"A chick sexer separates baby chickens into male and female," Grandma says soothingly.

Grandpa grunts something unintelligible.

"That's an interesting job," Oliver says. "I bet they're as difficult to differentiate as fish."

"It was a great gig for a while," Mom says. "But not as much lately. More and more hatcheries are using in-ovo sexing."

"Oh, honey," Grandma says. "I didn't know that."

Dad winks at Grandma. "Don't worry, Mrs. Butchski. I'll support your daughter."

Grandpa looks at Dad approvingly for the first time today.

"Oh, I'll find another way to make money," Mom says confidently. "I've been doing some husbandry around the farm and might start offering my services to others."

Cthulhu take me. She proceeds to tell a story that always makes me want to bleach my brain through my ears: how she once brought our pet pig Petunia to orgasm as part of her artificial insemination.

"It raises the chance of piglets by six percent," Mom says. "I hear some handlers at big farms don't feel comfortable doing it, so I could charge a decent rate."

Sheesh. Orgasms for money. I wonder what's more ancient, agriculture or the oldest profession in the world?

"Why don't you have Oliver give you some tourist-friendly ideas," Grandpa says, clearly as eager for a subject change as I am. "He did it for Lemon and Fabio, and they're having a blast."

Oliver plays the tour guide again, though this time

he doesn't just suggest attractions. He also mentions some amazing-sounding restaurants and the must-try dishes there.

"Wow," Mom says. "Some of the dishes you described are making my mouth water."

With that, she grabs herself a portion of each dish on the table.

When she's right, she's right. Oliver's descriptions (or is it his lips?) have made my mouth water too, so I grab myself all the non-seafood items. Dad follows suit, as does Oliver, the latter only partaking in the vegan entrees.

For whatever reason, Grandma and Grandpa exchange a guilty look.

"Yummy," Dad says when he tries Oliver's sweet-and-sour dish. "I can't believe it's tofu."

Oliver grins. "The trick is the sauce."

Dad rubs his belly. "Reminds me of dik-dik."

I nearly choke on my yams.

"You've eaten a dik-dik?" Oliver asks, eyes wide.

Eating your pet must sound barbaric to his vegan ears... or any ears.

"It's not what you think." Mom gives Dad a chastising look. "She died of natural causes first."

Oliver looks from Mom to Dad, probably hoping someone will say it's a joke. "I'm not sure that makes it better," he says after a pause. "Is it even safe?"

"You think it's starting?" Grandma asks Grandpa, but he hushes her.

"If the animal wasn't ill, eating them after they pass away is perfectly safe," Dad says. "It's a way to honor them."

Oliver gapes at Dad. "Honor them?"

Dad swallows a dumpling whole without chewing —a bit like a dolphin with a fish. "Some cultures used to eat their dead relatives for the same reason. Bambi was like family to us, and now she's part of our bodies. What greater honor is there?"

Is it shellfish that my takeaway from all this is that I'm glad I never met the dik-dik in question?

Listening to all of this, Grandpa pulls out a gun. After a glare from Grandma, he hides it away and locks eyes with my dad. "If you even think about eating me after I die, I'll go Poltergeist on your hippie ass and then shoot you."

"Honey," Grandma whispers through the side of her mouth. "You know it's the drugs talking."

I frown. "What drugs?"

Grandpa gives Grandma an exasperated glance. "She never could keep a secret."

Mom looks at Grandma. "What drugs are you talking about? Harry and I are all-natural."

"Remember when you insisted on helping me set the table?" Grandma asks.

Mom crosses her arms over her chest. "Go on."

Grandma sighs. "You shouldn't have taken out the peanuts."

Mom's pupils look extra wide as she narrows her eyes at Grandma. "Why not, Ma?"

I giggle. "Maple-chipotle peanuts. Of course. They were cannabis infused, weren't they?"

"It's medicinal," Grandpa says defensively.

I keep giggling. First, I almost slept with my boss. Then I peed on him, then I kissed him, and now my family has drugged him.

It's hysterical.

Yep. Now that I know what to look for, I see redness in Oliver's cyan eyes. "How high was the THC concentration?"

"High," Grandma says sheepishly. "As in *you* are high."

Mom and Dad begin chuckling, and the fact that I find it contagious further confirms what we've just learned.

"Might as well enjoy it," Grandma says. "That or ride it out."

"How?" Oliver asks. He doesn't look happy at all.

"Desserts help me come down from the high," Grandma says. "I have some in the fridge."

Yum. I could go for some dessert. And nachos. Do my grandparents have nachos? Oh, and can I have nachos *with* cheesecake?

"Drink a lot of water, too." Grandpa grabs a pitcher from the table and tops it off by the faucet in the kitchen.

"From my experience, cardio is good," Mom says with a giggle. "Especially certain kinds." She follows this with a disturbing wink at Dad. "It's a double whammy."

Oliver chugs a large glass of water while my parents and I stuff our plates with the remainder of the savory dishes to make room on the table for dessert.

"We could order a pizza," Mom says after she devours everything on her plate. She winks at me. "With olives."

Dad nods. "And put fries on top."

Grandma clears her throat. "What about that dessert I made?"

Mom frowns. "Caramel sauce on top of fries?"

"No, we should get Oreos," Oliver says. He doesn't look nearly as unhappy now. If anything, he looks hungry. The THC must be really kicking in.

"Is that vegan?" I ask.

"Yep," he says. "So is Vegenaise. I have some in my fridge. I bet they'd go perfectly together." He licks his lips, which almost makes me forget food and think about cardio—the kind my mom had in mind. "I also have an avocado that we can mix with chocolate," Oliver continues. "Maybe add some sriracha. And peanut butter." He looks at my parents. "Can I borrow some basil from your pizza?"

Grandma bangs a plate on the table. "This is a *vegan* key lime pie."

"Wow," all four of us say, then attack the pie like a pack of ravenous wolves.

"Is there agar-agar in this?" Oliver asks my grandma after his plate is clean.

She shakes her head. "What's that?"

"A gelatin made from seaweed." He grins. "If you'd used it, this would've been a kelp cake."

I fan myself. He's openly talking about wanting to eat me.

It's official.

We're high.

CHAPTER
Twenty

DAD RAISES a finger in the air. "We should do 'Dark Side of the Rainbow.'"

Mom nods enthusiastically. "And get more food."

"What's 'Dark Side of the Rainbow?'" Grandma asks.

"Bring munchies, and I'll show you." Mom leaps to her feet and runs into the living room.

Grandma sighs. "I guess we should follow." She hands everyone snacks.

I start helping, but standing up makes me even more high—that or time jumps. All I know is I somehow find myself in the living room, cozying up next to Oliver.

Hey. High me has the right idea. Now if only my family members would leave...

"Watch and listen," Mom says, grabbing another piece of key lime pie. "This is Pink Floyd's 'Dark Side of the Moon,' played to *The Wizard of Oz*."

At first, I'm too preoccupied by the wave of hormones generated by Oliver's nearness. Eventually, though, I notice the music and look at the screen.

Wow.

In a rare moment of lucidity, I realize they match eerily well. Did Pink Floyd write the album with the film in mind, or is this confirmation bias?

Somewhere midway through the movie, the music and the cannabis conspire to get me higher than I've ever been, and the plot of *The Wizard of Oz* becomes difficult to follow even though I've seen it before. A few times, I think I even forget how watching TV is supposed to work, but I snap out of that quickly.

Hmm. Maybe I'm like the scarecrow—need a brain?

Tons of questions spin through my head, and they all seem so profound I want to write them down—except I think I've forgotten how to write for the moment.

Why did the Tin Man rust? He's made of tin, not iron, and tin doesn't rust. Also, how horrible was it for him to stand there unmoving before Dorothy rescued him? And, returning to water damage, how did the Wicked Witch melt? Did she also eat a peanut, or was she made of something meltable?

"If water is her weakness, why did she have a bucket of it so conveniently in her castle?" I ask out loud.

"I know, right?" Dad says. "Why did she want to kill Toto? He wasn't a threat."

Yeah. Dad makes sense for the first time that I can

remember—though my remembering is impaired right now, to say the least.

Time perception too. In an eyeblink, the song and the movie are over, and apparently, the whole movie was "just a dream," which is very easy to believe in my current state.

Suddenly, a scene from hard-core tentacle porn flashes on the screen.

"Oops," Grandma says. "That's not what I wanted to play."

Is it weird that I'm horny now? Does it mean I like hentai?

No. Oliver has his arm around me—that's why.

Ignoring my mom's encouraging comments about porn and my grandparents' sex life, I press closer to Oliver and float on a cloud of euphoria.

Oliver hugs me back, making what's left of my brain cells short-circuit.

A new movie starts, without Pink Floyd this time.

I struggle to make sense of it. I think it's one of the later *Harry Potter* films because Hermione looks grown up in it.

But where is Harry? And who is that guy hitting on Hermione?

Hmm. His name is Gaston. Was he in Slytherin?

Also, I don't remember this werewolf with horns...

Wait a second. I get it now: this must be that live-action adaptation of *Beauty and the Beast*.

Yeah. The "Be Our Guest" song confirms it—and it's

just as psychedelic here as it was in the cartoon version, though it could just be the THC.

Now some of the earlier scenes make less sense... unless they were hallucinations. For example, did I see Hermione—I mean, Belle—invent a washing machine in eighteenth-century France? Also, if there are no werewolves in this, why were those wolves so large? And making lion noises?

"I'm hungry," Mom says, distracting me from my attempts to process the movie.

"There's no more food left," Grandma says with a chuckle.

"Want to go shopping?" Dad asks no one in particular.

"You're not driving like this," Grandpa says sternly and pats his gun.

"Bummer," Mom and Dad say in unison.

"I've got grub at my place," Oliver says an inch away from my face.

Oh yeah. He's hugging me. No wonder I'm feeling so cozy.

Also, who needs food when I can lick his lips?

No. Witnesses.

"Let's go to your house," my parents say.

"You sure about this?" Grandma asks Oliver.

He nods. "Tofu probably misses me."

"Yummy," Mom says. "We miss tofu too."

———

I don't remember the trip to Oliver's house in detail, but when we walk in, a hot dog runs over and yelps at us with glee, tail wagging too fast for my addled brain to process.

"This is Tofu," Oliver says to my parents. "He's not on the menu, but sweet-and-sour tofu is."

I giggle and pet Tofu's wet, pointy nose.

"The kitchen is this way," Oliver says, leading us through a minimalist-looking hallway.

The kitchen is also pretty sparse, with clean, modern appliances and a glass table.

"Do you have gravlax?" Mom asks.

"Or gnocchi?" Dad adds.

"Oliver is vegan," I say, and feel proud I've managed such a chain of logic. "No fish or egg-based dishes here."

"Here." Oliver takes something out of the fridge, and we attack it as a team until nothing is left.

"What was it?" I ask belatedly. "Nachos?"

Oliver laughs. "Oreos but with salsa, so I can see how you'd get confused."

The culinary adventures continue until Oliver's fridge is empty, which is when my parents excuse themselves and leave.

I blink at Oliver. "Where did they go?"

"I'm not sure," he says. "Let's go find them."

Sure. Just have to remember how to walk.

With herculean effort, I stand up.

Great. This whole walking thing might come back to me now.

Before I take a step, Tofu runs into the room and begins to prance around and whine.

Oliver casts a guilty look at his wiener. "I usually feed him when I get home from work. Can't believe I forgot."

Tofu cocks his head, as if saying, *Will you feed me, or am I going to have to kill a badger for dinner? That's what they bred us hot dogs for.*

Oliver chuckles. "I bet if he could talk, he'd sound just like that."

I frown. "Did I say that out loud?"

He scratches the top of his head. "I hope it was you. If I'm so high that Tofu is speaking to me, I may need to go to the hospital."

"No, it was me," I say. "I think."

"Whew. In that case, you should know that a Dachshund—especially a modern one—can't really kill a badger. They only help with the hunt. The humans do the killing."

I snort. "What's a Dachshund?"

He sighs. "A hot dog."

"Right. Right. In Latin, it's *canis pēnis*. Colloquially, though, it's wiener dog. Or sausage dog. Shlong dog? Shlong dog millionaire. Cock—"

A loud bark from Tofu interrupts me.

I don't appreciate being mocked.

Oliver smirks. "My wiener is ravenous."

The image of Oliver's massive Aqua-manhood flits before my mind's perverted eye.

It's official.

I'm as ravenous for his wiener as his wiener is for dog food.

Oliver reaches over to a nearby shelf and grabs a can with a picture of a (possibly) stoned dog on it. When he cracks the thing open, I smell something yummy and my stomach growls.

Tofu looks up at me worriedly.

When I'm hangry, I could bite a bitch.

With a chuckle that could indicate I spoke that out loud again, Oliver pours the food into a bowl on the floor.

Tofu gobbles it down extra fast, like he's afraid someone might fight him for it.

My stomach growls again. When was the last time I ate?

Oliver grins. "Munchies?"

I dart a glance at the dog bowl. "It smells so nice."

He snorts. "You'd eat dog food?"

I lick my lips. "You've never wondered what it tastes like?"

He looks intrigued. Grabbing another can, he cracks it open, takes out a spoon, and ladles a bite into his sexy mouth.

Is it weird that I want him to feed me that dog food, like a daddy bird?

"Not bad," Oliver says after he swallows. "Could use some salt, though."

I snort. "You're so stoned you just ate dog food."

Oliver waves his spoon—and a droplet of dog food

flies into Tofu's bowl. "I wouldn't feed Tofu something I wouldn't eat myself."

I giggle. "You know you've broken the sacred vegan covenant. Your psychic powers won't work anymore."

"Not true," he says. "This is vegan dog food."

"It is?" I blink at him. "Aren't dogs basically wolves —as in carnivores?"

He waves the can in the air. "I get these so Tofu has more variety. Dogs are omnivores and can eat vegan meals so long as they're properly formulated."

I grin. "He's a vegan hot dog?"

Oliver shakes his head. "Tofu isn't exclusively vegan —he likes meat-based food too much for that. Still, he enjoys an occasional vegan dish, and it gives him a chance to reduce his tiny carbon pawprint."

Hearing his name repeated over and over, Tofu looks up.

Actually, I could reduce the world's methane emissions singlepawedly by eating all the farting cows. And pigs—if that's what bacon is made from. And chickens—assuming they know how to fart. I'll eat anything that farts, really; that's why we dogs have such a good sense of smell.

Oliver chuckles and hands me the can and the spoon. "Interested?"

I sniff it. Smells yummy.

"I won't tell anyone," Oliver says. "It will be our little secret."

Hesitantly, I take a spoonful of dog food and stick it in my mouth as Oliver looks on hungrily.

Does he want more?

Then the taste reaches me. By Cthulhu's tastebuds, I like it! There's rice in this, maybe oats, some barley for sure, and either peas or chickpeas.

Tofu whines again, and I look down to see him staring at the can in my hands in panic.

Humans eat my special food now? What's next—me on the menu?

I giggle. Silly Tofu. "Will he overeat if I give it to him?"

Oliver shakes his head. "He can have it."

Mournfully, I pour the rest of the deliciousness into Tofu's bowl, and the wiener attacks it like a phallic-looking wolf.

Aww. I was hoping he'd leave me some.

Tearing my gaze away from the rapidly disappearing food, I look around. "I've got this feeling something is missing, but I can't exactly put my tentacle on it."

Oliver directs a confused glance at the door. "Yeah. Do you remember what?"

I close my eyes and strain my brain as hard as I can.

Dolphins?

No, they're at work.

Snacks?

Ate everything already. Tofu helped.

Music?

Nope. That was back at my grandparents' house—

Wait. I got it. Opening my eyes, I smack myself on the forehead. "Parents."

"Oh, yeah," Oliver says. "Where are they?"

"No clue." I sidle up to him and snake my arm into the crook of his elbow. "Want to go look for them?"

"Let's." He leads me out of the kitchen and into the living room.

I examine the comfy couch and the big-screen TV.

What was I looking for again?

"They're not here," Oliver says.

Oh, right. Parents.

"Let's go look somewhere else," I say and turn toward the hallway.

"Yeah." Oliver leads me down the hall and sniffs the air, like Tofu might. "Is that peanut butter?"

I take a big inhale. Mm, nutty. "It's either that or a spadefoot toad. When stressed, it exudes a secretion that smells like peanut butter."

Oliver's eyebrows furrow. "I think it's coming from my bedroom."

I try to make sense of that statement. Is *he* nutty? What was the nuttiness again? Oh, yeah, the smell. "You think my parents snuck peanut butter into your bedroom so they wouldn't have to share?" The bastards. How could they?

Oliver blinks at me. "They seem too nice to do something so heinous. Maybe they're testing each other for Alzheimer's?"

They are? How old are my parents? Wait, what year is this? "Did you say Alzheimer's or Alka Seltzer?"

He holds up a finger that seems to dance in my vision. "Patients with Alzheimer's aren't able to smell peanut butter as well through their left nostril as their right one."

Nostrils. Right. Versus left. I press my finger to one side of my nose. Wait, what were we talking about again? Oh, yeah, nutty parents and that yummy smell. "They're too young for Alzheimer's. I think they decided to bogart the peanut butter." Whew. I think that made sense.

Oliver looks horrified. "They wouldn't."

"Let's see," I say determinedly, and with an indignant huff, I pull open the door to the bedroom, ready to storm in and repossess the peanut butter.

Except I can't.

Next to me, Oliver sucks in a sharp breath, similarly frozen in place.

The shock of what I'm seeing is so strong it makes the pot haze recede.

Holy Cthulhu and the rest of the Great Old Ones.

Mom is riding Dad in reverse cowgirl.

Both of them are as naked as the day they were born.

Oh, and both parental units are smeared in enough peanut butter to feed an army of stoners.

CHAPTER
Twenty-One

LEAPING BACK, I slam the door shut and strongly debate poking out my eyes.

Nope. Not strong enough.

I let my feet carry me away. A second later, I find myself sitting on the couch, my palms over my eyes.

Did I poke them out, after all?

A strong arm wraps around me. "Are you okay?" Oliver murmurs in my ear.

I shake my head. "I think I'm traumatized."

He hugs me tighter. "Sealand's health insurance plan covers therapy."

Is it hot in here, or is it just him?

I remove my palms from my face. "It does?"

Oliver nods. "In a pinch, you could also talk to Rose."

I giggle. "You realize she's a fish shrink?"

He's staring at me, as if mesmerized. "Have I ever told you that you have a gorgeous smile?"

Has he? I can't recall. Probably not. If I'd ever felt this light and fluttery in my heart, I'd remember.

He's still staring.

I wonder why. Does he expect me to respond to something?

Also, why am I feeling so warm and nice?

Oh, yeah, he's got his arm around my shoulders. My eyes fall on the hand that's touching me.

Gorgeous. Yes, there was something said about that. "You've got a gorgeous thumb," I breathe, eyeing his fingers.

Then I remember what he said. I guess I accidentally nailed it. Total tit for his tat. Speaking of tits, mine feel like they're suffocating in my stupid bra, and the fact that my nipples are on point isn't helping.

Oliver's eyes are hooded as he leans closer. "You've never given me a compliment before."

How could I not have? If a compliment were a human, it would be him.

I moisten my lips. "Don't let my compliments go to your head. I'm not exactly running on all cylinders."

Carp. Should I have used a more environmentally friendly metaphor? Running on all horses? Do horses fart? Maybe running on—

Oliver's lips clash against mine.

Oh. My. Cthulhu.

I'm high, but not even remotely dry.

Whatever remaining cylinders I've been running on come to a screeching halt. In fact, if I were an engine, I'd be exploding now.

Feeling faint, I fall back, and Oliver follows without breaking the kiss.

He's got impressive mouth-eye coordination skills. Especially if he's as stoned as I am.

As soon as I get comfortable on my back, his octopus hands are all over me in the most wonderful way. One is holding my chin, the other the back of my head, and the third—

Wait. He's not actually an octopus, so that third thing pressing against my belly isn't a hand. It's something else.

But what?

Oh, I know.

His Aqua-manhood.

I snake my hand down and feel him. Yep. That's what that is, and I want it, bad.

He pulls away, breathing raggedly. His eyes are dark with heat. "Are you okay?"

I nod mutely.

He reaches for the hem of his shirt and pulls it off in a jerky motion.

I stare at his magnificence in hazy stupefaction.

He unbuttons my shirt, exposing my bra. His nostrils flare as he rakes his gaze over me.

Yes! I like where this is going—except I feel like there's something I'm forgetting. Something distant, but kind of important… I think.

He leans forward and presses his lips against the tender skin of my neck—and I forget everything, maybe even my own name. Cthulhu, that feels good.

His lips are soft and warm, his skin roughened with a hint of stubble that scratches me in the most delicious way.

I moan, and he licks my collarbone as some of his hands unzip my work shorts.

Work shorts... I feel like that might be a clue to something I'm forgetting—

His lips and tongue dip lower, to the tops of my breasts and then below them, traveling over my heaving ribcage to my belly button. Then down and down, and I forget that I've forgotten anything.

Is he about to—

Yep.

His breath is on my wunderpus. Lifting his gaze to meet mine for a moment, he murmurs, "Time for kelpcake."

Before I can answer, he gives my pearl a slow, luxurious lick.

A moan is wrenched from my lips.

He licks me again. And again. Then he does something genius, but I'm not sure what. It feels like he's suddenly sprouted eight tongues, and they're all competing for the honor of making me come.

Maybe he *is* part octopus?

My moans increase in rhythm.

Oliver keeps his relentless licks steady.

The cloud of euphoria I'm floating on is unlike anything I've ever felt. It's intense and almost frightening, as it makes me think I'll want to feel like this again and again going forward. He's getting me hooked on pot, or himself, or both.

"Will you come for me?" His voice is low and rough, coming at me as if from a distance.

Another moan is my reply, and it must encourage him to get even cleverer with his tongues. Four seconds later, I come undone, my toes curling as I cry out his name.

When he pulls away, there's an expression of male satisfaction on his face that is almost smug.

Oh, yeah? He thinks he's the only one who can drive someone crazy?

Grabbing fistfuls of his long hair, I pull him up to my face and kiss him, hard. As our tongues dance, I unbutton his pants.

He stiffens—in both senses of the word.

I push his pants down over his hips and tear my lips away from his, panting as I scoot down.

He looks hungry. Ravenous.

So does his Aqua-manhood.

I grab the latter by the shaft, then lean down and give it a slow, torturous ice-cream lick.

"Fuck," Oliver grunts.

That's right. I can operate heavy machinery even while high as a kite.

I'm about to slide him into my mouth when a strange noise intrudes on my consciousness.

Annoyed, I turn toward it, not bothering to release my grip on his Aqua-manhood. Because I'm not letting that baby go.

It's a decision I swiftly regret.

Because it's my parents.

They're here.

That's the thing I forgot.

CHAPTER
Twenty-Two

I LOOK at the cock in my hand.

I look at my mom.

I look back at the cock in my hand.

I look at my dad.

Both parental units are sporting bedroom hair and clothes that were pulled on haphazardly. There are also traces of something brown on their faces. And I smell peanut butter.

Oh, Cthulhu.

How could I have forgotten the peanut butter?

What's worse is that they're both looking at me with strange expressions. Approval? Encouragement? Either way you slice it, I want to fall through the couch and keep falling until I reach Australia.

I realize Mom is talking.

"I'm so, so sorry," she says. "Please continue. We were just leaving."

Oliver grunts, and I realize I might've squeezed his hardness a bit too hard.

Mom must concur because she says chidingly, "You've got to be gentler with male organs. I usually don't even use my hands with your dad's, instead opting to—"

I drop Oliver's male organ like it's burning my fingers and scramble off the couch. My frantic gaze falls on my shirt balled up on the couch, and I snatch it.

I catch Oliver's discombobulated gaze.

"Sorry," I mouth.

He looks down at his cock.

Then at me.

Then at my mom.

Then at my dad.

Then back me and mouths, "I understand."

He does?

I don't. I just know I have to flee, and that's what I do.

As I run away, I hear Dad encouraging me to get back to what I was doing, assuring me that I was doing a good job and that he and Mom would leave to make me more comfortable. Speaking over him, Mom goes on about something to do with the transcendental power of orgasms, but I don't make out the details.

Once outside, I pull on my clothes and beeline for my grandparents' house, where I sprint to the guest room and lie down in the hopes of clearing my head.

Instead, I pass out.

CHAPTER
Twenty-Three

THE SUN IS SHINING on my face when I wake up.

Motherfucking cocksucker balls of fire. Why does the sun want to give me skin cancer so badly? It's like it knows I didn't apply sunblock before bed.

I check under the blanket.

Not only did I not put on sunblock, I didn't undress either. Or brush my teeth.

Come to think of it, how did I get under the blanket?

Wait a sec. It's like Grandma's favorite song: it's all coming back to me now.

Did I dream what happened right before I fled Oliver's house, or did I actually experience the most embarrassing moment of my life?

"Namaste, sunshine," a voice says next to me, almost giving me a heart attack.

I whip my head around and see Mom's smiling face.

She crashed with me? I guess that explains the blanket.

"What are you doing here?" I ask, my voice strangely hoarse.

"We weren't in any condition to drive back to the Hymans," she says. "So, we stayed over."

I guess I should be grateful that Dad isn't in bed with us, or that I didn't wake up to them smeared in peanut butter and reenacting the Kama Sutra.

Cthulhu help me. I actually saw that last night—and then forgot about it minutes later.

I'm never, ever touching marijuana again. If the "Just Say No" campaign warned people that drug use would lead to seeing their parents naked, the war on drugs would've been short.

"About last night," Mom says. "I wanted to say how sorry your dad and—"

I scramble off the bed. "I don't want to talk about it."

Mom sits up. "Orgasms are the perfect—"

"Seriously, I don't want to talk about it," I growl.

She frowns. "I've got decades of experience when it comes to toe-curling, mind-boggling, tantric orgasms, so it would behoove you to use such a resource."

Grr. "I'm late for work. Picking your brain will have to wait." What I don't add is that this conversation makes me want to pick out my own brain through my right nostril and give it a good scrub with my toothbrush.

"But we're heading back to the Hymans after breakfast," Mom says.

"I can call," I lie.

"Fine." Mom swings her feet to the floor. "When you see Oliver, tell him your father and I liked him very much and hope to see him again."

Was it his erect penis that won them over?

Trying to hide my red face, I change into fresh work clothes. "If Oliver ever talks to me again, I'll make sure to mention that he has new fans." Not.

"Be positive," Mom says, and kisses my cheek. "Namaste."

I head downstairs, where I dodge Dad's attempt to chat with me. I'm not sure when or if I'll be able to look him in the eye again.

Relatedly, I'm never again eating peanut butter.

———

As I drive to work, I realize I'm not hungry in the slightest. Well, it's no wonder. I pulled a manatee last night and ate fifteen percent of my bodyweight.

The closer I get to my destination, the more my anxiety grows.

What will Oliver say to me when I see him?

Am I as good as fired? Or will he drag me into his office and finish what we started?

If it's the latter, do I want him to?

When I get to Sealand, I'm both relieved and disappointed that Oliver isn't waiting to fire me in the parking lot.

Like a coward, I go about my workday.

At four-thirty, I'm still employed, but I haven't seen Oliver, so I have no clue where we stand.

Just as I finish feeding Beaky, I feel a presence in the room and catch a whiff of ocean surf.

My heart leaps.

"Hi," Oliver says from behind me.

I turn, trying to look all cool and casual and not like my parents saw me holding his Aqua-manhood in all its yummy glory. "Hi, yourself."

His expression is again unreadable. "I wanted to talk to you."

Here we go. Am I fired or—

"Have you heard of the SOS?"

I blink at him. "The famous 'Save Our Souls' message you use when your ship is sinking, or the Save the Ocean Society?"

"The latter," he says.

"The SOS that holds annual fundraisers nearby?" I clarify.

I know this because I stalk Octoworld, which is a big sponsor of these fundraisers. I don't mention this to Oliver, though. I don't want to remind him of that faux pas when Fabio and Lemon blabbed about my desire to work for Sealand's competitor.

"Yes. *That* SOS," he says.

I smile. "Nope. I've never heard of it."

He neither smiles nor shows a single crack in his

unreadable poker face. "There's a fundraiser in a few weeks."

"Right," I say as the piranhas in my belly begin sharpening their teeth. This isn't going where I think it's going, is it? "Will Sealand make an appearance at the fundraiser?"

He nods. "I go every year and usually take a member of the staff with me."

The piranhas smell blood. "That's nice. I bet the competition for that plus-one spot is fierce."

"Not really. Some folks, like Dex, conveniently had 'family commitments' when I invited them."

Dex could have gone to the SOS fundraiser and didn't? He doesn't just look like an otter; he must have the brain of one.

Wait, that's not fair. Otters are actually highly intelligent. They use rocks to open clams, and if a boss were to ask them to go to an important event, I bet they'd go —or make up a better excuse than "family commitments."

"So," I say, trying not to show how much I want this in case it'll hurt my chances. "Who are you taking this time around?"

Please pick me. Pretty please.

His stony façade finally cracks, and he frowns. "Why would I bring this up if it weren't to invite you?"

To taunt me?

I shrug, hiding my elation. "I didn't want to presume."

"I see." The poker face returns. "Consider this your formal invitation. Do you think you can make it?"

I even out my breathing. "I think I can clear my schedule."

"Great. I'll email you the details." He turns on his heel and walks away.

Wait, what?

That's it?

I mean, I'm happy about going to the fundraiser of my dreams, but wasn't there something a lot more important we should've discussed? Something like— and I'm just throwing this out there—his Aqua-manhood returning to my mouth, or the withdrawal my wunderpus is suffering without his tongue(s)?

Maybe he didn't want to talk about such private things at work?

I look back at Beaky, as if for answers.

We don't expect our clergy to be austere, but still, when we honor someone with the title of High Priestess, we don't mean she should literally get high.

———

When I get home, Fabio and Lemon are waiting—and laughing at me. And this is before I tell them the whole story of last night.

"You got stoned with your parents?" Fabio asks, chortling. "People who act like they're stoned even without drugs?"

"She drugged her boyfriend, too. Don't forget that," Lemon chimes in.

I cross my arms over my chest. "I didn't drug him. That was Grandma. I think."

"Well," Lemon says with a huge grin. "What happened? Grandma said you left to raid Oliver's fridge."

With a sigh, I spill the beans, pausing only when they mock and make fun of me—as in, after every other word.

"Thanks for being so supportive," I grumble. "You realize I might still get fired, right?"

Lemon looks mildly repentant, but Fabio, grinning like a dolphin, seems anything but.

"I doubt he'd ask you to go to that fundraiser if he was going to fire you," Lemon says.

"Unless it's a date," Fabio says.

I frown. "I don't think it's a date. He's asked Dex before."

Fabio licks his lips. "I'd take Dex on a date."

"Me too," Lemon says.

"Our sour sweetie is being such a Samantha today," Fabio says. "What about the ballet dancer?"

Lemon looks down. "You're right. I shouldn't cheat on the Russian."

"It's not a date," I say firmly.

Fabio examines his perfectly manicured nails. "If it is a date, it might mean he wants to have sex with you before he fires you. That's what would happen at my job."

Lemon rolls her eyes. "You work in the porn industry. Sex is what happens before every one of your jobs ends."

"Speaking of, I'm leaving tomorrow," Fabio says. "I've got a shoot in Miami."

The alarm on my phone blares to life.

I look down at it in confusion.

Ah. Right. Garbage day reminder.

"I'll be back," I tell them without an explanation.

If they knew about my stalker-ish plans, I wouldn't hear the end of it.

Grabbing the trash bin, I drag it out—and just in time.

Oliver is passing by, Tofu in tow.

"Hi," I say breathlessly.

"Hello," he says.

I look at Tofu. "Should I pretend I'm not here before he counts me, and I have to join your walk?"

"It's too late." Oliver's face is once again impossible to read. "He's already 'counted' you."

Yay. I manage a casual shrug. "I guess I'm joining."

Oliver nods curtly. "Thanks."

We begin walking, and he doesn't say anything.

I clear my throat. "Does Tofu care what we talk about?"

"He doesn't," Oliver says. "But I wanted to discuss something with you, if you don't mind."

I nod and take a deep breath. Finally. We'll get to clear the air about last night.

"I know you're not on the clock," Oliver continues.

"But would you mind telling me some of your near-future plans for enclosure enrichment?"

He wants to talk shop? Now?

"I'm almost done with my manatee ideas," I say, struggling to hide my disappointment.

"What about the others?"

Yep. He wants to talk about work—as in he isn't planning to discuss last night at all.

Well, at least it seems like I'm keeping my job... unless this line of inquiry is to help him decide how inconvenient it would be to sack me.

Suppressing a sigh, I tell him what I plan to do for the seahorses tomorrow, and for the European chub the day after that.

"What about after that?" he asks.

I tell him, and just like that, we end up talking about toys for fish for the rest of the walk—and not a word about us.

When we stop in front of his driveway, Tofu having been sufficiently exercised, I feel that magnetic pull toward Oliver, stronger than ever, and I'd be willing to bet my right ovary he feels it too. But, to my huge disappointment, he doesn't lean down to kiss me. He just says, "Good night," and leaves.

At home, Lemon and Fabio are waiting for me with knowing expressions on their faces.

"That was pathetic," Lemon says. "You guys acted like strangers."

I'm sure I'm not the only one of my sisters who sometimes wonders why I didn't absorb the others in the womb. If I had, Lemon would be a mole on my shoulder right now—and moles don't kick you while you're down.

"I'm going to bed." I push between them, forcefully.

"Now you've upset her," Fabio says sternly.

"Hey, Olive, I'm sorry," Lemon calls after me. "I wasn't trying to be mean. I swear."

I stop and turn to face her. "I'm not angry with you. Not really." I shove my fingers through my hair. "Why is he pretending like nothing's happened?"

Lemons shrugs. "He's your boss?"

"Who has a bad history with work romance," Fabio says. "And trust me, I know what that's like."

"No more talk about fluffers," Lemon hisses at Fabio. Turning to me, she gently suggests, "Maybe Oliver just needs time?"

I sigh. "Maybe."

———

If Oliver needs time, he sure needs a whole lot of it.

For the next week, I barely see him, and any time we do talk, it's all professional—and it's driving me insane.

After his porn shoot, Fabio comes back for a day, then goes back to New York, freeing the couch. Lemon starts sleeping there, making it easier for me to take care of Oliver-related frustrations whenever I have a wet dream about him—a nightly occurrence, by the way.

Another week goes by, and Lemon is still here, vacationing. Not for the first time, I wonder what she does for work. Whatever it is, it allows her to have *really* flexible work hours. When I press her for answers, she's cagey, which makes me wonder if Blue's theory on this is true: Lemon has watched so much *Sex and the City* she's decided to write an anonymous sex column for some newspaper somewhere.

A couple more weeks pass by with work and family to occupy my time. Then, a few days before the SOS fundraiser, I "accidentally" bump into Oliver by the manatee exhibit.

"Chief," I say, hiding my bitterness.

"Hi," he says. "I'm glad I ran into you. There's something we need to discuss."

Nice try. I'm not getting my hopes up anymore. This will be work related, I'm certain.

He doesn't meet my gaze. "I'm not sure if we've talked about it, but Sealand doesn't make enough money from the tours."

Wait, what? Is it possible he's taken this long to get around to firing me? I guess it makes sense. He was looking for a reason and has come up with this: budget cuts.

Frowning, I say, "Okay. And?"

This time, he does meet my gaze, and I instantly feel myself drowning in those cyan depths. "And it takes important donors to keep things afloat."

Hmm. So maybe not a "budget cuts" conversation. I feel a surge of relief.

"Donors?" I ask.

"Yeah, like Tampa Electric," he says.

"Tampa Electric?" Apparently, I've turned into a parrot today.

"Florida's top producer of solar energy," he says, sounding like a TV commercial.

"Great," I say. "What does any of this have to do with me?"

He steps closer, enveloping me in his ocean surf scent. "Have you heard of Tampa Electric's Manatee Viewing Center?"

I shake my head.

"Since 1986, the company has been using water from Tampa Bay to cool something called Big Bend Unit 4. Afterward, the water—which is still clean but warmed up—flows into a discharge canal and then back into the bay."

I nod, beginning to see where this might be going.

"Manatees like warm water, so since that year, they've been hanging out at the discharge canal—especially when the Tampa Bay water cools down."

"Wow," I say. "That must save lives in cold winters."

He nods. "The site is now a federally designated manatee sanctuary. It's called the Manatee Viewing Center and is open to the public."

I glance at Betsy and the other manatees. Those of them that will be released back into the wild might end up hanging out by that power station—a heartwarming thought.

"Anyway," Oliver says. "Tampa Electric is a big

sponsor of the SOS fundraiser. They reached out to me and said they were looking for ideas on how to make the manatees even more comfortable at the MVC—without feeding them or otherwise jeopardizing their ability to thrive in the wild, of course."

I scratch my chin. "They could build underwater scratching posts." I point at my made-out-of-brushes contraption.

"Exactly," he says. "Think of a list of ideas. We'll present them in a couple days when we go to a meeting in Tampa."

"A meeting in Tampa?" I take an involuntary step back. "We?"

He nods. "I'll need you there."

"You will?" I hold my breath. The "we" he mentioned means what I hoped it would—the two of us.

The piranhas in my belly get agitated.

"You have to come," he says. "I wouldn't feel comfortable taking credit for your ideas." He glances at Betsy, who happens to choose that moment to scratch herself sensually on one of my posts.

That's right. This is what curves look like on real mermaids. Eat your heart out, human.

"Besides," Oliver continues. "They may have questions at the meeting, and you'd be the best one to answer."

"When is this trip?" I ask.

"In two days."

The piranhas begin their attack. "How will we get there?"

Please say by driving together.

"I'll need you to meet me there," he says. "I'm leaving today because I have a few other meetings on that coast."

"Oh," I say, hiding my disappointment. "And where are we staying?"

"The Grand Hyatt Tampa Bay hotel," he says.

The piranhas swoon. Sure, he doesn't want to take a road trip in the same car, but the two of us in the same hotel sounds very promising. We'll probably share meals together. And maybe he'll take me sightseeing. He's so good at being a Florida travel agent, after all.

"I guess I can go," I mutter.

For the first time in a while, he smiles—and I'm glad I have sunblock on, or else I would melt into a puddle from the blinding intensity of it.

Speaking of sunblock, I'm running low. I have about two tubes left, maybe three. I'll have to make sure to get more, especially given the upcoming trip.

"It goes without saying you'll be on company time for this trip," he says.

As in a paid vacation? With the guy I've been having wet dreams about?

Sign me up.

CHAPTER
Twenty~Four

ON MY WAY to the meeting in Tampa, I get stuck in traffic—the first time such a thing has happened since I came to Florida.

Carp. This New York staple is as welcome as giant rats. I hope I won't be late for the meeting. Had I fathomed there might be traffic, I wouldn't have settled in at the hotel first.

Nah, who am I kidding? I needed to make myself look presentable before facing Oliver, not to mention the people from Tampa Electric.

By the time I pull into the parking lot, my cortisol levels are through the roof and I'm a minute late.

After a mad run, I'm panting as I explain why I'm here to the security lady. Since this is the first of several meetings, she gives me a temporary ID. Grabbing it, I hurry deeper into the air-conditioned building, the sweat on my skin feeling like it's turning to icicles.

I'm about to make a great first impression.

Sprinting for the elevator, I jam the button and wait for what feels like an hour.

"Hello," a familiar deep male voice says, startling me.

I turn and face Oliver.

He's wearing a bespoke suit, and his hair is up in his neatest man bun to date.

Cthulhu eat my heart. I know that this hammering in my chest is due to the earlier sprint and the stress of the traffic, but seeing Oliver tricks some deeper part of me into feeling that the effect is all due to his gorgeousness.

This is how a lover might feel reuniting with her beloved. Or a horny octopus risking his life (and limb) to mate.

Oh, and the most maddening part is that his recent poker face isn't on. If I didn't know any better, I'd think he was examining me with a purely male appreciation.

Does he have a fetish for sweaty messes that I don't know about?

"You're late," I pant.

The corners of his lips tilt up. "Wouldn't that make you late as well?"

Damn those lips. They're making my panties damp. "Unlike you, I'm not the walking-and-talking embodiment of Sealand."

The elevator opens, and he gestures for me to go first. "Actually, it's you they've come to hear from, so you're the Sealand icon today, not me."

"Then why did you even come?"

He presses the button for the second floor. "Moral support."

The elevator ride is quick. When we get out, a man in a suit greets us with a smarmy smile.

"I'm Jason," he says, extending his hand. His palm is clammy as I shake it, and I can't help but notice he is leering at me.

When it's Oliver's turn for a handshake, I catch a pained expression flitting over Jason's face before Oliver lets go of his hand.

Did Oliver squeeze it too hard? If so, why?

Could he have noticed the leering?

Before I can explore that line of thought further, Jason leads us to a meeting room where a group of people are already waiting. He does the introductions, and it turns out that he's a project manager, while the rest of the folks are an assortment of bigwigs from the company.

"Now let's give Olive the floor," Jason says magnanimously.

Gulping in some calming air, I go into my spiel, starting with the scratching posts. When I'm done, they ask me a million questions, the majority of which revolve around costs.

"This is a great start," Jason says after the Q&A is over. "Why don't we all process this, discuss offline as needed, and reconvene here tomorrow?"

"Sure," I say, and look at Oliver, who hasn't spoken once throughout.

"Sounds good to me," he says. "Thanks, everyone."

We all get up, but some executive asks Oliver a question, leaving me in a strange situation where I'm not sure if I should wait for him or not.

Probably not. We came in different cars, after all.

I smell half-digested garlic and turn to see Jason standing a bit too close to me.

"Let me walk you out," he says.

"Sure," I say uncertainly.

I follow Jason to the door, which he holds open for me.

"So," he says as we exit into the hallway. "Is this your first time in Tampa?"

I pick up my pace. "I moved to Florida from New York fairly recently, so I haven't had a chance to explore the Sunshine State."

Reaching the elevator, I desperately summon it.

Jason grins, exposing a grill of toilet-white chompers. "You must let me take you out tonight. I know this amazing restaurant that—"

"Olive already has plans," a deep voice growls from behind us.

I turn and see Oliver. His jaw is tight, and his eyes are flinty.

"Plans?" I fold my arms across my chest. "Remind me what they are, exactly?"

I have no idea why I'm so pissed at my boss all of a sudden. I was about to have to awkwardly decline Jason's advances, so I should be grateful for the save.

Then it hits me.

Oliver is acting as Brett might have in this situation. And he's doing so after pretending for weeks that there's nothing between us.

The nerve.

"Dinner at Dim Subtraction," Oliver says, his eyes gleaming. "Seven o'clock."

I arch an eyebrow. "And why can't Jason join us for dinner?"

Jason steps back. "I'm not sure I—"

"Jason can't join us because we're going on a date." Oliver narrows his eyes at Jason as I stand there, shell-shocked. "Unless you want to be a third wheel?"

"No, no," Jason says. "You two enjoy your dinner."

The elevator arrives, and as soon as the doors open, I stumble into it.

What on earth does he mean, a date?

Wait, no. It was probably a bluff. If so, I'm even more pissed off.

"So." I turn on Oliver as soon as the doors close. "What's the dress code for our dinner?"

My boss sighs. "You don't have to actually go."

So it was a bluff. The bastard.

"No, no. I'm looking forward to it. Should I wear a cocktail dress to match your suit?"

His gaze grows heated. "If you insist."

"Should I meet you at the restaurant, or will you drive me?" I ask before he can back down. My heart picks up its pace as I wait for his answer.

The elevator opens, and he steps out. "I'll pick you up at six-thirty. Don't be late this time."

Holy Cthulhu and all his arms. This date is happening. "You were late too," I say with what remains of my composure, then tell him my room number.

His lips quirk. "I know that. We've got adjacent rooms."

"Oh. Okay. I'll see you," I manage to say after the concept of our beds being just a few feet apart fully penetrates my dirty mind.

"Later," he says and strides to his Tesla.

I watch him with that hungry piranha feeling in my belly that I've grown to associate with anything Oliver-related.

There's no doubt about what I've just done.

I've strong-armed my boss into taking me on a date.

CHAPTER
Twenty-Five

As I DRIVE to the hotel and get ready for dinner, I keep telling myself how bad of an idea this date is.

For starters, he could turn out to be the next Brett. There are a few red flags already, like his jealous behavior toward Jason today and Dex before that. The fact that I find his possessiveness hot is another red flag, as is the fact that I was highly attracted to him when we met. I clearly have a type that leads to no good.

Worse still, he's my boss who's against any workplace romance.

Yet I dress to the nines, perfect my makeup, and wait by the door, watching the minutes tick by on my phone.

As soon as it's six-thirty, I open the door and see that he was just about to knock.

"See? Late," I say, ignoring the way my heart leaps at the sight of him in that suit.

He looks me over from head to toe, his gaze reminiscent of a hungry barracuda stalking its prey. "You look amazing, kelpcake."

Gulp.

"You think flattery will get you anywhere?" I ask, playing it cool. On the inside, I'm floating like a helium balloon, my earlier concerns all but forgotten.

A wicked smile twists the corners of his lips. "Where do you want me?"

Boss? What's a boss?

"I want you seated in front of me in a restaurant," I somehow squeeze out. Hey, it's better than, "Pick a hole, any hole."

I float down to the lobby on a cloud of hormones, which skyrocket when Oliver shoos away the porters and valets to make a point of holding all the doors open for me himself.

When he starts the car, the music from the opening credits of *Pulp Fiction* blasts through the speakers, matching my heartbeat.

Or is this "Pump It" by The Black-Eyed Peas?

"Are you a big Tarantino fan?" I ask when Oliver lowers the volume. "Or are we about to rob the restaurant instead of eating there?"

He pulls out onto the road with a smile. "Rob it, for sure. No one ever does, so it's a golden opportunity. Do you want to be Honey Bunny or Pumpkin, or stick with kelpcake?"

"Kelpcake," I say. "And you'll be Aquaman."

His eyebrow shoots up. "Not Namor?"

"Who the haddock is Namor?"

"Namor the Sub-Mariner?" He shoots me an exaggeratedly exasperated glance. "He's Marvel's King of Atlantis, who predates Aquaman and can fly."

Well, "Namor-hood" doesn't quite have the same ring to it as Aqua-manhood, but I'm not going there. Keeping my gaze safely away from said manhood, I ask, "You like the comics?"

"I like anything related to the ocean or the sea." He ups the volume. "Like this song."

I eye him curiously. "What does the *Pulp Fiction* theme have to do with the sea?"

He grins. "This is 'Misirlou' by Dick Dale and His Del-Tones. A surf rock classic. And this melody comes from a folk song that originated in the Eastern Mediterranean—a sea."

I laugh and quiz him on his other musical preferences, which are all surf-related, unsurprisingly.

"How about you?" he asks. "Do you like that band Octopus, for obvious reasons?"

I shake my head. "I really like Jawaiian."

"Is that a band?"

"No. It's a genre. Hawaiian-style reggae."

He fiddles with the screen controls in his car, and soon a Jawaiian station is on.

"Sounds beachy," he says as we pull over to the restaurant. "I like it."

Damn it. As he opens the door, I wish I could jump on him and take a ride, like Aquaman on a giant seahorse. Instead, I check out the swanky exterior of the restaurant.

"This place used to be called Dim Sub," Oliver says, following my gaze. "They renamed it Dim Subtraction because too many people thought it was a BDSM club."

The old name would be more fitting given how I feel—like a bad girl who should be spanked... preferably with Oliver's Aqua-manhood.

A blond, model-esque hostess seats us near a window, and then her clone hands us the drink menu and asks what we want.

"Sex with an Alligator." I wink at Oliver. "It sounds like a Florida Man headline."

"I'll have a Smart-Ass Manhattanite," Oliver says. "It's made exactly like The Leg Spreader on your menu but in a manly glass." He pauses, then adds, "If you could keep my drink and the food vegan, that would be great."

"Same here," I say, figuring if I eat meat, he might not want to kiss me later—not that I'm plotting or anything.

"I'll speak to the chef and the bartender for you," the waitress says to Oliver in a husky voice that seems to imply that *her* legs are available for spreading. She then grabs the menus and lingers near him a bit too long for my liking.

To Oliver's credit, he doesn't look at her as she sashays away. Instead, he leans in and says in a conspiratorial tone, "I think the drink names here may have contributed to the whole 'sex club' misconception."

I grin. "Where's the food menu? I'm starving."

"There isn't one," he says. "The dim sum will all be the chef's choice."

Intriguing.

I'm about to question him further when a cloud blocking the sun moves away, and a sun ray from a nearby window lands on me.

Carp. I don't want to act like a diva and ask them to move us, but if we stay, I'll need to reapply sunblock, pronto.

With a sigh, I pull the sunblock bottle out.

Oliver doesn't blink, so I begin the application, which is when the waitress comes back with our drinks and looks at me like I'm a syphilitic war criminal.

"Sun exposure is bad for you," I say to Oliver in a defensive tone when the waitress is gone.

"Even at this time of day and through glass?" He tastes his drink and nods approvingly.

"I'd say the UV index here is half a point," I say. "But that means UV-A rays coming through the glass can still wreak havoc on my DNA, not to mention the aging effects of blue light, infrared light, and so on." To stop myself from launching into a TED talk on sun exposure, I sip my drink and learn that it's yummier than the name would imply.

"I should wear sunscreen when I surf," Oliver says. "I've been hesitant because some of the ingredients hurt coral reefs."

I dive into my bag and take out one of my spare

tubes. "Here." I thrust it into Oliver's hands—and as my fingers brush his, I nearly orgasm from the pent-up lust. Somehow, I still manage to sound semi-coherent as I say, "The active ingredients in this are minerals, and it doesn't have anything like oxybenzone, which is probably the chemical you're thinking of."

He eyes my purse warily. "How many of these do you carry with you on a regular basis?"

This again?

"Don't you know that the contents of a woman's purse are intimate and private?"

"My bad." He pockets my gift. "I won't pry again."

I resist urging him to apply some protection right now. I don't want to sound like my germophobic sister, Gia, when someone makes the mistake of bringing up viruses, bacteria, or sausage.

"So," I say. "You're worried about coral reefs?"

"Who isn't?" he says. "But I don't want to talk doom and gloom tonight."

"So nothing about environmentalism then."

"Not necessarily. Some stuff can be uplifting—like the prospect of floating cities." He circles his hand in the air, index finger pointing up.

Would it be so wrong if I sucked on that finger? Just for a few seconds, that's all.

With effort, I put on a deadpan expression. "Cities on floating islands, like in *Avatar*? That sounds uplifting indeed—literally."

His mouth quirks with a faint smile. "Current technology can barely handle making cities that would float on water—so we'd start there."

I regard him with interest. "Do any of those exist yet?"

"Some villages are in the early stages of development. When a fully developed floating city exists, it'll be great for humans and sea creatures alike. For example, the bottom of such a city could be an artificial reef."

I chuckle. "That's going to give a new definition to 'city underbelly.'"

He smiles. "If a floating city existed, would you want to live on it?"

I sip my drink. "What would it be like?"

"Modern. They'd use the coolest technologies, like OTEC and—"

"Slow down. What's OTEC?"

"Ocean Thermal Energy Conversion," he says. "It uses the temperature differential between the cold water deep in the ocean and the warmer water near the surface to generate power."

"Huh. I feel like I should know this, but it's the first time I've heard of it."

His eyes gleam with excitement. "That's just one of many renewable technologies a floating city could use. There's also wave energy, solar—you name it."

I eye my glass. "Would I have to drink any recycled urine, à la Kevin Costner in *Waterworld*?"

He shrugs. "I wouldn't worry about that sort of thing. Every single glass of water you've ever drunk has contained molecules that have passed through some living creature—most likely a dinosaur."

Great. If I ever want to kill Gia, I can share this factoid with her.

I clutch my nonexistent pearls. "You really know how to stimulate a lady's appetite."

He studies my lips. "Are we talking about food?"

Well, I walked right into that. Before I can reply, I'm saved by the Nordic-looking waitress—who sashays over with a huge tray filled with small bamboo steamers.

"All organic and plant-based," she tells Oliver. "Enjoy."

Suppressing the urge to growl at her, I shove a morsel into my mouth.

Not bad.

I try another.

Decent—though I think it's from the wrong cuisine. Spanish, to be exact.

Oliver seems to savor whatever he tries a lot more, and I enjoy that expression on his face.

After trying a couple more entrees, I ask, "Is this a fusion restaurant?"

He swallows whatever he was chewing. "Why?"

"Well, most of these remind me of dim sum, but some taste more like tapas."

He shakes his head. "This is authentic Chinese dim sum."

"Sure, it is. And I'm a real mermaid."

He arches an eyebrow. "You don't like it?"

"It's okay, but it's certainly not authentic." I glance at the blond waitress and the equally blond hostess. "Just looking at the staff, you can tell."

He frowns. "Is that racist?"

"How? Maybe foodie-ist. A random, dingy dim sum restaurant in Chinatown is a million times better than this place. Not to mention, even the way they serve—"

"Not this again," Oliver says with a sigh. "Are you about to tell me you've found yet another way New York is superior to Florida?"

I grin. "If the shoe fits."

He extends his hand as if for a handshake. "I bet I can show you something here in Florida that isn't available in New York."

Is that something in his pants? Because yes, please.

Outwardly, I scoff. "Like what? A naked guy wrestling a python? That'll be something that isn't available in New York—thankfully."

His hand doesn't waver. "You know what I mean. I can give you an amazing experience here. Something where you'll say, 'Oliver, thank you. That's not something I could ever get in New York.'"

"I highly doubt you can make me say that." Unless it *is* related to his Aqua-manhood, in which case I'll lose with pleasure.

"Then you risk nothing by taking my wager." He grabs another inauthentic dim sum with his free hand.

"Fine." I shake his hand, cinching the bet—and the zing of pleasure that shoots down to my nether regions makes me wish we *were* talking about something inappropriate. "What does the winner get?"

Please say oral.

A sexy smirk appears on his lips. "If I lose, I'll wear one of those 'I heart NYC' T-shirts."

I pull my hand away before I have an orgasm. "And if I lose?"

"I'll make a custom shirt for you," he says with a devious smile. "It will say, 'I heart Florida Man.'"

Hmm. The stakes couldn't be higher, but how could he possibly impress me that much... outside of the bedroom?

"You've got yourself a bet," I say. "Under one condition."

He arches an eyebrow.

"If I win, I also get to braid your hair."

He frowns.

"Hey, take it or leave it."

"Fine," he says with a sigh. "We'll go after the meetings are over."

Alrighty then. If this meal isn't a date, the mythical place he plans to take me to sure sounds like it will be.

Not for the first time, I can't help but wonder if maybe, somehow, something could happen between us. Despite him being my boss and all the other stuff.

It's scary how much I want it—which in itself almost makes me want to put a stop to it before it can even begin.

"So." I clear my strangely dry throat. "Tell me more about floating cities."

He does. After that, we talk about anything and everything, and before I know it, we're on our way back to the hotel.

The closer we get to saying goodbye, the more I wonder if he'll kiss me good night... or more. By the time we step out of the elevator and approach my room, my skin feels flushed and my panties decidedly damp.

Swallowing, I run my tongue over my lips. Seductively, I hope. "So..."

His face goes taut as his gaze falls to my mouth. "So I'll make the arrangements for the trip. As soon as tomorrow's meetings are over, we can set out."

I bite my lip this time, in case that works better. "Are you *that* eager for me to win our wager?"

More importantly, why am I not being kissed yet?

His eyes darken, and he lifts his hand.

Yes, yes, touch me.

And he does. He tilts my chin up with his curved knuckles, sending a lightning bolt straight to my pearl. His cyan eyes hold mine captive as he says in a low, rough voice, "I'm eager to say, 'Told you so.'"

"In your dreams," I breathe, my heart hammering madly.

His nostrils flare. "Oh, kelpcake. In my dreams, I do so much more to you than talk."

It's official. I'm having serious trouble breathing, like an octopus out of water. "Like what?"

Whatever it is, yes, please.

227

"We should get some sleep," he says, lowering his hand with obvious reluctance.

Wait, what?

What's it going to take to get our lips to lock? Should I grab him by his perfect-for-such-a-maneuver hair and pull him down to me?

If he weren't my boss, I'd totally do it.

He's about to turn away, so I desperately blurt, "I have tea in my room... Want some?"

He stills for a second, then ruefully shakes his head. "We had drinks earlier."

Is he serious right now? "I'm barely buzzed."

His gaze drops to my mouth for a millisecond, giving me hope, but then he takes a half-step back. His voice is low and tight as he says, "If the tea offer is still there when alcohol isn't in the picture, I'll take it."

Damn it. If everyone experienced this much torment over a drink, there would be no need for twelve-step programs.

"I'm sober enough to brew tea," I insist.

His hands twitch at his sides before he shakes his head again. "Maybe you are, maybe you aren't. I must be sure."

Sure about what? Before I can ask, he turns and disappears into his room. A second later, a lock clicks on his door.

"Fine," I growl, fighting the urge to kick his door down like a member of a SWAT team. I raise my voice so he can hear. "Maybe you'll never have my tea again!"

CHAPTER
Twenty-Six

A DISTANT KNOCK reaches my ears.

I open my groggy eyes and cringe. I've got a headache. Is it a hangover? Nah. More like SMMDS— Severe Man Meat Deprivation Syndrome.

"Who is it?" I yell.

"Oliver," he says. "Do you know what time it is?"

Carp.

I grab my phone and check it.

Yup. Late for the meeting.

Also, there are a dozen missed texts from Oliver.

"One second," I shout, and get ready as quickly as I can.

Opening the door, I give him a sheepish look. "I'm not sure what happened."

He raises his eyebrows. "Still think you're impervious to alcohol?"

My hackles rise at that, but I hold back my retort. I did oversleep.

"What do we do now?" I ask instead.

"Nothing. I told them to move the meeting so you and I could check out the Viewing Center first thing, in case that gives you some new ideas."

"Thanks." I blow out a relieved breath. "It's actually a good idea for me to check the place out."

He nods. "Let's go."

————

The Viewing Center is what one would expect—a large factory-like structure with stacks spewing out vapor. What's unusual about it are the happy manatees frolicking in the bay below.

"Are you sure that water is clean?" I ask Oliver, peering at the murky depths.

"Positive," he says. "The electrical company's only impact here is the warm water."

Before I can say more, Jason and a few other people from yesterday's meeting show up and begin talking about the sanctuary status of this place, and how proud they all are of this "symbol of environmental commitment."

"So, Olive," Jason says. "Do you have any new ideas now that you've visited this place?"

"Tons." I point at the wooden pier we're standing on. "For starters, you could attach some brushes to these underwater wooden stilts and create scratching posts much easier than the way I suggested yesterday."

Jason and the rest of them love the cost-saving

implications of this, and I tell them a few more things they could do.

"Should we take this to the meeting room?" Jason asks when he notices me reapplying sunblock.

Oliver and I agree, so we return to the air-conditioned space, where I pitch a few pricier ideas and field a bunch of follow-up questions.

"Looks like we have everything we need," Jason says eventually. "On behalf of everyone, I want to thank Olive and Oliver for coming down and helping us out."

Why do I suddenly have that children's nursery rhyme stuck in my head? *Olive and Oliver sitting in a tree, K-I-S-S-I-N-G...*

Why do the kissers always sit in a tree, by the way? Are they environmentalists who refuse to let said tree get cut down? I guess I could see Oliver in that role—

"—buy you lunch?" Jason finishes saying as I realize that I zoned out and missed the rest of his colleagues scattering from the meeting room.

"She can't." Oliver's voice is cold enough to freeze an Antarctic toothfish, a creature that has special proteins that act like antifreeze. "We have plans."

"Right. Bye," Jason says hurriedly and scurries away.

For some reason, I can't bring myself to be annoyed at Oliver's high-handedness. Probably a bad sign.

I arch an eyebrow at him. "I take it lunch is on you?"

He nods. "I'll get it for you on the way to our destination."

Ah, right. The mythical place that he thinks will win him the bet.

I can't wait to prove him wrong.

———

We drive for an hour on a Florida highway, and just as we pass a town called Brooksville (not to be confused with Brooklyn), Oliver turns into a rest area parking lot and looks at me with slight concern.

"Do you have any idea where we are?" he asks.

"Florida?"

With a wicked smirk, he reaches over to the glove compartment—which puts him so close to me that I nearly faint.

I take deep breaths in and out, which helps, especially when I notice what he pulls out.

It's a sleeping mask, the kind you get on planes. Or, if your mind is dirty—which mine is primed to be by his nearness—it's a sexy blindfold to put on a willing lover.

"My plan depends on an element of surprise," Oliver says, handing me the mask. "Don't worry. It's brand-new."

I take it gingerly. "You want me to put this on?"

He shrugs. "Or you can just admit I've won."

With a huff, I put the mask on, which hides a monstrous eye roll that might not be appropriate to direct at one's boss. "I never surrender."

Did that sound too sexual? Also, I should probably never say never. If he wanted to play a sexy game where I'm a blindfolded submissive who surrenders to his—

"I didn't think you'd make winning that easy," he says. "Ready?"

I nod, and we resume driving.

Sitting there blindfolded, I feel like I've turned into Daredevil... or my sister Lemon. With sight out of the picture, my other senses are heightened. I can smell Oliver's delicious ocean surf scent and feel the warmth wafting off his muscular body. Also—though this could be my imagination—I think I hear his powerful heartbeat... at least until he puts the Jawaiian music back on.

After a few songs, he lowers the volume. "We're almost there."

I say nothing as I feel the Tesla turn. I'm trying not to let curiosity get the best of me, but it's hard.

We stop.

"Stay in your seat," he says. "I'll get the door."

Huh. It might be this blindfold, but him being bossy makes me think more and more about BDSM scenarios... and I kind of like what I'm picturing.

His door closes, and the one next to me opens.

"I'll take your hand," Oliver murmurs. "You ready?"

I nod so enthusiastically I nearly sprain my neck. I was really, really hoping things were leading to this.

A strong, callused hand takes mine. My pent-up sexual energy goes through the roof.

"Watch your step," he says as he helps me out.

"Okay," is all I trust myself to say.

As he leads me through what's probably a parking

lot, I feel the sun on my face and see some of its light seep through the mask.

Hey, the mask provides extra sun protection around my eyes—a bonus.

He squeezes my hand.

By Cthulhu's mighty beak. Who knew blindfolded handholding could be this arousing? My brain is a hormonal mush, which is my only excuse for wondering if maybe he's taking me to a kinky sex club... in the middle of the Florida countryside.

Given how I feel right now, if that were to happen, I just might say, "Oliver, thank you. That's not something I could ever get in New York."

No. I can't lose. Besides, there must be sex clubs in New York. To wow me, this needs to be uniquely Floridian.

Speaking of which, have I ever heard any stories that start with, "Florida Man blindfolds date and...?"

Hmm. I sure hope the rest of that headline isn't "he eats her, and not in a good way."

But no, Oliver is vegan. And even if he weren't, I trust that he's not a cannibal. Then again, if he were a secret cannibal, wouldn't veganism be the perfect cover?

"I'm going to get the tickets," he says, startling me. "Please stay here."

To my huge disappointment, he removes his hand from mine... and I miss it instantly.

Once I hear him walk away, I decide to be naughty and slide down my blindfold to sneak a peek.

We're standing next to what looks like a park entrance, and the sign on the ticket booth proudly states, "Weeki Wachee."

Hmm. There's a symbol, a mermaid inside a seashell. So far, so good—not that I'd tell Oliver that. Wouldn't want him to think he's winning and needlessly get his hopes up.

"Cheater," Oliver says sternly, and I realize he's walking back, tickets in his hand.

Carp. Busted. I pull the blindfold back up. "Sorry."

"Please follow directions, or I'll consider the bet forfeit," he says with mock sternness.

"Yes, sir," I say in my best imitation of a sex slave.

"You ever heard of this place?" he asks.

"No. What is it?"

He sounds smug as he says, "You'll see."

I shrug and let him lead me inside. As we walk, I hear some people murmuring about my blindfolded condition, but I couldn't care less thanks to Oliver's hand holding mine.

After a short walk, he tells me to wait again.

Unable to help myself, I peek once more.

Interesting. There are water rides in the distance. Is this some sort of theme park? We've got those in New York and in nearby New Jersey, so there's no way this will impress me enough to lose the bet.

Also, there are kids running around, which puts the nail into the coffin of my sex club idea/fantasy.

I spot a woman approaching Oliver. A woman that's far too attractive for my peace of mind.

Is the surprise a threesome? If so, I'll be pissed. When it comes to my boss, I have zero inclination to share.

I watch them talk furtively for a few seconds. Then Oliver starts to turn back, so I pull the blindfold back on.

"The surprise isn't ready," he says. "Would you like to do something while we wait?"

"Like what?" I ask.

"You'll see," he says and leads me deeper into the park—or whatever this is.

We stop a few times, and Oliver speaks in a low voice to some people, but I don't dare peek again.

The next time we come to a stop, Oliver tells me that I can take the mask off "for now."

Freeing my eyes, I examine our surroundings.

Huh. We're standing next to an orange two-person kayak, and there's a serene body of water in front of us, beckoning.

"What do you think?" Oliver nods at the spring, or river, or whatever it is.

I peer at a log floating downstream. "Remind me… is it gator mating season?"

Because if humans had mating seasons, mine would be right here and now.

He grins. "Typical New Yorker. Worrying about the gators."

I back away from the kayak. "That sounds like a yes."

"It's a no. The mating season hasn't started yet. But even if it had, you've got me to keep you safe."

My heartbeat speeds up. Clearly, the genes I've inherited from those cavewomen ancestors are letting themselves be known. What else could explain how excited I get at the prospect of him being my big protector?

Pulling out my phone, I look up statistics on gator attacks. From the late seventies until now, fatalities are only in the mid-twenties. Scary but not too bad, considering all the articles in which a Florida Man wrestles a gator, beats it up, keeps it as a pet, or tries to have sex with it.

Oliver peeks at my screen and scoffs. "You're more likely to get hurt by a coconut falling on your head than by a gator."

Great. I examine the shoreline for palm trees too close to the water but find none.

I put my phone away. "Fine. Let's kayak."

He nods approvingly, and before I can blink, he takes off his shirt.

I audibly gasp as my entire body catches fire.

Even though I've seen him in all his muscular glory before, I'm so sexed up that this new exposure makes me feel like my wunderpus might implode.

Oliver grabs a paddle and walks over to the kayak.

"Are you insane?" I ask, finally recovering my powers of speech.

He pulls on his ear. "What?"

"You haven't put on sunblock."

Oliver's sexy mouth opens, but nothing comes out. He just stands there silently, watching me as I pull out a tube from my purse and slather myself the way he should have done.

"Like this," I say. "Bear in mind, the surface area I have to worry about pales in comparison to yours… No pun intended."

Was that a slight headshake? Hey, at least he didn't mock me like most of my sisters would have. Instead, he surprises me by saying, "Can you help me?"

There's a tingling in my chest and other regions of my body. "You want me to cover you in sunblock?"

He grins. "If you don't mind."

If I don't mind? Would an octopus mind gobbling down a juicy clam? Would a manatee mind taking a dip in a Jacuzzi?

I sunblock my hands and hurry over.

Oliver's nostrils flare when I touch his chest.

Wow. His heart is beating like a drum. Would it be wrong to spread the sunblock with my tongue instead of my fingers?

Settling for digital application, I focus on spreading the sunblock and keeping the drool inside of my mouth.

His eyes track the movement of my hands hungrily, his chest heaving. The bulge in his pants is unmistakable.

An evil part of me is glad. Why should I be the only one who suffers?

Not to mention, hot.

Done with his pectorals, I move down to cover his abs, and if it were possible to faint from horniness, I'd be out cold right now.

When I'm done with the front, I command him to turn.

"You know," he murmurs when his back is to me. "When I asked for your help, I actually just meant my back."

Well, he sure as hell didn't stop me from doing his front.

I squeeze out more sunblock and begin applying it to his powerful back, all the while wondering if I could sneak an orgasm in while no one is looking... or ask him to ravage me right here on the kayak.

As if waiting for this exact moment, a blue kayak glides down the water, and a happy elderly couple wave at us with that signature Florida friendliness.

Cock-blocking fuckers.

"Do your arms yourself," I say grumpily when I'm done with his back.

He takes the sunblock and applies it to his arms, and I wish I'd kept my stupid mouth shut. It could've been my hands gliding over those chiseled biceps and triceps.

"Ready?" he asks.

I nod, gulping down my drool, and he carries the kayak into the water—which makes his gleaming muscles bulge and reminds me of the first time I watched *Magic Mike*.

He sits in the front, and as soon as he starts

paddling, I'm further reminded of male strippers—which makes it very challenging to care about the wildlife we pass by, including lots of pretty birds, some not-yet-as-horny-as-me gators, and a snake.

Toward the end of the kayak ride, I start to consider capsizing us and diddling myself under water.

"What do you think?" Oliver asks, pulling us to the shore with another easy flex of his muscles.

I wipe the sweat off my forehead as I climb out. "I think we could've done something similar in New York's Central Park. If your main surprise is anything like this, you're going to lose, big time."

He chuckles as he drags the kayak out of the water and hands me the blindfold. "It's time."

A handgasm follows as he leads me away. This walk is the longest one yet, but I'm enjoying his touch so much I don't want it to end.

Eventually, we enter some building, and I'm allowed to take the blindfold off.

"For the record, this is only half of the surprise," Oliver says. "Enjoy."

I eagerly examine my surroundings.

We're part of an audience standing in front of a theater curtain. A spotlight falls on a woman who claims we're about to see a spectacle the likes of which we've never seen before.

Hmm.

Strip club music begins blasting from the speakers, and the curtain slowly rises.

What the hell?

The curtain unveils a giant water tank.

Whatever this is, it already looks interesting.

Then I see the surprise—and realize that I just might lose this bet.

The water is not filled with octopuses, which was my first theory and would've been trouble enough.

This is even worse.

This tank is filled with real, live... mermaids.

CHAPTER
Twenty-Seven

OKAY, maybe they're not the actual mythical creatures, per se. But these women are wearing high-caliber tails and swimming deep underwater, so this is as real as you can get.

I grab Oliver's hand and squeeze it in gratitude, watching in fascination as the mermaids float about. I'm not sure if it's their majestic tails, or Oliver's nearness, but my poor libido revs up with a vengeance.

Then, as if to add insult to a homoerotic injury, I notice that each mermaid is holding a phallic tube in her hand. They start sucking on said tubes very temptingly. Of course, what they're really doing is getting oxygen, but still.

Everyone claps, me most of all.

The mermaids do a loop in the water.

They turn tricks too? Damn.

At one point, a lady without a tail begins talking under water—or lip syncing, because science. She mentions some guy who found the springs (which is how I learn where we are) and then decided to open an underwater theater… with mermaids.

Whoever that guy was, he was a visionary, on par with Steve Jobs and Elon Musk.

To the sounds of "Do You Believe in Magic," the mermaids perform more underwater tricks, and then they seemingly eat and drink under water.

More feats of amazing synchronized swimming follow, and then we hear about the history of this venue—which is extremely impressive, as is the list of celebs who have visited the springs.

As if for Oliver's benefit, they talk about the problem of pollution—singling out nitrates from fertilizers, perhaps in the hopes that this gross association will lessen everyone's horniness before we leave. Doesn't work in my case.

"Do I win?" Oliver asks when the mermaid show is over.

If I were honest, the answer would be yes, but I'm a bad girl, so I lie through my teeth as I say, "It was nice, but—"

"Hold that thought," he says. "The surprise is not over yet. Come."

He leads me into a back room.

My eyes widen when I see mermaid tails and other mermaid paraphernalia lying about.

He got me a VIP backstage visit with the mermaids? If so, it'll be very hard to pretend he hasn't won.

The woman he spoke to when we entered the park

walks into the room, and I realize she was one of the mermaids in the show.

"Oliver," she says with a smile. "Is this the student?"

Student?

Does that mean what I think it means? That I have the opportunity to learn how to be a mermaid from a real expert? That's so much cooler than VIP access. It's a dream, on par with—

"She *might* be the student," Oliver says, then turns to me with a devilish expression. "Assuming she wants to be."

I narrow my eyes at him. "Why would I not want to be?"

He lifts my chin with his index finger, so our eyes meet. "Oh, I know you want to. The question is, do you want it badly enough to admit you're impressed? Admit that this *isn't* something you can get in New York?"

I gulp, his touch burning through me. "Fine." The word comes out breathless. "You win. If I'm honest, you won when I saw the show. This is just amazing gravy."

He removes the finger, and my chin misses it instantly. "I thought so."

He's so smug, but what he doesn't realize is that wearing a T-shirt that says "I heart Florida Man" is a small price to pay for the chance to learn mermaid tricks. Not to mention, given this experience he's set up for me, his hotness, and our interactions, there might just be a Florida Man that I heart, so the T-shirt will just be an accurate representation of reality.

"Come with me, grasshopper," the mermaid sensei says. Or at least that's what I assume she says. I'm so excited my brain is a little foggy.

"Wait here," she tells Oliver. "Mermaids only."

She then takes me into another room.

Wow.

Rows and rows of brand-new, premium mermaid tails are all around us. There are also bikinis of all sizes, but that's less exciting.

"Pick one," my mermaid sensei says with a knowing twinkle in her eye. "It'll be yours to keep."

This is how a horny virgin must feel when they enter a brothel. The tails are amazing, and it's very hard to choose just one—but eventually, I manage.

"Put it on," the sensei says. "And some swimwear."

I do as she instructs.

Have I mentioned that I get strangely turned on while wearing a mermaid tail? That's under normal circumstances. Since I'm already high on Oliver's presence, by the time the tail is on, I'm glad Oliver stayed behind. Otherwise, tomorrow's news story might've read: "Florida man sexually assaulted by nympho mermaid in a public park."

My sensei pulls out a wheelchair and tells me to take a seat. "It's hard to walk with the tail," she explains.

I sit on my honorary throne, and the sensei wheels me out and over to the spring.

Here's how excited I am at this point: the idea of reapplying sunblock doesn't even cross my mind.

"Was there anything you saw during the show that you'd like me to teach you first?" my wise sensei asks once I'm wet (with spring water, not the other kind of wet—that ship sailed long ago).

"I want to learn it all," I say reverently.

She nods knowingly and starts the teaching— beginning with the all-important skill of breathing through an air hose, a Weeki Wachee mermaid's greatest weapon.

What follows are the best hours of my life, except maybe for my make-out session with Oliver the other day.

Right about when my lips and nails turn blue from being in the water for so long, the sensei says, "That's it for today, but you're welcome to come back. Oliver arranged for you to learn our full curriculum."

He did? I'm speechless as she takes me back to Oliver, and I'm still overwhelmed as we walk to the car, though I distantly realize that Oliver is telling me how the whole surprise came to be. Long story short, the Weeki Wachee mermaids once performed at Sealand, which is how they ended up owing him a favor.

When we stop next to his car, I meet his gaze. "I don't know how to thank you."

A sensual curve appears on his lips. "I won. That's reward enough."

"It's not. That was amazing."

He opens my door and gestures for me to get inside.

Once we're both in the car, he says, "I have a confession to make. I watched you in that water."

I arch an eyebrow as a trickle of heat moves through me. "And?"

"And I feel like I've won twice over."

He liked what he saw? That right there is the kind of flattery that would get him into my panties if he hadn't already earned a season pass there, twice over.

He starts the car.

"How come I've never heard of this Weeki Wachee?" I ask as we pull out of the parking lot.

"I have no idea. In 2008, they became a state park— that's how important they are. Weeki Wachee is one of Florida's oldest roadside attractions and home to one of the deepest underwater caverns in the country."

I turn back and wave Weeki Wachee goodbye before asking, "Are there other hidden gems here in Florida that I should know about?"

Since I've already lost, I might as well go all the way and let him brag about his home state as much as he wants. Not to mention, there's always a chance I'll get another date or two out of it.

I don't have to prompt Oliver twice. If he ever tires of being Sealand's owner, he can always start a travel agency—he's that good. The whole ride back, he showers me with interesting Florida road trip ideas, though by the time we park and take our hotel elevator up to our floor, my mind has shifted to other things.

Things like "what do you do after the best date of your life?" and "what positions do you do it in?"

"So," Oliver says when we reach my door. "Here we are."

I nod, determined to seize the moment. "Indeed. And with zero alcohol in our blood."

His eyes grow hooded. "What are you saying, kelpcake?"

I lick my lips. "I want to make you that tea. Hard."

CHAPTER
Twenty-Eight

MOVING FASTER than a swordfish on Adderall, Oliver swoops in and claims my mouth.

I drop the bag with my new mermaid tail and kiss him back with everything I've got. Our tongues tangle hungrily as we drink in each other's taste, smell, feel. His hands roam over my body with barely restrained greed, and my fingers dig into his shoulders, reveling in the feel of his powerful muscles flexing under my touch and the heat coming off his skin.

Breathing heavily, he pulls away. His voice is hoarse. "Your room or mine?"

Instead of an answer, I pull out my room key, unlock the door, and pull him in by his shirt.

As soon as the door closes, he rips off said shirt, and I ogle his muscular torso again. This time, no elderly couple in a kayak can thwart me. Hopefully.

Our lips meet again and stay locked as we rip the clothes off one another, all the while half-walking, half-dancing deeper into the room, inching closer to the bed. By the time I pull away to catch my breath, I'm in my bra and panties, and he's in his boxers.

His tenting boxers.

He runs a heated gaze over me. "You're stunning, kelpcake. You know that, right?"

"Shut up and strip," I say breathlessly as I unclasp my bra.

Pupils dilating, he drops his boxers.

My mouth waters as I stare at his Aqua-manhood in all its glory.

Almost as an afterthought, I peel off my drenched panties.

"Stunning," he says raggedly.

With that, he's on me again, his octopus hands roaming over my body as his tongue explores my mouth. In response, my nipples turn hard and pointy, like conch shells, and the breasts around them feel fuller and heavier. Unable to help myself, I reach for his Aqua-manhood and give it a light stroke.

Oliver grunts into the kiss, and my wonderpus practically shouts, "Yes, that. Slide that in me, now."

His hands scorch my body everywhere they touch, and as if he has more than two (eight?), he lifts me up and drapes me over the bed.

"Spread your legs," he orders roughly.

By Cthulhu's oxytocin release. Am I getting the opportunity to play the coy submissive after all?

Yay!

Blushing as befits my role—and because I can't help it—I do as I'm told.

His nostrils flare. "Touch yourself."

Yep. Bossy boss fantasy is becoming reality.

I lick my fingers to make sure they're nice and slick, then spread my folds with one hand as I locate my G-spot with the index finger of the other.

"Just like that," he says, cyan eyes gleaming.

I circle the spot, and a moan escapes my lips.

"Good job." The words are like a lion's purr. "Now hand me those fingers."

Obeying again, I watch, stupefied, as he licks them clean.

"Delicious," he murmurs. "I want more."

Oh?

Before I can ask him to explain, his mouth is next to my sex, his tongue going unerringly for my pearl as his beard rubs sensually against my folds.

Cthulhu help me. My entire body contracts on a wave of heat, my toes curling, and I come all over his mouth with a loud cry as sensations blast through me with such force that fireworks explode behind my tightly clenched eyelids.

"Yes," I hear him say when my senses are back. "Now taste yourself on my lips."

Blinking dazedly, I open my eyes and meet his devouring kiss. He tastes different than usual, and I love it—but I think I'd like anything, even cyanide, if it were delivered via those lips.

"Your turn?" I ask huskily as I pull away, and he

leans back in reply, his Aqua-manhood jerking in anticipation as his eyelids lower to half-mast.

Finally. With no parents or peanut butter in sight, I can do this uninterrupted.

Swooping down, I ice-cream lick him.

He grunts something unintelligible.

I look up, and my eyes lock with his cyan gaze as I slide his Aqua-manhood into my mouth.

His eyes are feral now.

I swish my tongue under the shaft.

He twitches in my mouth, and I taste precum.

Damn, this is turning me on. I never realized this before, but sucking a cock is even more arousing than wearing a mermaid tail. At least when it's attached to the right person—the cock, I mean, not the tail. Though come to think of it, Oliver with a tail might be hot in its own way.

He coils his hand in my hair, so I double my enthusiasm. He groans, his ass muscles flexing. Just as I'm really getting into the spirit of things, he pulls on my hair, and I free my mouth to look at him questioningly.

"Get on all fours." The husky command is equal parts dominance and lust.

I not only do as he says, but I also shake my naked booty to show him what a good girl I can be when properly incentivized.

Looking at his taut face over my shoulder, I ask, "Like this?"

In answer, he grabs my hips and his Aqua-manhood

prods at my opening before entering me in one smooth motion.

My breath vacates my lungs.

Wow. Wow. Wow.

He's so big it should hurt, but instead, he fills me perfectly, the slight stretch only adding to the heated tension building in my core.

"I want to come inside you," he growls.

"Fuck," I gasp. "Yes, please."

Oops. I might've just released the Kraken.

His next thrust is hard. The one after that is even harder—and I love it so much I let him know via a moan.

Oh. My. Cthulhu.

With a growl, he pistons into me with renewed vigor, and the tension grows so intense I claw at the sheets.

This is it. This is how Oliver's surfboard would feel if he rode her over a tsunami. This is also how I get ruined for any other man.

A scream is wrenched from my lips.

"Yes, kelpcake," he groans, pounding into me. "Come with me."

Yes.

Yes.

That's the best idea in the history of ideas.

I yelp out his name as a massive orgasm makes landfall.

He thrusts deeper into me, his Aqua-manhood

impossibly hardening as he shoots his release into me with an animalistic grunt.

Boom! His orgasm triggers another one of mine, and I moan over and over, until my arms finally give out and I drop limply onto the bed.

CHAPTER

Twenty~Nine

SPOONING ME FROM BEHIND, Oliver nuzzles his face against my hair. "That was amazing."

I exhale slowly. "Understatement much?"

"My apologies." I can hear the smile in his words. "It was astounding, remarkable, out of this world."

I sniff. "That still doesn't do it justice. I guess it's one of those situations where you had to be there to appreciate it."

A chuckle. "I was very much there."

I smile into the pillow. "Shower?"

"Sure." I feel myself lifted and carried into the bathroom.

Giggling, I enjoy the ride.

When we approach the shower stall, he asks, "Can you stand?"

I grin. "Someone is *really* cocky about his prowess."

He sets me on my feet and turns on the water.

I know how the water feels.

"Join me." He steps under the stream and pours body wash into his big hands.

I follow obediently, and he begins to soap me up, which feels amazing and decadent.

Carp. He's already ruined other men for me. Does he also mean to ruin the simple pleasure that is the shower?

Seems like it. The gentle strokes of his hands (all eight of them), the head massage he performs as he washes my hair, the way his muscles glisten under the spray—it's exactly the sort of thing I could get used to very quickly... and then not be able to live without.

"Your turn?" I ask when he's done with my back.

"I have something else in mind," he murmurs, and I turn to look him over.

Gulp. A shiny new erection winks at me.

Heh. Even after the gallon of soap he's just used up, I feel dirty—in a naughty kind of way.

I tickle the underside of Aqua-manhood as I would the chin of a cat. "I like where your head is at."

With a wicked smirk, Oliver claims my lips again, his tongue reaching deep to stroke every surface of my mouth.

It's a good thing we're in the shower, or else there'd be a puddle under me, for sure.

Pressing my back against the slick tiles, he grabs my ass, lifts me a few inches, and enters me again.

Gasping, I wrap my legs around his hips and clutch at his shoulders, holding on for dear life as he thrusts into me. This time, his pace is gentler, slower, like our earlier frantic session was the appetizer, and this is a mindfully savored main course.

Water is totally our element. This is even hotter than when he took me in the bed. The running shower muffles my moans, but not the slaps of wet naked flesh, and the sounds turn me on beyond reason. Growling, he deepens the kiss, and a powerful orgasm builds in my core as his thrusts speed up.

I guess we're back to the appetizer mode again. Or maybe this is the decadent dessert.

"I'm close," I pant into his mouth.

He sinks his teeth into my lower lip and thrusts deeper, taking me over the edge.

My cry of release is so loud it might be audible in the rooms nearby. My whole body spasms and releases, scorching hot ecstasy exploding through my nerve endings. I still haven't caught my breath when Oliver reaches his peak, groaning my name and grinding into me—an action that sets off an aftershock orgasm for me.

Wow. Double, triple wow.

My legs feel like noodles, but thankfully, he's there to hold me up.

"You okay?" he murmurs as he maneuvers me back under the spray and tenderly washes my sex.

"Officially and properly fucked," I say weakly. "Otherwise, peachy."

He gives me a look of pure male satisfaction. After leading me out of the shower stall, he towels me off and carries me back to the bed.

"Unfair," I say as he covers me with the blanket. "I didn't wash *you.*"

He winks. "You'll just have to make it up to me. Somehow."

I yawn. "Yeah. Tomorrow."

"First thing," he says with mock sternness. "Don't oversleep again."

Oversleep and miss *that?*

Never.

I tuck a strand of his hair over his ear and try to sound serious as I say, "Oliver, thank you." I look down at his Aqua-manhood. "That's not something I could ever get in New York."

My reward is hearing his belly laugh and watching his abs flex. Afterward, he gives me a gentle peck on the lips. "Sleep tight."

With a goofy grin, I close my eyes and instantly pass out.

CHAPTER
Thirty

I WAKE up to strong fingers touching my face. Opening my eyes, I see that it's Oliver, massaging something into my skin.

Did he come on my face?

I don't mind, but I'd prefer to be awake for that.

But no. He's fully dressed.

I rub my eyes as he pulls his hand back. "What's happening?"

He grins. "It's almost ten-thirty, and the sun was about to land on your pretty face."

Oh. That substance he was rubbing into me is sunblock.

I turn and see that he's right. The rays of sun have almost reached the pillow.

Fucking assholes.

Then my sleepy mind registers the most important point. Oliver was worried about sun exposure on my behalf.

Even if I hadn't just experienced the best sex of my life, I'd keep him based solely on that gesture.

He leans in to resume the sunblock application, but I pull back.

"I think I want to brush my teeth first."

He smiles. "Fair, but don't take too long. I actually have to leave soon."

I feel my heart sink. "You do?"

He nods. "I've got a long drive ahead of me."

"Oh?"

He squeezes my thigh through the blanket. "I'm heading to St. Augustine before the SOS fundraiser to meet a few of the attendees."

Carp. I can't keep the pout from showing on my face. "But I owe you a soaping."

He smiles ruefully. "You were sleeping so peacefully I didn't want to wake you."

Ugh, I *did* oversleep in the end. Had I known what was at stake, I would've set an alarm. Maybe two.

"When are you leaving?" I ask.

He looks at his watch, and his face changes. "Fuck. In ten minutes."

I leap to my feet and sprint into the bathroom to make myself presentable.

By the time I come out, Oliver only has five minutes left—so we spend them wisely, making out as if we depended on each other for oxygen.

Or maybe not so wisely. Last night, I satisfied my overactive libido, but I'm back to being horny and Oliver has to leave.

Why is life so unfair sometimes?

"So." Pulling back, I touch my swollen lips. "When will I see you?"

He sighs. "At the fundraiser. I'm sorry. I made the plans before we—"

"It's fine," I lie, but inside, I'm stomping my feet like it's my birthday and I've been deprived of cake.

Not seeing him until tomorrow feels like a punishment.

"Okay." He plants a gentle kiss on my cheek. "I'm going."

He leaves before I can ask a million questions.

Disoriented, I sit down on the bed to catch my breath.

I can't believe what happened.

I slept with Oliver.

Twice.

Is this as monumental of an event for him as it is for me? Or does he see this as a one-time thing?

Doubts darken my good mood, like the ink of a frightened octopus. Even if this isn't a one-night stand, can he and I properly date? I work for him, and he's got that HR policy against fraternizing for a good reason.

I groan inwardly. This is the sort of thing I should've cleared with him *before* issuing the "tea" invite, not after. Although, in my defense, I wore a mermaid tail yesterday for an extended period of time —which would be like a guy mainlining Viagra.

My stomach rumbles.

Right. I should eat.

As I head downstairs to get breakfast, I come up with more prosaic questions for Oliver, such as, "Do I have to go back to work, or can I enjoy Tampa for some time?"

On the one hand, he told me about the nearby Salvador Dali Museum, but on the other, it is a workday and our business in Tampa is finished. Oh, and since he left for work reasons, doesn't that imply work is back on?

When I'm done eating, I decide that texting him the work question would be as awkward as sleeping on the ceiling—and it doesn't escape me that this is but a tiny example of why genitals and bosses don't mix.

Oh, well. I'll just head back to work. I bet if he hears that I was at Sealand today, he'll be impressed with my work ethic.

———

On the drive back, I call Lemon and tell her what happened. I regret it immediately because she starts squealing like a teenage piglet.

I wait for her to finish and say, "So, I have no idea where we stand, him being my boss and all."

"Who cares?" She giggles. "He's hot enough to put up with a little awkwardness."

I roll my eyes. "Have you ever worked in a business environment?"

She scoffs. "Whatever. Here's an idea. We look identical, so he'd probably be just as happy to have sex with me as he is with you. And I don't work for him, so—"

I nearly swerve off the road. "Back the fuck off."

"See?" I can hear her grin over the phone. "Now you know how you really feel."

"I feel like I should've choked you with the umbilical cord when we were inside Mom," I say. "Besides, what about the Russian ballet guy?"

"I was obviously kidding," she says. "As hot as your guy is, the Russian is hotter."

"Right." *Keep telling yourself that.*

"Anyway, when will you be back?" she asks.

I shrug, realize she can't see me, and say, "After five. I'm headed to work."

"Okay, then I guess I'll see you tomorrow afternoon. I'm going to Orlando again."

"What attraction?" I ask.

"Harry Potter World and then the Blue Man Group."

I chuckle. "First you talk about sleeping with *my* man, now you're eyeing a whole group of Blue's?"

———

Just as I park in front of Sealand's main building, a text from Oliver arrives:

Forgot to mention something before I left. A recommendation. At the SOS fundraiser, dress to impress.

I stare at my phone with horrified fascination.

Seriously? Am I cursed, like those pirates on the

Black Pearl? The sheets we slept on are still warm, and he's already turning into Brett 2.0, telling me what to wear.

My reply is curt:

You worry about your own attire, and I'll handle mine.

I walk briskly and angrily into Sealand as I wait for his reply.

My phone dings.

Sure. If you want to recommend something for me to wear, I'll hear you out... exception being a T-shirt with "I heart NYC" on it.

Okay, so he's a little better than Brett at digging himself out of holes—but is that even a good thing?

"Hey, Olive," Dex says, startling me. "I'm glad you're here. I wanted to ask for a favor."

I shake my head to clear it. "What's up?"

"It's about the octopus tank. Turns out, it's not just octopus-proof." He grins sheepishly. "I don't know how to open it either."

Carp. It's a good thing I'm back to work today and can feed Beaky. He almost became a victim of his own cleverness—or human dumbness.

Dex rubs the back of his otter-like neck. "So, what do you say? Can you teach me how to open it?"

I purse my lips. "I really, *really* like feeding Beaky myself..."

He must understand the idea of calling dibs on a specific creature. He's the primary feeder of the otters for a reason. Still, I have no idea if "I'm the one who feeds the octopus" fits Sealand policies. I hope so, or else I'll fight tooth and nail to make it so.

"I understand." Dex bounces from foot to foot. "This is for later. You can't exactly feed him when you're not here."

I resist the urge to say something like, "Well, duh." Instead, I lead him to the tank so I can demonstrate what's what.

Throughout the lesson, I can't help the feeling that Dex is acting odd, but I'm not sure why.

"Thanks," he says when I finish listing Beaky's favorite treats.

I tear my eyes away from Beaky—who's been watching our conversation with those intelligent eyes of his. "No problem."

Dex turns to go. "Don't worry," he says over his shoulder when he's halfway to the door. "I can teach the others how to do this."

"Oh?"

"It's no problem," he says. "You must have so much on your plate."

I do? Before I can tell him that I don't really mind teaching everyone, he's gone.

That was definitely weird.

Oh, well.

Since the tank is already open, I drop a treat in there.

Oh, High Priestess, we couldn't help but notice you forgot to teach Otter Deacon the most important rule when it comes

to worshipping us, the God Emperor of the Bigger Tanks:
"The treats must flow."

Someone shuffles their feet behind me.

I turn and see that it's Rose.

She sighs and gives me a strange look.

Hmm. What are the chances she's so good at HR stuff that she's managed to smell "sex with boss" on me already?

"I'm glad I found you," she says. "I need a favor."

I blink. "What's up?"

She gestures at the tentacle dildo in Beaky's tank. "Could you document all the enrichment tools you've created thus far, as well as how to maintain them?"

Hmm. That's an odd request... Unless she's already planning on firing me based on what she's sniffed out with her HR super senses.

Nah. I'm being paranoid.

"When do you need it?" I ask.

She scratches her chin. "Any chance you could do it by the end of the day?"

"Sure." Feeding Beaky was my only real priority today.

"Thank you."

Is it just me, or does she look disproportionately relieved?

I head over to my computer and start working on Rose's request. Since she didn't say how detailed I should be, I dummy-proof the document —a lesson learned from Beaky's tank. I explain how to change the videos on the TV in the manatee tank, and even how to turn said TV on and off.

As I'm finishing up, I check the time. It's just after five, as in heading-home time.

Someone clears her throat behind me.

Swiveling my chair, I look up to see Aruba.

"Miss Hyman," she says. "Sorry to interrupt."

She's still here? I thought everyone at this place left at five on the dot.

"We agreed you'd call me Olive," I say.

"Sorry," she says. "*Olive*, may I have a moment of your time?"

"Sure." Curiouser and curiouser.

Aruba plops into a nearby office chair. "If I were interested in making toys for sea creatures, the way you do, is there a book you'd recommend I read or something like that?"

I cock my head. "I didn't realize that was something you were interested in."

That's an understatement. Her exact words were: "Anything is better than 'making toys' for goldfish."

Aruba turns her chair left and then right. "Look, I'm sorry if I was a bit prickly before."

Sure. We'll call it a bit... and prickly. "Water under the bridge."

She exhales a relieved breath. "All I've ever done here is train the dolphins. And as much as I love them, I figure if I learn to do what you do, it will give me a chance to stretch my job."

I frown. "You want to start helping me?"

As flattered as I am, and despite her apology, she's still not an understudy I'd choose voluntarily.

Aruba blinks dumbly. "I thought that with you gone —you know what? Never mind."

The whole chain of odd events clicks together, like a puzzle box meant for a particularly clever octopus.

I see red.

Jackknifing to my feet, I growl, "What do you mean 'gone?'"

She pushes her chair away from me. "Umm. There was that email from Dr. Jones. He said to prepare for when you're not at Sealand any longer, so I—"

I don't hear the rest because blood is pounding in my ears.

She's just confirmed my horrible suspicion, and it hurts like a punch to the liver.

Oliver and I had sex, and now he's decided to fix the HR snafu that act has created by using the most treacherous method possible.

He's going to fire me.

CHAPTER
Thirty-One

"I'll EMAIL you some book recommendations," I mutter before rushing out of the room as if I were a tuna and Aruba one of her favorite dolphins.

Everything fits. The way Rose asked me to write that document and how weirdly she acted. Why Dex wanted to learn how to take care of Beaky.

Oliver told everyone I'm going to get canned.

I bet he doesn't actually have any meetings in St. Augustine. He's probably in his office or at home.

Fueled by unadulterated rage, I rush to his office.

Luckily for him—and for my criminal record—he's not there.

I growl angrily and sprint to my car. Speeding like a maniac, I get to his house in an eyeblink and come to a screeching stop in his driveway.

I ring the bell and then pound on the door with my fist, pretending it's his face.

A man opens the door. For a second, I think maybe

it's Oliver after a haircut, but then I realize it's definitely not him. I don't want to kill this guy, or have my way with him.

"Hello," the stranger says.

"I'm here for Oliver," I grit out.

The guy flashes a sexy smile. "You must be Olive. What did he do now?"

I take a calming breath. "You must be one of his brothers."

"Ash, at your service." He glances at the dog at his feet. "Bro asked me to watch the snack—and teach him how to surf while I'm at it. Would you like to leave a message?"

I shake my head. "I need to speak to Oliver."

Ash runs his hand through his much-shorter-but-still-nice hair. "He's not due back today. He said he has some important meetings before the conference, and then drinks with some people. You must know by now how he is about drinking and driving."

"Okay." I back away from the door. "Thanks."

I stagger to my car and park in my grandparents' driveway.

The adrenaline spike that started in Sealand is turning into a crash of epic proportions.

I drag myself into the guest room, my legs feeling like jellyfish on Xanax.

My grandparents aren't home, it seems. Did they go with Lemon to Orlando?

It's for the best. I don't think I can face anyone right now.

Fighting the urge to cry, I crash onto my bed without taking my clothes off.

How could I have been so stupid?

How could I have let yet another man use my heart as a punching bag?

The red flag was there—my attraction to him. Assholes are apparently my type, so why am I shocked that Oliver turned out to be yet another one?

I bet he was planning to have sex with me one more time before pulling the rug out from under me. Why else would he invite me to the SOS fundraiser? He even had the balls to specify I should look nice for him.

Unbelievable.

The worst part is that I no longer have the energy to locate him and give him a piece of my mind. However, I also can't stand this limbo where I know that he doesn't know that I know.

Pulling my phone out, I type furiously:

I know you plan to fire me. Don't bother. I quit. Both you and your job. I never want to see your face again.

There. Like ripping off a Band-Aid. Except it feels more like waxing my whole body and soul, over and over.

Feeling oddly cold, I burrito myself in a blanket.

Despite all my comparisons of Oliver and Brett, this feels infinitely worse than that breakup... even though I've known Oliver for much less time, and he isn't officially my boyfriend.

It must be that mermaid surprise Oliver set up for me. Even if it was a ploy to get under my tail, it was nicer than all the kind gestures Brett and my other exes ever made, combined.

Cthulhu curse his coccyx. The sex was so amazing I'll probably never experience something like that again. And it wasn't just the sex. Just hanging out with him was—

What am I doing? Why torture myself like this?

What I should be worried about is Beaky.

Am I going to let him stay with Oliver?

My stomach feels frozen solid.

Has Oliver planned that far ahead? He did make it a point to say that if I left Sealand, Beaky would stay behind. Was he already planning to literally and metaphorically screw me?

I have no idea, and what makes this impossible to deal with is that Beaky is happy in his new tank, so the best thing for him might be to let Oliver keep him.

The room starts to spin, and I close my eyes, squeezing them shut against the burning sting of tears.

My entire body feels heavy, especially my chest, and despite my best efforts, the tears begin to flow.

They don't stop until exhaustion claims me, and I fall asleep.

CHAPTER
Thirty-Two

I WAKE up with a stuffy nose and a scratchy throat.

The sun is out, which means I've slept from dinner time until late morning.

I guess I was *that* emotionally drained.

Having slept, I feel a bit stronger—and I have a decision to make.

Do I go to the SOS fundraiser or not?

On the one hand, it might be a good place to network for my next job. On the other, Oliver will be there, and it will take a lot more sleep for me to feel like I'm ready to face him.

Okay, no fundraiser, which leads me to a secondary dilemma: should I even bother getting out of bed?

After a short deliberation, I go for it. In the past, whenever I've felt down, taking action, no matter how small, has always made me feel better.

I climb out of bed and go through my morning routine.

Nope.

Not feeling better.

I check my phone.

The fundraiser starts soon. If I were going, I'd have to run now.

Unable to help myself, I check on my text to Oliver.

Looks like he hasn't read it yet—probably too busy schmoozing with the other fundraiser attendees.

Carp. That means he still thinks he's gotten away with it.

Must stay sane.

Opening my laptop, I stalk Octoworld's website again. If there is any fairness in the universe, I'll find a job there to compensate for the shitty blow life has dealt me.

Nope. They have no new job openings listed. I do notice something interesting, though. According to their news tab, they're sponsoring the SOS fundraiser again this year. I wonder if…?

I check out Ezra Shelby's social media and confirm my suspicion. She's going to be representing Octoworld at the fundraiser.

Looks like the universe is not done kicking me in the teeth.

If not for this clusterfuck with Oliver, I could've met my idol today.

Then again, I still can… if I'm willing to bump into Oliver.

But no. I can't risk slapping his face in public.

Besides, at this point, I'm late for the meet-and-greet portion of the event anyway.

Unsure of what else to do, I open my email so I can send Aruba a list of resources she can use if she wants to do my job.

In my inbox are two unread emails from yesterday.

One is from Oliver, so I give it a middle finger, but the other is from a person who's never written to me before: Ezra.Shelby@Octoworld.com

My pulse leaps.

It can't be, can it?

I open the email from my idol with trembling fingers:

Dear Olive,

I'm greatly looking forward to meeting you tomorrow. A few weeks ago, your current employer and my good friend, Oliver, told me about the amazing work you've been doing at Sealand. He also mentioned how much you love octopuses and that you've applied for jobs here at Octoworld. I checked on this and saw that your resume never got past our HR department. My apologies. If all goes well tomorrow, I will be creating a job just for you—which will be very similar to your work at Sealand, but with an emphasis on the octopuses. If you don't mind, please bring any notes or designs you have tomorrow, so that—

I peel my eyes away from the screen, blink a few times, then read the first two sentences again.

Yep. I have an interview with Ezra Shelby herself... and it was Oliver who set it up.

Was it out of a guilty conscience?

No, couldn't have been. He told her about me "a few weeks ago."

In a daze, I open Oliver's email to see if it can shed some light on this.

Hi Olive,

I just heard from Ezra and learned that she's ruined what was supposed to be another surprise. I guess now you know why I invited you to join me at the SOS fundraiser. It was to meet with her. Oh, well. I hope you impress her as much as I think you will. On my end, I'm so confident she'll hire you that I told the folks at Sealand to prepare for when you're no longer—

I stop reading with a gasp.

By Cthulhu's claws, I've made a huge mistake.

Oliver didn't decide to fire me after we slept together. He just paid attention when Fabio and Lemon said my dream was to work with Ezra, and then he decided to make that dream a reality—even if it meant he'd be short-staffed.

That's why he asked me to dress to impress. It was for this interview.

And to thank him, I sent him that nasty text.

I check my phone.

He still hasn't read it.

I text him again:

Ignore what I said. You're the best.

Nice. I sound like a lunatic. And ugh, he's not reading that text either—obviously.

Chewing nervously on my nail, I call him. He

doesn't pick up. Probably too busy doing something else very nice for ungrateful old me.

I leap to my feet.

I have to do something. I have to go to him. I have to tell him I was self-sabotaging. I have to explain that I've had bad relationships, and that they sometimes make me see things through the opposite of rose-colored glasses. Oh, and I have to thank him. And kiss him. And most importantly, grab on and never let him go.

Also, it might be a good idea to not miss the interview he's set up for me.

The interview of a lifetime.

I dress up as fast as I can, but then I realize I have a huge problem.

With the Tampa trip and what followed, I completely forgot to buy myself more sunblock, and now I'm out.

Carp.

What do I do?

I rush downstairs to ask my grandparents for some. Their brand might not be optimal, but any sunblock is better than none.

"Ah, Caper," Grandpa says with a smile. "Ready for breakfast?"

I shake my head. "No time. I'm late for the fundraiser. Hopefully, they'll have hors d'oeuvres. Can you give me your sunblock?"

He sighs. "I was afraid this might come up. We don't have any."

I frown. "How do you go outside?"

He shrugs. "Our doctor told us sun exposure is good for vitamin D production, so we've been—"

"No. You can take supplements for vitamin D. When I'm back, we're going to discuss this at length—both the dangers of sun damage and the qualities you should look for in your new doctor."

"Great," he grunts. "I can't wait."

With a heavy heart, I rush into the garage and check to see if, by some miracle, there's some sunblock lying around in there.

Nope. It's all missing, and so is my car.

Wait. Where's my car?

Oh, right. I left it in the driveway.

I open the garage door.

The evil that is the sun shines threateningly outside the garage.

Carp.

I'm not sure I can do this.

No. I can. I must. It's just a few feet, and once I'm inside the car, the front window will block the worst of the UV rays—which is better than nothing.

Yeah.

Better to not think about it and just do it.

I take a step toward the light.

Then another.

Then one more.

I feel like I'm in the movie *Poltergeist* and someone is about to shout, "Do not go into the light!"

But I must, so I do.

Cringing, I step out—only to face something even worse than UV radiation.

A person I didn't think I'd have the displeasure of seeing ever again.

Despite being pursued by cops, despite the restraining order, and despite Blue's surveillance, here he is.

My ex, Brett.

CHAPTER
Thirty-Three

As I look at his face this time, the primary emotion I feel is annoyance, with a twinge of fear. There's also enormous relief that I broke up with him when I did. He's clearly unhinged. Plus, that way I was single when I met Oliver.

Shit. Oliver. I'm late as is, and I don't need Brett slowing me down.

Side note: now that I see Brett, I realize how foolish it was to compare him and Oliver.

Oliver is a better man, times a million.

"Hi, baby," Brett drawls.

How unoriginal. I glare at him. "Why are you here? The cops nearly caught you the last time. Are you sure you want to take that chance again?"

His jaw tenses. "Can't we just talk like two adults?"

"At most, we can talk like an adult and a half." Actually, I'm being generous by giving him that half.

He advances on me, and although he doesn't smell like a distillery today, something about his pupils is off.

Maybe he's high?

The twinge of fear grows into serious concern. He's attacked Blue and now stalked me here to Florida, so who knows what else he might do?

"Why can't we just talk?" he insists as I cautiously back up toward the garage.

"Because there's nothing for us to talk about," I say, throwing a glance over my shoulder to gauge how far I am from the door, in case I have to sprint to safety. "We're over. Get that through your thick skull."

"Over?" His fists clench and unclench.

"Finished. Through. Done. Now go, and maybe I won't tell Blue and the cops that you came." I force myself to stop backing away as I reach the garage door. "I have somewhere to be, and I'm late."

His face darkens. "You're going to finally hear me out."

I raise my chin, meeting his furious gaze. "Take another step, and I'll scream."

He sneers. "If you don't shut the fuck up, I'll *make* you scream."

Suddenly, there's the tell-tale sound of a shotgun being pumped, and Grandpa's stern, ice-cold voice growls from the front door, "Actually, it's you who's going to scream."

And with a deafening boom, Brett is thrown back onto the driveway.

CHAPTER
Thirty~Four

OH, Great Cthulhu! Grandpa shot Brett.

In a flash, I picture Grandpa in handcuffs and an orange jumpsuit. Then again, when it comes to shooting people, Florida is a "stand your ground" state, which I think means if someone threatens you and you're standing on the ground, you can shoot them.

Still. Killing Brett is—

Brett groans in pain and clutches his ass.

Oh. He's not dead?

"Not so tough now, are you?" Grandpa growls, looking satisfied. He then loads a bean bag round into his shotgun and pumps it again. "If you even think of moving before the cops arrive, I'll shoot you again."

Stunned, I stare at Grandpa. "You didn't kill him."

He takes his phone out. "Not yet. Maybe I'll get lucky, and he'll move a few times."

A relieved breath whooshes out of me. I take a step toward Grandpa, then remember where I was going.

Hesitantly, I ask, "Do you need me here for when the cops show up?"

"Nah, go to the fundraiser. This knucklehead threatened you right in front of my security camera. I'm sure that's all the police will need."

I bite my lip. "Right. He also broke a restraining order, skipped out on bail, and trespassed on private property—again."

"They'll sort him out," Grandpa says. "Go."

I gingerly step over whimpering Brett and get into my car. "Tell Blue about this as well," I say before I close the door.

Grandpa nods, and I start the car.

Blue has connections with security agencies, so whatever Brett has coming to him, she might be able to make it even worse—and at this point, I think I'd feel most comfortable if he went to jail. And became somebody's bitch.

Pushing all thoughts about Brett aside, as well as my resurfacing worries about the UV radiation, I peel out of the driveway and reenact a scene from *Fast and the Furious* all the way to St. Augustine.

To my huge disappointment, the parking lot is outside and a block away from the building.

Not this again.

I check my glove compartment in the hopes that some sunblock was left there, forgotten.

Nope.

None.

I step out of the car and take a valiant step toward my destination. Then another. Then one more.

I can't help but picture solar flares and plasma rains falling on the surface of the fiery orb above me, with rain drops the size of a country. I can practically feel my skin burning, my cells mutating, and my collagen and elastin being damaged.

In the future, I should at least keep a parasol in the trunk of my car, just in case. Maybe a ninja outfit as well. Then again, if we're talking "just in case," I might as well keep a dozen spare sunblock tubes in there too.

Unsure if it will help, I break into a run.

My face is warm. Way too warm. I imagine that's what the first responders at Chernobyl felt on that fateful day after the reactor exploded. At least twice, I think I'm just going to give up and take cover in the nearby shade, but I don't.

If there is any fairness in the universe, Oliver should forgive me just for braving all this UV on his behalf.

Feeling like I've survived an ordeal worthy of Greek myths, I dash into the building that is my destination and spend a few precious seconds catching my breath.

"Name?" a lady at the entrance asks.

I rattle it out, and she checks me off the list in front of her.

"How late am I?" I ask, still breathless.

She looks up. "These things are like weddings. Nothing ever starts on time."

When I step inside, I see that she's right. Everyone is still mingling.

Yes! Now to find Oliver.

Passing through crowds of unfamiliar people, I scan all the faces.

Nope.

Nope.

There.

He's standing by himself next to an ice sculpture.

Oh, no. He's raising his phone to his face.

Carp.

He can't be checking—

He must be. Like the sky during a storm, his face transforms, darkening dangerously.

I check my own screen and curse.

He's just read my text.

My vague hope was to get here before that happened, snatch his phone, and delete the text—but that's out the window now. Maybe groveling will help? It's worth a shot.

I start toward him when someone taps me on the shoulder.

I turn and blink at the elegant woman in front of me. It takes me a couple moments to recognize who she is because she doesn't wear this much makeup in her social media photos.

"Olive?" she asks.

I nod dumbly.

She extends her hand. "Ezra Shelby."

I shake her hand a tad too vigorously. "Of course. I recognized you."

She smiles kindly. "Thanks to social media, no one is a stranger anymore."

I bob my head, still starstruck.

She glances at her watch. "Can we have that chat now?"

Carp.

How can I say no? She's doing me a huge favor.

I dart a glance at Oliver.

No, I can't talk to anyone but him right now. I have to make this right.

Gulping in air, I tell Ezra, "I'm so sorry, but I can't talk now. I have something urgent to say to Oliver."

If this means I don't get my dream job, so be it.

She looks confused as she nods. She must not have had anyone act this unprofessional with her before.

So much for good impressions.

Whatever. The most important thing is telling Oliver I didn't mean what he's just seen on his screen. The chances of him forgiving me are slim, but I have to at least try. I'd never forgive myself if I didn't.

Leaving Ezra standing there, I sprint over to him, ignoring the faint ping coming from my phone as I run.

When Oliver spots me, his eyes widen.

"Hey," I blurt. "Before you tell me to go fuck yourself, let me speak."

His eyes widen further.

"I'm sorry I didn't get here before you got the

chance to read that stupid text," I rattle out. "Brett turned up and—"

Were his features this stormy before?

He looks scary. Murderous, even.

"Your ex showed up?" he growls. "That fu—"

I wave my hand. "Forget him. Grandpa shot him in the ass with a bean bag."

Oliver's stormy expression doesn't alter, so I speak faster. "Look, I didn't mean what I said in the text. I mean, I obviously meant it at the time, but I don't mean it now. It was stupid. I obviously have some issues, but I'm working on it. It was basically a misunderstanding. Everyone acted like you fired me and I—"

He shuts me up in the best way possible: by pressing his soft lips to mine. The kiss is deep, hot, and extremely inappropriate for the venue—and exactly what I didn't realize I needed.

I feel like a manatee has just slid off my chest.

When he finally lets me go, I'm gasping for breath.

"Does that mean you don't hate me?" I manage to ask.

He tenderly cups my face. "Kelpcake, how could you even ask that?"

My sigh of relief would do a yogi proud.

"Now." Dropping his hand, Oliver glances at the place where I was standing a few seconds ago. "How did your conversation with Ezra go?"

I follow his gaze. "I haven't talked with her yet," I admit. "Apparently, I had to kiss you first."

He shakes his head, and I'm not sure if his disapproval is real or in jest. "What are you waiting for? Go get her. We'll continue what we started afterward."

I beam at him. "Okay."

I doubt she'll be as happy to talk to me now, but it's worth a shot.

As I head over to where she's standing, I check my phone. Turns out, I have texts from a few people, Oliver among them.

Where are you? is what he replied to my psycho texts.

Warmth spreads in my chest. I can read between the lines of that reply. He was going to come find me and talk/kiss me into sanity.

Yay.

Another text is from Blue:

Brett is with the police now. Don't expect him to see freedom for a while.

Yet another text is from Grandpa, with basically the same message as Blue's but with more expletives about Brett.

I feel light on my feet. For someone who might've messed up her chance at the Octoworld job, I'm feeling exceedingly happy.

When I reach Ezra, she shocks me by giving me a wink that's all BFF and not at all potential employer.

"That looked like some tremendously urgent business you had to take care of," she says with a grin, fanning herself. "The temperature in the room might've risen a few degrees."

I smile sheepishly. "I hope you can see why it might be best if I worked somewhere other than Sealand."

"Let's talk about that," she says, and the conversation quickly turns into a casual interview.

In no time at all, we're bonding over our love of octopuses—a great start. Midway through it, I seem to have impressed her with my inventions and ideas, or at least I assume I've impressed her, because in the end, she offers me a job.

"I'll take it," I blurt.

She grins. "Don't you want to know how much it pays?"

Carp. I sigh. "I guess that didn't help my negotiating position, did it?"

Her face turns serious. "I believe in paying people fairly. How would this sound?" She takes out her business card and writes a number that's thirty percent higher than what Sealand is paying me—and they're generous.

Since I didn't play it cool before, I don't bother hiding my excitement now—though I do resist the urge to jump up and down in glee.

"If that doesn't convince you," she says. "I understand you have your own octopus that you'd want Octoworld to house? I'll be happy to make that happen and cover all the moving costs."

I gape at her. "How did—"

"Oliver," she says. "He requested I provide him one of Octoworld's denizens in return, which isn't a problem."

I can't believe this. I'll be surrounded by octopuses, making more money, and seeing Beaky every day.

"You're very persuasive," I say with a wide grin. "If I had any hesitations about working for you—which I didn't—I'd definitely take the job now. Thank you so much."

She grins back. "I'm looking forward to working with you. Now, I think there's more of that tremendously urgent business awaiting you."

I turn to follow her gaze and meet Oliver's cyan eyes.

"I'll go take care of it now," I say to Ezra and hurry over to him.

"Want to take a walk?" he murmurs, extending his hand. "We're near a gorgeous spot I wanted to show you."

"Sure." I take his hand. As he leads me out, I grab a couple of hors d'oeuvres and swallow them without chewing.

When we reach the exit, I realize there's a huge problem and stop. "I'm not sun-blocked."

He arches his eyebrows. "How is that possible?"

"I ran out. You could say I've been distracted."

He smiles knowingly. "I think it's fate." To my shock, he pulls out a tube of sunblock from his pocket —and it's my favorite brand. "I took your words to heart and will now be using this on a regular basis," he explains.

I just stare at him. Can someone really be this perfect of a male specimen?

"Do you want my help applying this?" he murmurs.

Speechless, I nod, and he slathers me in sunblock, touching my face, my neck, and my arms in the process—and causing orgasmic explosions along the way.

"Is that good?" he asks when I'm covered in a thick double layer.

"Amazing," I breathe. "The best I've ever had."

He grins, puts the sunblock away, and grabs my hand once more.

Our destination turns out to be a little bridge over a koi pond surrounded by greenery, with giant fish that have likely been overfed by tourists.

In other words, a spot romantic enough for wedding pictures.

I look up from the pond and into Oliver's eyes. "We should talk."

"Sure." He pulls me by the hand he's still holding into another panty-scorching kiss.

"Wow," I breathe when we pull apart. "You've made some great points there. Still, I wanted to apologize for—"

"Don't." He presses a finger to my lips. "Consider the matter forgotten."

"Okay, but can I at least say thank you? For the mermaid surprise, and for setting that up with Ezra. I got the job, by the way."

"You're welcome. As for getting that job, I had no doubt you would."

This time, I kiss *him*—and if we weren't in a public

place, my gratitude would be way more X-rated. As is, I reluctantly pull away and readjust his tie.

"There's something else," I murmur, looking up at him.

His eyes twinkle. "I also have something else to say, but ladies first."

"Well." I clear my desert-dry throat. "I've realized that I have feelings for you. Feelings not unlike the way an octopus feels about shrimp."

A sexy smirk curves his lips. "What a coincidence. I was going to tell you that I have feelings for you as well. Mine are not unlike what a manatee feels for romaine lettuce."

Wow. Manatees *love* their romaine lettuce—

He cradles my face with his palms. "Olive you."

O.M.G.

Fabio has managed to corrupt yet another victim with his puns from hell.

I lightly pinch Oliver's shoulder. "If you expect me to say, 'Olive you too,' or, 'I Oliver you,' that's not happening." I place my hands over his, pressing them tighter to my face. "But I will say that I love you too."

To seal the deal, we kiss again.

And again.

And about a hundred more times.

Epilogue

OLIVER

WHERE THE FUCK IS HE?

I scan the lobby once more.

Nope. My brother is still nowhere to be found.

Maybe he's confused about the meeting place?

I head into Octoworld at a brisk pace. The last thing I want is to be late because of my brother.

As I pass through the halls of Octoworld, not for the first time, I really, really hope that no one in Olive's family has chapodiphobia—the fear of octopuses. I'm pretty sure my relatives are fine, though I doubt my knucklehead brothers would admit to being scared of cephalopods, be they clams or octopuses.

Then again, is that why Ash is missing? Is he cowering in a corner, paralyzed by the gaze of some octopus? Witnessing that just might be worth being late.

I decide to return to the lobby. On my way, I see my kelpcake's work everywhere. My favorite is probably the setup currently on my left, where two octopuses in adjacent tanks are throwing Frisbees at the glass that separates them. Olive arranged that after she discovered how much her charges enjoy assaulting fellow members of their species with random objects. Ezra is lucky she's not actually Jane Goodall because that would make this place Chimpworld, and the Frisbees would be feces.

Correction. *Here's* my favorite invention. Beaky zooms by in a small mobile tank that he's able to control with his arms, like an otherworldly bicycle. In a feat worthy of a NASA engineer, Olive built this tank-vehicle in a way that allows it to dock with the bigger tank that is Beaky's actual home—and many people now come to Octoworld just to see this wonder.

When I return to the lobby, I still see no sign of my best man.

Why did I think today would be different? Why did I imagine he'd finally take something seriously?

An ecstatic moan coming from the nearby utility closet interrupts my increasingly angry musings.

Seriously? This again?

Fuming, I stride over and yank open the closet door before I can think through my actions.

Thankfully, I was right. Looking smugly over his shoulder is my brother, and not, say, one of my soon-to-be in-laws.

Atypically for Ash, he's being a gentleman—that, or he's blocking his conquest from my view by mere chance.

Then I see a bridesmaid's dress on the floor. Shit. It doesn't take Sherlock to figure out that he was just banging Ezra. I told my brothers and friends that if they so much as gawk at someone who even remotely looks like Olive, I'll have their balls, so Ezra is the only bridesmaid who's not strictly off-limits.

"We're late," I bark and close the door.

After a minute, Ash saunters out of the closet. "Bro, mind coming with me to the bathroom?"

I frown. "Since when are you so in touch with your feminine side?"

He nods at the closet. "Don't be a dick."

Ah. He wants to give his lady friend—who'd better be Ezra—a chance to sneak out without facing me.

Fine. Without replying, I walk to the nearby bathroom.

"Thanks," he says loudly before joining me.

Since we're here, I use the facilities, and so does he. When we're done, I glare at him. "That better not have been one of the Hyman sisters."

"I don't kiss and tell," he says. Then, seeing the murder in my eyes, he adds, "It wasn't."

Poor Ezra.

"We're late," I growl. "Hurry up."

Pushing open the door, I take long strides in the direction of the atrium.

"Slow down," Ash says, catching up. "They can't exactly start without you."

Shaking my head, I step onto the red carpet someone rolled out for just this occasion.

Whew. She's not here yet. Ash gets to live another day.

Stepping on a petal, I grin. Tofu was the flower dog, and it looks like he did his job like a good boy.

As I walk, I see my family and friends on the right and Olive's peeps on the left.

In the back of the room is my other brother and the rest of the groomsmen, and facing them are Olive's sisters and Ezra—whose disheveled appearance confirms my earlier suspicion.

I avoid looking head-on at the five identical Hyman sisters. Though I can easily tell Olive apart from them, the rest look creepily alike despite different hairstyles and makeup. The older Hyman twins resemble them closely as well, especially in the matching bridesmaid dresses they're all wearing, so it's more like there are seven of them.

Oh, and where a priest would be standing is Fabio —our officiant.

Wait. I'm not being fair. Fabio *is* a priest today. As a joke that went a bit too far, he was ordained by the First United Church of Cthulhu—a real religious organization registered in Arizona.

Yeah, and they make fun of Florida.

Spotting me, Fabio performs an official Cthulhic greeting called "the chin tentacle salute." He covers his mouth with his fingers splayed and makes them tremble.

I take my place and join everyone in staring at the entrance from which the bride will come forth.

My heart begins to hammer in my chest.

This is it. All those other steps—admitting our love, moving in together, getting engaged—have led to this, a wedding surrounded by our loved ones... and octopuses.

Pleasantly eerie guitar riffs ring out in place of the usual Wedding March. It's Metallica, and the song is called "The Call of Ktulu." They spelled the name of the Great Old One incorrectly because doing it properly is supposed to bring the beast closer, and they decided against tempting fate.

Olive's parents walk in first. Then her dad holds the door, and my bride steps majestically into the room.

Everyone gasps as I gape at her. She didn't let me see her before the ceremony, so all I knew was that she loves her dress.

Now I can't tear my eyes away.

She's as gorgeous as when I first met her, but today, there's an ethereal radiance to her beautiful features. Her strawberry-blond hair shimmers in its intricate updo, her green eyes shine, and her pale skin has a pearly glow to it that makes me want to lick her all over.

As for the dress, I love it too. It shows off her every curve so expertly that a rush of unwelcome blood shoots into my cock.

Down, boy. Too many people watching. Auspicious occasion. You'll get your chance in a few hours.

For our wedding night, my kelpcake and I are going

to figure out how mermaid reproduction is supposed to work. Spoiler alert: no caviar is involved.

Nope. Thinking of the wedding night is not the best idea.

I start to think of unsexy things, like oil spills, red tide algae, and blobfish. This seems to work. Code-name Aqua-manhood rests for the moment, so I risk checking out the rest of my bride.

Not surprisingly, she's wearing a mermaid-style dress, though not the typical kind. This one has scales below the waist and is the closest you can get to wearing a mermaid tail at your wedding while still being able to walk.

I smile. I doubt I'm the only one battling my libido right now. When my kelpcake puts on a mermaid tail, she turns into a horny beastie, in the best possible way. There's a reason I've given her so many of those things as gifts—one for every holiday, even Flag Day.

When they reach me, Olive's dad winks at me, triggering a flashback to his Thanksgiving Day massages. Her mom whispers something encouraging to us both that I can't make out. Probably something like "marriage is about giving and receiving as many orgasms as humanly possible," or "orgasms help pigs conceive, so why not humans too?"

"If I may have everyone's attention," Fabio says into a microphone in the solemn voice of a Cthulhu priest. "The hour of reckoning is upon us."

I look back at Olive, and my heart feels like it may

leap out of my chest, like a salmon during spawning season.

"Dear ethereal beings," Fabio says to the crowd. "We have gathered here today to witness the joining of two celestial entities in an ageless tradition that us human meat sacks refer to as 'marriage.'" His air quotes look like the writhing tentacles from one of Olive's grandmother's cartoons.

Olive and I exchange knowing grins. Fabio was clearly yearning for some non-porn acting opportunities and is really getting into his role.

"Eighty-five percent of our vast universe is dark matter"—Fabio moves the mic from hand to hand—"and we are but tiny specs of light glimmering in that infinite cold void."

Yeah. Nice and cheerful, just as officiations should be.

Fabio brings the mic closer to his face, as if he's about to ceremonially lick it. "Our feeble minds should boggle at the improbability of celestial entity Olive and celestial entity Oliver arriving at this point, but here we are, about to witness the uncaring universe become just a bit warmer and infinitesimally less hostile."

Moving the mic away, he says in his normal voice, "The rings people. Chop, chop."

Ash brings me the ring, while Ezra does the same for Olive.

Fabio speaks into the microphone again. "As we learned from the famous documentary about hobbits and Sauron—who is really but a minion of the True

Lord, Cthulhu—rings have great power." In an eerie impersonation of Gollum's voice, he adds, "Exchange each other's Preciouses."

I step forward and slide my ring onto Olive's delicate finger. Oops. Our palms brush, and I have to compose another calming soliloquy for my dick as Olive places the ring on my finger.

Our eyes meet, and there is a giddy finality to it. A feeling of something like fate.

"Now," Fabio continues. "Does the entity known as Olive accept the entity known as Oliver to be her lawfully wedded husband?"

Her eyes glow brighter. "I do."

"Does the entity known as Oliver accept the entity known as Olive to be his lawfully wedded wife?"

I feel ultra-aware, as though I've mainlined amphetamines. "I do."

Fabio nods solemnly and does the chin tentacle salute once more. "So be it. By the power vested in me by the State of Florida, the God Emperor of the Tanks, and of course, the Blessed Tentacles of Cthulhu, I pronounce you man and wife."

I grin, warmth radiating throughout my body.

This is it.

It's official.

She's mine.

"You may kiss the bride entity," Fabio says, and I do.

I kiss her and give it my all as everyone hoots and cheers.

Sneak Peeks

Thank you for participating in Olive and Oliver's journey! If you loved their romance, you'll definitely want to pick up *Sextuplet and the City*, the story of Lemon and her hot ballet dancer.

Looking for more laugh-out-loud rom-coms? Meet the Chortsky siblings in *Hard Stuff*:

- *Hard Code* – A geeky workplace romance following quirky QA tester Fanny Pack and her mysterious Russian boss, Vlad Chortsky
- *Hard Ware* – The hilarious story of Bella Chortsky, a sex toy developer, and Dragomir Lamian, a potential investor in her next big business venture
- *Hard Byte* – A fake date romcom featuring Holly, a prime-number-obsessed Anglophile

who makes a deal with Alex Chortsky (aka the Devil) to save her dream project

And if you can't get enough of the Hyman sisters, you should also check out:

- *Royally Tricked* – A raunchy royal romance featuring daredevil prince Tigger and Gia Hyman, a germaphobic, movie-obsessed magician
- *Femme Fatale-ish* – A spy romcom starring aspiring femme fatale Blue Hyman and a sexy (possible) Russian agent

We love receiving feedback from our readers, and we are always interested to know what you'd like to see in books to come. Want your favorite side character to have their own book? Mention it in a review! We take all suggestions into consideration, and if you sign up for our newsletter at www.mishabell.com, you'll be the first to know who will be featured next!

Misha Bell is a collaboration between husband-and-wife writing team, Dima Zales and Anna Zaires. When they're not making you bust a gut as Misha, Dima writes sci-fi and fantasy, and Anna writes dark and contemporary romance. Check out *Wall Street Titan* by Anna Zaires for more steamy billionaire hotness!

Turn the page to read previews from *Royally Tricked* and *Femme Fatale-ish*!

Excerpt from *Royally Tricked*

BY MISHA BELL

A daredevil prince wants to pay me mega-bucks to train him to hold his breath underwater for ten minutes? Sign me up.

Except I'm a magician, not a stunt consultant. My record-beating dive without air was a trick. Of course, I can't tell that to my client, the royally hot Anatolio Cezaroff, a.k.a. Tigger. Not if I want to be able to pay my rent.

Also, I'm not exactly comfortable around germs. All germs, including those lurking on uber-attractive men. So falling for my gorgeous client is out of the question, and I fully intend to keep my distance.

That is, until he offers to train *me* in bed.

———

"Holly?" an unfamiliar male voice says from the street.

I glance at the newcomer, and suddenly, it's my turn to gape.

I didn't realize this kind of masculine perfection existed outside of Hollywood.

Chiseled features. A Roman nose. Vaguely feline hazel eyes that zero in on my face predatorily, making me feel like an about-to-be-devoured gazelle.

I swallow the overabundance of saliva in my mouth with a loud gulp.

The stranger's broad-shouldered, muscular torso is clad in a tight white t-shirt, and despite the raggedy jeans riding low on his narrow hips, there's something regal about him—an impression supported by the strange design on his belt buckle. It resembles a crest that a medieval knight might put on his shield.

I've been told I compare people to celebrities too much, but it's hard to do with this guy. Maybe if the love between Jake Gyllenhaal and Heath Ledger in *Brokeback Mountain* had borne fruit?

Nah, he's even better-looking than that.

Realizing that I'm staring at his face too intently for it to be considered polite, I drop my gaze lower and notice that he's holding two leather straps in his fists. Leashes, presumably.

Half expecting to see willing sex slaves on the other end of those leashes, I instead find two weird dogs.

At least I think the creatures are dogs.

One sports black-and-white spots that make it look like a panda. Actually, given the creature's ginormous size, I can't rule out the possibility that it *is* a bear. And, if looking like an endangered ursine species wasn't odd enough, the beast is wearing goggles.

Is it because of bad vision, or is the panda about to go snowboarding?

The second creature is eyewear-free and reminds me of a koala, just much bigger and with a lolling canine tongue.

I force my gaze back to their ridiculously handsome owner. "Hey," is all I can manage. My overactive hormones seem to have robbed me of the ability to speak.

The stranger narrows those hazel eyes. "You *are* Holly, right?"

This is your chance, my inner magician pipes up. *Trick the hot stranger. Fool his pants off.*

Banishing lust with a heroic effort of will, I inwardly rub my hands together, à la evil villain. Until I adopted my current pale-skinned, raven-haired stage persona, I was mistaken for my identical twin on a regular basis, even by people closest to us. Our oval-shaped faces are exactly the same, right down to sharp cheekbones and a strong nose. I was literally born for this particular deception.

Adding the slightest touch of poshness to my voice, I say, "Who else would I bloody be?"

There. If he knows that Holly has a twin named Gia (as in, me), he'll voice that guess now and I'll stand down.

Maybe.

I bet I can bluff him out even if he does know I exist.

He stares at me intently. "You've changed your hair."

"*Addams Family* cosplay," I say in my best Morticia Addams voice. It's not my most convincing lie, but the guy looks like he's about to buy it anyway. Then I see a problem. Waldo, who's blinking in confusion, is about to speak. I kick his leg under the table and cheerfully ask the stranger, "Have you met Waldo?"

I'm hoping the hottie will extend his hand and introduce himself, thus letting me learn his name.

My evil ploy is thwarted by the panda. It pulls on the hottie's pant leg with its teeth. Seeing this, the koala does the same on the other side, except its movements are clumsy, puppy-like, leaving a hole in the pants.

If this is how the dogs get his attention, no wonder he wears something so raggedy. Also, yuck. I hope he washes that dog saliva off his pants ASAP.

"One second, guys," the stranger says to his furry friends in a warm, paternal tone that tugs at something in my chest. "Can't you see I'm talking to Holly?"

Score! He believes I'm Holly.

Looking up from the dogs, the stranger gives Waldo a once-over. Does he also think my friend looks like Willem Dafoe, only when he played Aquaman's mentor, not the Green Goblin from *Spider-Man*?

Before I can ask, the stranger's gaze returns to me. "That's not your boyfriend."

I blink. He knows Holly's boyfriend? Where does

my sister find all these hunks? This one is even hotter than her Alex.

"Indeed," I say, channeling her again. "This bloke is just a *friend* friend."

The stranger's wicked smirk is like a flick on my clit. "I don't think men and women can be just friends."

They so can. My sisters and I have been friends with one particular guy forever, and he's never made a move on any one of us. Granted, he's gay, but still.

Waldo stands up, all wounded dignity. "Look, chum, I'm allergic to dogs, so if you don't mind…"

"Chum?" The stranger's feline eyes are mocking as they capture mine. "See? He doesn't like me horning in on his territory."

The heat that flashes through my body is no longer lust. The nerve on this guy. "I'm nobody's territory." And certainly not Waldo's. He's never made a move on me either, not in the entire eighteen months we've known each other.

Waldo's face reddens, and he tightens his grip on the knife that he never gave back.

Seriously? Can testosterone make you *that* stupid?

"She's right, chum," Waldo says in his most menacing voice, which, if we're honest, sounds a bit like he's doing a Cookie Monster impersonation. "You'd better skedaddle."

The stranger curls his upper lip at him. If he's aware of that knife, he doesn't show it. Another testosterone-poisoning victim, no doubt.

"Skedaddle?" He looks back at me. "Where did you find this Waldo?"

Okay, that's it. I'm the only one allowed to make "Where's Waldo?" jokes at my friend's expense.

The hot stranger has just crossed a line.

I push my chair back and rise to my full five-foot-five height. "How about 'get the fuck out of here?' Is that a better choice of words for you?"

This is when the panda growls at Waldo—a threatening sound one wouldn't expect to come out of such a cute, if overlarge, dog. It reminds me of this news report about a man who tried to hug a panda at the zoo, only to end up in the hospital after the frightened bear mauled him.

Paling, Waldo sets the knife on the table. There are clearly at least ten brain cells inside that thick skull of his.

The stranger pats the bespectacled beast's head and murmurs something soothing in a language that sounds Eastern European.

Huh. He didn't have any accent when he spoke to me, but English must be his second language. Otherwise, he wouldn't address his dogs in that foreign tongue.

Crap. With our luck, the hottie is some Russian mobster.

"Sit down," I hiss at Waldo, and to my relief, he does as I say.

Make that twenty brain cells.

The stranger's beautiful eyes roam over my face before narrowing again. "You're not Holly. She's nice." A touch of that wicked smirk returns to his lips, and his voice deepens. "Whereas *you* are naughty."

That does it. No more Mrs. Nice Magician.

I slowly saunter over to him.

Although… maybe this isn't such a good idea.

Now that I'm closer, I realize just how tall he is. And wide-shouldered. The giant dogs threw off my perspective, creating a visual illusion that their owner was normal-sized. He's not. Worse yet, he smells divine, like ocean surf and something ineffably male.

A trick under these conditions will test all of my abilities.

Hold on. Will the dogs get mad that I'm so close?

As if reading my mind, the stranger gives them a stern command, and they sheepishly fall behind him.

Was that command intended to make *me* want to behave like a good, obedient bitch? Because I kind of want to.

No, screw that. I'm sticking with my plan, which requires me to get within pickpocketing distance.

"Do you want to see just how naughty I can be?" I ask in the sultriest voice I can muster.

Is it normal for human eyes to go all slitty like that, as if he were a lion?

"How naughty is that, *myodik?*" the stranger murmurs.

Did he just say "me dick?" Nah. It was something in

whatever language he used with the dogs. Still, his dick is now firmly on my mind, which doesn't help the hormonal overload situation.

Forcing away the X-rated images, I purposefully lick my lips. "I'll steal your wallet. Or your watch. Your choice."

The supposed choice is misdirection, obviously. My real target is neither of those things, but he doesn't need to know that.

His nostrils flare as his gaze drops to my lips. "Is it stealing if you warn me?"

If it were possible for me to forget my concerns about germs and consider placing my lips on someone else's, I'd do that now. It's the strongest such urge I've ever felt.

"What's the matter?" I say breathlessly. "Chicken?"

He pats the right pocket of his jeans. "How about you steal my wallet?"

I take in a steadying breath. "Thanks for showing me where it is."

Before he can reply, I delve into that pocket. I need major misdirection for what I'm really trying to steal.

By Houdini's eyebrows, is that what I think it is?

Yup. There's no mistaking it. As I brush my gloved fingers over the wallet, I feel something else behind the fabric of the pants.

Something big and very hard.

Well. Someone is overly happy to be pickpocketed.

Maybe he *was* saying "me dick" before?

I do my best to hold his gaze and not clear my suddenly dry throat. "Can you feel me stealing it?"

As I speak, I work on unclasping the fancy buckle—his belt being my real target.

His lids lower to half-mast, and his voice deepens further. "Your nimble fingers are exactly where I want them."

Crap. Between my gloves and his ridiculous sex appeal, I'm having trouble with the clasp.

But no. I can't get caught. That would be like revealing a magic secret—the biggest taboo I can think of.

"These fingers?" I ask huskily and gently stroke his hardness through the layers of fabric, using the misdirection this slutty move creates to pull harder on the clasp with my other hand, finally opening it.

I'd like to see David Blaine do *that*.

The stranger's low, guttural groan is animalistic and makes my nipples so hard they feel on the verge of turning inside out. He now looks like a lion about to pounce.

Gulping, I yank my hand out of his pocket and try to give him a sneaky smile. It comes out faltering instead. "I changed my mind. I'll steal your watch."

I grab his wrist and give it a tight squeeze while pulling out the belt with my other hand.

Yes! Got it. Hiding the belt behind my back, I pout at the watch. "On second thought, I think I'll let you keep your possessions."

He looks triumphant, probably convinced that his

sex appeal has defeated my pickpocketing skills. Since it almost did, I can't really fault him for thinking it.

I carefully back away. "Oh, by the way, did you lose this?"

I show him my prize.

Eyes wide, he shifts his gaze back and forth between my hand and his pants.

"How?" he asks.

The question is music to my ears.

"Extremely well," I say, but I can't manage my usual bluster.

He extends his hand to get the belt back. "You're a dangerous woman."

Two things happen simultaneously as I step toward him to return the belt.

The panda tries to get his attention again by pulling on his left pant leg. Not wanting to be outdone, the koala does the same thing on the right side—only this time, there's no belt holding the pants up, and they slide down.

All the way down.

Fuck. Me.

The biggest erection in the history of phalluses juts out and—though this could be my imagination—winks at me.

He's been commando all this time?

Me dick indeed.

I gape at the ginormousness. Even though I touched it and felt its size when I was rummaging in his pocket, I never would've imagined it like this.

Smooth. Straight. Delectably veiny. It just begs to be touched, or sucked, or licked—but I can't for reasons that are difficult to recall right now.

A concealed carry license should be required to pack that kind of heat. And also whatever license you need to operate heavy machinery. And a hunting license. Maybe even a 007-style license to kill—

Behind me, I hear Waldo gasp. Poor thing. I bet even *he* is ready to get on his knees for a taste, and to the best of my knowledge, he's straight.

I can't tear my gaze away.

If that cock were a magic wand, it would be one of the Deathly Hallows—the one Voldemort wielded at the end. And if it were a banana, it would be just the right-sized snack for King Kong.

The stranger should be turning red with embarrassment and scrambling to cover himself, but instead, a cocky smirk lifts the corners of his lips. "Like what you see?"

I do. So much so I want to pull out my phone and take a selfie with it.

To my huge—and I do mean *huge*—disappointment, he pulls up his pants. His voice is husky. "Like I said. Naughty. Very naughty."

Snatching the belt from my nerveless fingers, he loops it back into his pants and saunters away with his dogs, leaving me standing there, mouth agape.

"Can you believe that guy?" Waldo asks somewhere in the distance, his tone outraged.

No. I can't.

I can't believe what just happened, period.

All I know is this wasn't what I had in mind when I set out to fool that guy's pants off.

———

Go to www.mishabell.com to order your copy of *Royally Tricked* today!

Excerpt from Femme Fatale~ish

BY MISHA BELL

My name is Blue—insert a mood-related joke here—
and I'm a femme fatale in training. My goal is to join
the CIA. Unfortunately, I have a tiny issue with birds,
and the closest I've come to my dream is working for a
government agency that's disturbingly up-to-speed on
everyone's sexts, rants in private Facebook groups, and
secret family chocolate-chip cookie recipes.

I know I'm a spy cliché, that agent who works at a desk
but craves fieldwork. However, I have a plan: I'm going
to infiltrate the secretive Hot Poker Club, where I've
spotted a mysterious, sexy stranger who I'm convinced
is a Russian spy.

And once I'm in? All I have to do is seduce the
presumed spy without falling for him, so I can expose
his true identity and prove my femme fatale bona fides
to the CIA. I never lose concentration at work, so

that'll be an absolute breeze for me. Oh, and did I mention he's sexy?

I'm doing it for my country, not my ovaries, I pinky swear.

WARNING: Now that you've finished reading this, your device will self-destruct in five seconds.

————

I stick my finger into Bill's silicone butthole.

"What the hell?" Fabio exclaims in a horrified whisper. "That's poking. You have to be gentle. Loving."

Grunting in frustration, I jerk my hand away.

Bill's butthole makes a greedy slurping sound.

"See?" I say. "He misses my finger. It couldn't have been *that* bad."

"Look, Blue." Fabio narrows his amber eyes at me. "Do you want my help or not?"

"Fine." I lube up my finger and examine my target once more. Bill is a headless silicone torso with abs, a butt, and a hard dick—or is it a dildo?—sticking out, at least usually. Right now, the poor thing is smushed between Bill's stomach and my couch.

"How about you pretend it's your pussy?" Fabio's nose wrinkles in distaste. "I'm sure you don't jab *it* like an elevator button."

"I usually rub my clit when I masturbate," I mutter as I add more lube to my finger. "Or use a vibrator."

Fabio makes a gagging sound. "You're not paying me enough to listen to shit like that."

With a sigh, I circle my finger seductively around Bill's opening a few times, then slowly enter with just the tip of my index finger.

Fabio nods, so I edge the finger deeper, stopping when the first knuckle is in.

"Much better," he says. "Now aim between his belly button and cock."

I cringe. I hate the word "cock"—and everything else bird-related. Still, I do as he says.

Fabio dramatically shakes his head. "Don't bend the finger. This isn't a come-hither situation."

I pull my finger out and start all over.

My digit goes in rod straight this time.

"Huh," I say after I'm two knuckles deep. "There's something there. Feels like a walnut."

Fabio snorts. "That *is* a walnut, you dum-dum. I shoved it in there for educational purposes. The prostate—or P-spot—is around where you are now, but the real one feels softer and smoother. Now that you got it, massage gently."

As I pleasure Bill's walnut, Fabio shakes the dummy to simulate how a real man would be acting. Then he starts to voice Bill as well, using all of his porn-star acting ability.

"Bill" moans and groans until he has, as Fabio puts it, "a P-gasm to rule them all."

I remove my finger once again. I have mixed feelings about my accomplishment.

Fabio grabs my chin and tilts my face up. "Show me your tongue."

Feeling like I'm five, I stick my tongue all the way out.

He shakes his head disapprovingly. "Not long enough."

I retract my tongue. "Long enough for what?"

"To reach the walnut, obviously." He sighs theatrically. "I guess I'll work with what I've got."

Ugh. Can I slap him? "How about we work on his peen?"

With another sigh, he turns Bill over. "Did you take those lozenges, like I told you?"

Not for the first time, I field doubts about my instructor. The goal for this training is simple: I want to be a spy, which means gaining skills as a seductress/femme fatale. Think Keri Russell's character in *The Americans*. According to her backstory in that show, she attended a creepy spy school that taught seduction. In fact, such schools are common in movies about Russian spies—the latest was featured in *Anna*. Alas, these schools are harder to find in real life. So I figured I'd hire a professional instead, but the prostitute I solicited for help refused. Ditto with the female porn stars I reached out to on social media. As my last resort, I turned to Fabio, a childhood friend who's now a male porn star. Being in gay porn, he claims he's able to please a man better than any woman can.

"Yes, I sucked on the lozenges," I say. "My throat is numb, and I can barely feel my tongue."

"Great. Now get that whole shlong down your throat." Fabio points at Bill.

I scan Bill's length apprehensively. "You sure about this? Wouldn't the lozenges make the penis numb? If Bill were real, that is."

He lifts an eyebrow. "Bill?"

I shrug. "Figured if I'm having relations with him, he shouldn't be anonymous."

Fabio pats my shoulder. "The lozenges are just to give you some confidence. Once you see that it fits, you'll be more relaxed for the real thing and won't require numbing. Don't worry. I'll teach you proper breathing and everything. You'll be a pro in no time."

"Okay." I take off my sexy wig and put it on the couch. Before Fabio says anything, I assure him I'll keep it on during a real encounter.

Now comfy, I lean over and take Bill into my mouth as far as I can.

My lips touch the silicone base. Wow. This is deeper than I was able to swallow any of my exes—and they weren't this big. My gag reflex is sensitive. Typically, even a toothbrush gives me issues when I use it to clean my tongue. But thanks to the numbing, the silicone dildo has gone in all the way.

This is interesting. Could lozenges also help one withstand waterboarding? If I'm to become a spy, I need to learn to withstand torture in case I'm captured. Of course, waterboarding isn't my biggest concern. If the enemy has access to a duck—or any bird, really—

I'll spill all the state secrets to keep the feathery monstrosity away from me.

Yeah, okay. Maybe the CIA did have a good reason to reject my candidacy. Then again, in *Homeland*—another one of my favorite shows—they let Claire Danes stay in the CIA with all of *her* issues. Which reminds me: I need to practice making my chin quiver on demand.

Fabio taps my shoulder. "That's enough."

I disengage and swallow an overabundance of saliva. "That wasn't so bad. Should I go again?"

He shakes his head. "I think you need a motivation boost."

I know what he's talking about, so I take my phone out.

"Yeah." He rubs his hands like a villain from the early Bond films. "Show me the picture again."

I pull up the image of codename Hottie McSpy.

An undercover FBI agent took this photo because he was after one of the men in it, but not my target. No. Everyone thinks Hottie McSpy is just a rando—but *I* believe he's a Russian agent.

Fabio whistles. "So much premium man meat."

It's true. In the image, a group of extremely delicious-looking men are sitting around a table inside a Russian-style *banya*—a hybrid between a steam room and a sauna—wearing only towels and, in the case of Hottie McSpy, a pair of non-reflective aviator sunglasses that must have some kind of anti-fog coating. With the sweat beading on everyone's glistening muscles, they look like a wet dream come to life.

"They're playing poker," I say. "That's why I've been taking poker lessons."

"Yeah, I figured as much, since the picture is called Hot Poker Club." Fabio giddily enunciates the last three words. "You realize that sounds like the title of one of my movies?"

I shrug. "An FBI agent named this image, not me. They were after another guy who was in that room, and I was helping out as part of the collaboration between the agencies."

Fabio taps on the screen to zoom in on Hottie McSpy. "And he's the one you're after?"

Nodding, I drink in the image once more. Hottie McSpy has the hardest muscles of this already-impressive bunch, and the strongest jaw. His chiseled masculine features are vaguely Slavic, a fact that first made me suspicious of him. His hair is dark blond and shampoo-commercial healthy. Not even my wigs are as nice.

If I were to learn that this man was the result of Soviet geneticists trying to create the perfect male specimen/super-soldier/field agent, I wouldn't be surprised. Nor would I be shocked to find out that he was the inspiration for the Russian equivalent of a Ken doll (Ivan A. Pieceof?). Even if I didn't think he was a spy, I'd infiltrate that poker game just to rip those stupid glasses off of him and see his eyes. Though I picture them—

"You're drooling," Fabio says. "Not that I can blame you."

I nearly choke on the treacherous saliva. "No, I'm not."

"Yeah, sure. Be honest, are you going after him because he might be a spy, or because you want to marry him?"

"The first option." I hide my phone. "Spy or not, marriage is out of the question for me. My current attitude toward dating shares an acronym with the name of the agency I work for: No Strings Attached. But that's not what this is about, anyway. If I single-handedly expose a spy, the CIA is bound to take notice and rethink their rejection of my candidacy. And even if they don't take me, I will have made America safer. Russian spies are still among the biggest threats to our national security."

"Sure, sure," Fabio says. "And his hotness has nothing to do with you focusing on him, specifically."

I frown. "His hotness is why he's the perfect agent. Think James Bond. Think Tom Cruise in *Mission Impossible*. Think—"

Fabio raises his hands like I'm threatening to shoot him. "The lady doth protest too much, methinks."

I gesture at the silicone phallus. "Should I go again? I think the numbing is wearing off."

For some unknown reason, I feel super motivated to deep-throat someone.

Fabio takes out his phone. "Sure. You work on that, but I've got to run. My Grindr date awaits."

He shows me a dick pic.

"Dude," I say. "Don't you get enough action at work?"

Fabio playfully flicks at Bill's erection, and it swings back and forth like a naughty pendulum. "This is why I thank heavens for being attracted to men. Their sex drives are so much stronger."

"That's sexist. Just because women don't hump everything that moves doesn't mean we have weak sex drives."

He flicks Bill's manhood—or is it his dummy-hood? —again. "If your cock and asshole aren't always sore, your sex drive is lacking. That's all there is to it."

I cringe again. What do roosters—killing machines that they are—have in common with penises? Why not call the male organ a python, a bratwurst, or a honey dipper? Any of those would be more appropriate.

Fabio grins and flicks the appendage in question once again. "Sorry for saying 'cock.' I'm such a—"

Before he can finish, a blur of fur streaks by. A giant feline lands on Bill's washboard abs and swats razor-sharp claws at the pendulum-like phallus.

Screaming in falsetto, Fabio pulls away from the scene of the unfolding hate crime.

The owner of the claws is my cat, Machete, and apparently, he's not done—because he rakes his claws over what's left of Bill's dummy-hood.

"That's just obscene." Fabio stands crossed-legged, as if he needs to go tinkle. "You should get your cat to a therapist."

As if he understands what my friend has just said, Machete shoots him a feline hate-filled glare.

As usual, I can picture what Machete would say in a nightmarish world where cats could talk:

The silicone male couldn't escape Machete. The softer, fleshy one will be next.

"Come here, sweetie," I croon and swoop down to grab the cat.

Machete must be feeling extremely magnanimous today because he lets me hold him and keep my eyes.

Fabio chuckles, and I give him a quizzical look.

"Your cat was trying to kill Bill," he explains.

Machete hisses at Fabio.

Machete is not amused. Uma Thurman has a lot of range, but she can't play Machete.

I grin. "He must've heard you call that a cock." I gesture at Bill's misfortune. "My sweetie protects me from birds." I pet Machete's silky fur and get rewarded with a deep purr. "When I first got him, he killed what turned out to be a goose pillow for me."

Fabio eyes the door. "All I know is he looks like he'd fought in a lot of illegal street fights before you adopted him. And lost a lot."

It's true. Machete actually looked even worse when I came across him at the shelter. It was also the only time I can recall seeing him vulnerable in any way.

Needless to say, I used my work resources to track down his prior owners, and soon after, they mysteriously ended up on a no-fly list... just before a big vacation.

I stop the petting for a moment, and Fabio gets hissed at again.

"I'd better go," Fabio says, backing away.

I follow him. A videocall window pops up on one of my wall monitors. Yes, I have multiple wall monitors. My home setup is inspired by all the movies where spies watch someone from a surveillance room.

Forgetting the cat danger, Fabio stops and looks at the screen. If my friend were one of Machete's kind, his curiosity would've killed him long ago.

"It's my video conference with Gia and Clarice," I explain. "You can go."

Fabio purses his lips. "Who's Clarice?"

"My poker teacher," I say. "Go."

He looks on the verge of stomping his foot. "But I want to say hi to my girl Gia."

"Fine." I accept the call, and both Gia and Clarice show up on the screen.

———

Go to www.mishabell.com to order your copy of *Femme Fatale-ish* today!

About the Author

We love writing humor (often the inappropriate kind), happy endings (both kinds), and characters quirky enough to be called oddballs (because... balls). If you love your romance heavy on the comedy and feel-good vibes, visit www.mishabell.com and sign up for our newsletter.